"Electrifying and sus̲ ̲eviews

"[An] action-packed a̲ ̲the reader on a roller-coaster ride or emotional highs and lows. With dynamic characters, intensely erotic action, and an extremely solid storyline, it makes for a resoundingly good read. *Chosen Prey* will keep the readers's eyes glued to its pages until the very end!"

—*Road to Romance*

"One of the rare and special books for which a five-heart rating seems inadequate . . . characters are so well-developed they seem to come alive."

—*The Romance Studio*

"With *Chosen Prey* Cheyenne McCray has moved to suspense with flair and savvy, and readers will certainly hope that move is permanent. Readers will stay on the edge of their seat as they follow her characters on their wild race for their lives."

—SuspenseRomanceWriters.com

"A riveting tale of danger and passion . . . one of those books where evil lingers but good has one bad-ass hero who will do whatever it takes to protect the woman he has grown to love."

—Romance Junkies

Seduced by Magic

"Blistering passion and erotic sensuality are major McCray hallmarks, in addition to a deft and exciting storyline. This magical series continues to develop its increasing cast of characters and complex plotline; the result is erotic paranormal romance liberally laced with adventure and thrills."

—*Romantic Times BOOKreviews* (4 ½ stars, Top Pick)

"The slices of humor, the glimpses of the characters' world through fantastic descriptions, not to mention fascinating characters, landed this book on . . . the keeper shelf."

—*Romance Divas*

Forbidden Magic

"A yummy hot-fudge sundae of a book!"

—MaryJanice Davidson, *New York Times* bestselling author

MORE . . .

"Cheyenne McCray has crafted a novel that takes the imagination on an exciting flight. Full of fantasy, with a touch of darkness, a great read for anyone who loves to get lost in a book that stretches the boundaries!"—Heather Graham, *New York Times* bestselling author

"McCray's magical tale will thrill and entrance you!"
—Sabrina Jeffries, *New York Times* bestselling author

"Explosive, erotic, and un-put-downable. Cheyenne McCray more than delivers!" —L.A. Banks, bestselling author of the Vampire Huntress Legend series

"Magical mayhem, sexy shapeshifters, wondrous witches and warlocks . . . in *Forbidden Magic*, Cheyenne McCray has created a fabulous new world. You won't be able to get enough!"
—Lori Handeland, *USA Today* bestselling author

"Fans of dark paranormal fantasy will enjoy the fast-paced, spine-tingling twists and turns of Cheyenne McCray's *Forbidden Magic*."
—Toni Blake, author of *In Your Wildest Dreams*

"Cheyenne McCray's *Forbidden Magic* is a rich mix of witches, demons, and fae in an epic tapestry full of conflict and desire."
—Robin Owens, author of *Heart Choice*

"Chock-full of emotion and action, Cheyenne McCray's *Forbidden Magic* will find a spot on the keeper shelf of every reader who enjoys a touch of the paranormal along with her erotic romance. I highly recommend it!" —Ann Jacobs, author of *A Mutual Favor*

"McCray has written a tempting, exciting novel rich in magic and pleasure." —Lora Leigh, author of *The Breed Next Door*

"McCray's knowledge of Fae, Fomorii, elves and ancient Irish magics shines in this book of witches, warriors and dangerous desires."
—Linnea Sinclair, author of *Gabriel's Ghost*

"McCray delivers a scorching tale of modern witches and ancient Fae, a winner rich with lore, fantasy, gritty action, and heart-gripping romance." —Annie Windsor, award-winning author of *Sailmaster's Woman*

"This modern-day tale meets ancient world paranormal isn't just a book, it's an event. The elements all come together in this paranormal romance. You start reading for the story and end up reading for the characters. You're left at the edge of your seat needing more until the very last satisfying word. You won't be able to put it down once you start reading!"
—Sheila English, CEO of Circle of Seven Productions

St. Martin's Paperbacks Titles by
CHEYENNE McCRAY

Wicked Magic

Seduced by Magic

Forbidden Magic

Chosen Prey

MOVING
TARGET

CHEYENNE McCRAY

St. Martin's Paperbacks

This is a work of fiction. All of the characters, organizations and events portrayed in this novel are either products of the author's imagination or are used fictitiously.

MOVING TARGET

Copyright © 2008 by Cheyenne McCray.
Excerpt from *Shadow Magic* copyright © 2008 by Cheyenne McCray.

ISBN: 0-312-93764-4
EAN: 978-0-312-93764-5

Printed in the United States of America

St. Martin's Paperbacks edition / January 2008

St. Martin's Paperbacks are published by St. Martin's Press, 175 Fifth Avenue, New York, NY 10010.

10 9 8 7 6 5 4 3 2 1

To the wonderful critique partners who stood by me, supported me, and held my hand when I needed it. Here's to you, Annie Windsor, who encourages me to blow things up; Mackenzie McKade, along with her husband, Bill, and daughter, Ashley, for setting me on the right path; Tara Donn for invaluable feedback and great apple martinis; and Patrice Michelle, who brings me back to reality. This book wouldn't have happened without you. Lots of love and hugs!

ACKNOWLEDGMENTS

I had fabulous assistance with WITSEC, the Witness Security Program, from Nikki Credic of the United States Marshals Service Office of Public Affairs. A huge thank-you to Nikki for finding the answers to my many, many questions.

Charge Nurse Tom McAdams of the Oregon Burn Center provided me with invaluable information regarding burn victims that is used in *Moving Target*. Much appreciation for all of your help.

Thank you, thank you to Special Agent Tara Donn, who helped me tremendously with many aspects of law enforcement among other important details used in this book. She also graciously led me on a tour of Federal Plaza and locations in New Jersey and New York City that are used in *Moving Target*. I owe her more chocolate than money can buy.

I can never forget Dr. Susan Vaught for her help with psychological trauma and answering a zillion questions, and for being there whenever I needed her.

Thanks to Lev Krystal for his help with Russian words, even though he wouldn't give me any Russian curse words. (So I had to find them on my own!) And thank you, Lev, for allowing me to make you a hit man.

In addition, thank you to my hometown councilman for patiently putting up with all of my off-the-wall questions.

And I can never forget my editor, Monique Patterson!

I used a great deal of creative license. Any mistakes, perversions, twisting of reality—you get the picture—are mine and mine alone.

AUTHOR'S NOTE

For over two hundred years, since 1789, U.S. Marshals and their Deputies have served as the instruments of civil authority by all three branches of the U.S. government.

The U.S. Marshals Service provides protection for the federal judiciary, transports federal prisoners, protects endangered federal witnesses, and manages assets seized from criminal enterprises.

The Marshals Service is responsible for over 50 percent of arrests of federal fugitives. In 2006, the U.S. Marshals arrested more than 38,000 federal fugitive felons, clearing 41,300 federal felony warrants—more than all other law enforcement agencies combined. Working with authorities at the federal, state, and local levels, U.S. Marshals–led fugitive task forces arrested more than 46,800 state and local fugitives, clearing 54,300 state and local felony warrants.

As mentioned, the U.S. Marshals Service provides

for the security, health, and safety of government witnesses—and their immediate dependents—whose lives are in danger as a result of testimony against drug traffickers, terrorists, organized crime members, and other major criminals.

The Marshals Service has had over 17,000 witnesses and their families in the program. To this date, no program participant who has followed security guidelines has ever been harmed while under the active protection of the U.S. Marshals Service.

CHAPTER ONE

Who wouldn't go out on a limb to help a child who was fighting for his life?

"Can you please help us, Ms. King?"

Ani's gaze shifted from the desperate man and woman to the almost perfectly intact fourteen-centimeter-high bronze and gold statue of Tyrion III. With reverence she held the piece that came from the tiny country of Masia. She studied the art as early morning sunshine poured into the antique shop's fifteen-foot-high windows, highlighting the statue's delicate gold inlays.

If she wasn't mistaken—and she was pretty sure she wasn't—the statue was from the twenty-second dynasty, circa 900 B.C. She'd seen only one other like it, and it was in the Brooklyn Museum in New York.

Formerly an art curator for a major metropolitan museum in New York City, Ani now ran a dinky antique shop in Bisbee, Arizona. The Witness Security Program wouldn't allow her to be in the same field as she'd been in before, but at least the U.S. Marshals had put her into an environment she could relate to. Even if most of the "antiques" in the place were junk.

But this . . . this was a priceless treasure.

A lead weight settled in her belly. It was likely also a very illegal treasure. It was against the law for any artifact to be taken out of the country where it had been excavated unless bequeathed to a museum.

Ani looked to the husband and wife who had brought her the artifact to ascertain its value. It was early morning and the Harrisons had been waiting for the shop to open to talk with her. They wanted to see if they could sell the statue to help pay medical bills for their son, a burn victim, and get him to a top-notch center that could treat burns of such magnitude. The mere thought of what the child was going through made her own twisted scars itch from the small of her back to her shoulder blades.

Ani barely kept her hands steady as she settled the small statue into the intricately carved ebony box Mr. and Mrs. Harrison had brought it in. The velvet-lined box itself looked to be of some value. It smelled of aged wood and dust, but was in beautiful condition.

"Where did you get this artifact?" Ani asked the couple, wondering how something so priceless and illegal had ended up in Bisbee.

"My older brother just arrived from Montana." Mr. Harrison shuffled his feet and glanced down before looking back up at Ani. "He gave it to us to see if we can sell it to help our child." The hollow-cheeked, emaciated Mr. Harrison fidgeted, then stuck his hands in his jeans pockets. "Our great-grandfather was an archeologist." His voice was scratchy as he spoke. "This statue was passed down through our family. His other findings went to museums and Masia."

Ani studied him, her heart breaking apart for the family. "I can't do anything with this piece. It's illegal to possess an artifact from Masia unless it has been donated to a museum."

Mr. Harrison cleared his throat. "In a secret drawer at the bottom of the box is a letter from Masia's King Aronan awarding the statue to my great-grandfather. It was a gift of appreciation for discovering the tomb of Tyrion III."

Ani raised an eyebrow. Mr. Harrison stepped forward and showed her an almost invisible indentation in the wood at the bottom of the box. She pushed the catch, and a drawer slowly opened.

Nestled inside more velvet lay a yellowed parchment. She withdrew it and carefully unfolded the parchment, which felt rough and brittle between her fingers. She scanned the page and her belly did a little flip. A letter from King Aronan himself awarding the priceless treasure to James Harrison for the exact reason the younger Mr. Harrison had said. It was stamped with a red wax seal and the letter looked as authentic as the statue. The letter by itself would be worth a fortune.

Ani looked up from the paper and met Mr. Harrison's pleading gaze. She tried to keep her voice from wavering with excitement. "I know a collector who might be interested in purchasing this artifact. If you'll give me two weeks, I'll see what I can do." In two weeks she'd be done with her testimony, the trial would be behind her and she'd feel safer contacting someone from her former life.

"We don't have that much time." Mr. Harrison interrupted her thoughts as he looked from his wife to Ani. "We only have enough money left to pay for a few more nights at the motel we've been staying in since our home burned to the ground."

"Do you think that statue will bring enough to pay Jamie's medical bills?" Mrs. Harrison asked, her brown eyes bright with unshed tears.

Now? Could I do it now? The trial's already started—it's as good as over in a few days. Why couldn't I help this poor boy? Isn't it the right thing to do?

Heart aching even more for the family, Ani said, "I can't promise anything, and the statue and letter will have to be authenticated. But I think this may be of some value."

More than you can imagine.

Mr. and Mrs. Harrison looked at one another then back to Ani. "Please find out as soon as you can," Mr. Harrison said.

Ani had been in the Witness Security Program for almost two years—two quiet, uneventful years. She had the contacts from her past life to help these people, and her gut told her she should. Definitely the right thing.

"I'll do my best." Ani slipped the parchment into the drawer and shut it, then put the lid back on the wood box and extended it to them.

"No." Mr. Harrison waved it off with a pained expression. "You'll need the statue to make this happen for our boy, Ms. Carter." She could see in his eyes how strong his love was for his son. The treasure meant nothing compared to Jamie's welfare.

Ani offered him a smile even though her soul was wrenched in two for the little boy. "Let me get you a receipt." She set the box on the counter. "And call me Ani, please." She'd been Ani Carter for two years, and the name rolled easily off her tongue. But she still couldn't think of herself as anyone but Anistana King.

Even though they usually recommended keeping the same first name, the U.S. Marshals couldn't allow her to use hers, Anistana, because it was too unusual. But they did allow her to use an abbreviation of it.

Once the Harrisons were gone, Ani braced her hands on the glass countertop and stared at the ebony box. It had gold inlay within the carvings. Likely it was as old as the letter, over a century.

Priceless.

A fortune.

All that little boy would need to cover his treatment, but . . . did she *really* dare call George Hanover?

"I have to," she said aloud. "I can't live with myself if I don't."

Two years was a long time for her to be off the radar, but Hanover was a good guy. He wasn't part of the Russian Mafia—and it wasn't likely the Mob had contacted her old clients. It had been so long, and the Mob probably didn't know about Hanover anyway. George would buy the piece, and if she asked him to, he'd keep his mouth shut. She'd be careful. She'd go about this the right way, and she'd be able to help Jamie Harrison before she went to New York City to testify.

The trial . . .

She held her hand against her belly where it felt as if an ice block had frozen. The FBI case agent, experts, and other witnesses were already testifying. She was on call and was to be flown in a couple of days before she had to get up on the stand in order to be prepped by the associate U.S. attorney, AUSA, John Singleton. He, as well as the FBI and U.S. Marshals, wanted to keep her out of New York City until the last possible moment. According to the AUSA, she was the one piece that would pull the entire puzzle together.

Now, here she stood with the welfare and life of a child in her hands. It wasn't likely the Russian Mafia would have contacted her old clients. It had been so long. How would they even know about George?

Tears stung the back of her eyes at the thought of Jamie Harrison. Second- and third-degree burns covered eighty percent of his tiny body. The family's home had burned down and the eight-year-old boy had been trapped in his bedroom until firefighters rescued him. The tragedy had been on TV, but as small as Bisbee was, everyone knew about it and many had been donating clothes, food, and other items. Even with monetary donations, they didn't come close to fulfilling the need for Jamie to be sent to the best burn center in the U.S.

The burns Ani had received in the fire two years ago were nothing compared to Jamie's. Her scars only covered her lower back up to her shoulder blades. It had been the most painful experience of her life . . .

No, losing her entire family had been.

Ani clenched her fists on top of the counter and closed her eyes. The little boy *needed* her, and she had the ability to make this happen. All she had to do was contact a friend from her old life.

With steely resolve, she raised her chin and tucked back an errant brown curl that had escaped her up-swept hair. The Russians wouldn't have a clue if she called George. He'd been one of the kindest men she'd ever known. The billionaire had an extensive collection of art, all legally obtained. He'd always struck her as honest and upfront and had become a good friend over the years they had worked together.

Plus, she'd use her cell phone. Then she would be sure her call couldn't be traced. Her number was un-listed, so the possibility of the Russians identifying her location was next to nil.

With a lump in her throat, she pulled her cell phone out of her pocket and called information. When the operator came on the line she asked for George Hanover in Brooklyn, New York. There were three listings, but she recognized one of the ad-dresses. Ani grabbed a pen to scratch the number on a notepad by the phone.

She took a deep breath. Her fingers trembled as she gripped the cell and punched in the number for the customer-turned-friend, and her hand shook when she brought the phone to her ear. She immediately recognized his voice when he answered.

"This is Anistana King." It seemed weird saying her real name again instead of Ani Carter. "How are you doing, George?"

A brief moment of silence was followed by, "Anistana, what happened to you? I tried getting a hold of you at the museum, but they said you'd more or less disappeared. Are you all right?"

It felt so good to talk to an old friend and to hear the concern in his voice. Yet at the same time Ani's gut churned. Maybe this hadn't been such a good idea.

But the Harrison family needed what she could give them.

She gripped the phone tight enough that her knuckles ached. "When my parents died, I just had to get out of town."

"Such a tragedy." George's voice softened. "I've thought of you often since then."

"I'm glad we have this chance to chat." A smile touched her lips. "Even if I have a motive behind it."

He gave a low chuckle. "Go on."

She toyed with the pencil in her free hand. "I'm calling because I've come across something that will fit perfectly in your collection."

George cleared his throat and she could imagine the balding man tipping back in his office chair and studying the artifacts in his den. "Shoot."

Ani heard excitement in George's voice when she told him what she was certain she had. "It still needs to be authenticated," she added. "But I don't think that will be a problem."

They negotiated a fair price that would more than help the Harrisons with Jamie's bills, and then some. Before disconnecting the call, Ani gave George her cell phone number, swearing him to secrecy and asking him to not give out her number or tell anyone about her call. He sounded puzzled, but agreed.

For a moment, memories of other friends, coworkers, and acquaintances flowed over Ani and her chest ached. She hadn't been able to say goodbye to anyone. One day she was in a burn center in New York City, and the next day she as good as disappeared from everything and everyone she'd ever known.

Ani missed terribly the three friends she'd lived with in the old carriage house in Brooklyn. Jules, Erica, and Lexi had probably been frantic with worry when Ani vanished. She'd lost her family to a murderer, then lost everything from her old life when she signed the contract to enter WITSEC.

No connections to her past, no information about people from her former life, no trail that the Mafia could follow. WITSEC was absolute on that point, and the loss on top of loss had been brutal. Still, the hit the Russians put out on her was enough to convince her to enter the Witness Security Program. She intended to live to testify and put the man who murdered her family behind bars for manslaughter, among other crimes.

Just the thought of that bastard made her chest ache with rage and fear.

Ani caught her breath as she opened the box to peek

at the figure of King Tyrion III again and marveled at its beauty. She carefully touched the blackened bronze, feeling its coolness beneath her fingertip. She could never get enough of true art, even if she couldn't work in a museum because the Russian Mafia could possibly track her down in such an obvious occupation. And the Russians wanted her badly enough they'd do anything to get to her.

Not that anyone would recognize her now. She was the same cultured, refined, sophisticated woman she had been in New York. But with all of the trauma in her life since that night, she'd had a hard time eating and had lost eighty-something pounds, most of it in the last year. She'd gone from a size twenty-two to an eight, which was a bizarre feeling. She'd always been heavy and had been comfortable in her own skin. Now she had a lot less skin and it just felt strange. She had to start eating again, or there would be nothing left of her.

Her black slacks hung loose on her hips as she took the box containing the statue to the back room, her high heels ringing against the tile floor. She locked the box in the old-fashioned but very secure vault. They kept what few valuable treasures they had in the safe along with the store's daily take of cash. Which wasn't much considering the price tags Tammy put on the merchandise. Ani had furnished her own small house on the street above Castle Rock with some of the nicer pieces that came into the store.

After she finished locking the safe, she went back

to work in the shop. From the time the store opened at nine A.M., starting with the Harrisons' arrival, it continued to be a busy day. Tourists picked through the collectables and not-so-collectables, most taking their time to browse the shop that included a huge lower level. Bisbee was an artists' community with tourism supporting the economy, and the tourists definitely supported this store.

In between interruptions, Ani worked on the inventory program she'd convinced Tammy to buy. Even though she was constantly interrupted by customers, she still managed to get work done.

Her friend Lyra stopped by on her lunch break to see if there was anything new and interesting, specifically old lunch boxes and other old tin items. Lyra worked up the street in a shop where she sold metal sculptures she made out of pieces of tin and aluminum from various items. Ani had several of Lyra's pieces in her own home. Lyra was one of the few friends Ani had made in Bisbee along with Lyra's husband, Dare, a private investigator.

Around noon, her cell phone rang. "This is Ani," she answered. The line crackled. "Hello?"

It crackled again, but she didn't hear anyone. Probably one of the few friends she had in Bisbee, calling from a cell phone out of range. Happened all the time with Bisbee being in the Mule Mountains. The caller ID said "not available," so it could have been anyone.

She punched off when no one on the other end responded.

The rest of the day flew past and Ani fielded a few

calls on the antique store land line, along with another out-of-range call on her cell that didn't come up on her caller ID. By the end of the day her feet were killing her and she had a headache.

Her cell phone rang again.

She glanced at her watch. Six o'clock. Time to close the store, and it was Friday. Also time for Daniel's call—maybe he'd been the one trying to reach her earlier, even though he never called her that early in the day.

Her heart raced as she slipped her cell phone out of the pocket of her slacks. On the caller ID it said "unknown," but she was certain it was Daniel.

She answered the phone with a breathless, "Hello."

"Hi, Ani." Daniel's deep, sensual voice affected her the way it always did. It sent a twist of sensation in her belly and caused her heart to beat faster.

"Hey." Ani closed her eyes, imagining Daniel's lean, muscled physique, his slightly wavy brown hair and warm coffee-brown eyes. It had been an entire year since she'd seen the Deputy Marshal, the Inspector, who was her contact, but she could picture him in his Stetson and Wranglers, down to his boots. "Anything exciting today?" she asked.

"Not until you answered the phone." His voice was smooth and sexy, like warm buttered rum, but the man never said anything he didn't mean.

Ani almost sighed out loud at the feelings he stirred within her. "Same here," she said as she opened her eyes and saw only Daniel in her mind's eye. He'd been there from the beginning, moving her to the Oregon

Burn Center, to rehab, to a safe house, and then to Bis-bee. She'd been in Bisbee for a year now.

He used to call every now and then to check in on her, but those calls became more frequent and more personal, until they talked almost every Friday. Sometimes on the weekend. She'd fallen in love with everything about him.

She'd fallen in love with a man she could never have.

"How 'bout you? Anything interesting happen to-day?" Daniel asked in his lazy drawl.

She shook her head even though he couldn't see her. "Same old same old." She walked to the front door, locked it, and turned the OPEN sign to CLOSED.

"Oh, wait." A buzz of excitement quickened her pace as she returned to the front register that sat on a long glass case. "A man and woman came in first thing this morning with a priceless treasure." Her de-light in handling such an object faded as she realized why it had ended up in her possession in the first place. "Their son is a burn victim, Daniel. Eighty per-cent of his body." The large scar on her back itched again, but she tried to ignore it. "They need the money to pay his medical bills, so I helped them bro-ker the piece."

Daniel was quiet for a moment. "Honey, what did you do?"

"Well, ah . . ." Heat flushed Ani. "I called an old client who collects Masian artifacts and hashed out a deal."

"Shit!" Daniel's voice came out so loud and harsh

she held the cell phone away from her ear. "Goddamnit, Ani. You know the rules."

"They have to have the resources for their son's treatment." She blinked back tears. "It's been two years. George Hanover is an old friend—and he's very discreet. How could the Mob find me through him?"

"I'm coming to get you." Daniel's voice steeled and suddenly she didn't recognize him. This man's tone was harsh and unforgiving. "Do *not* leave the store. Stay in the back room, away from the windows. I'm sending in local police. Do not open the door for anyone except the police—if you're absolutely positive it's the cops."

Ani said in a rush, "I used my cell. You and I use our cell phones all the time."

"I'm not a contact from your past—your friend was," Daniel said in a voice that sounded like a low growl. "He's the point of reference the Mafia could start with and work backward until they found you."

"But—"

"It's a four-hour drive from Phoenix. I don't have a Deputy Marshal available who's close enough to you, so you'll need to wait at the police department until I get there."

"Daniel—"

"Like I said, don't open for *anyone* but the cops, and there'd better be sirens and flashing lights. Do you understand?"

"Yes, but—"

"Are all the doors and windows locked?"

"Yes—"

"You are not to call *anyone* that you know, *anywhere*. Understand?"

She sucked in a deep breath, but the tears wouldn't stop flowing and she couldn't stop the tremble in her voice. "I'm sorry," she whispered.

"I don't have time to talk. I have arrangements to make."

He severed the connection. She brought the cell phone away from her ear and held it in both fists as she flipped it shut. She leaned her head back against the wall and slid down it until her butt hit the floor. Tears ran freely from her eyes as she dropped the phone, wrapped her arms around her knees, and buried her face against her slacks.

With one little phone call she'd screwed up everything. She could possibly have put herself in danger, and she hadn't even *thought* about placing Daniel at risk.

She raised her head and dried her tears with the backs of her hands, then thunked her head against the wall when the tears continued to flow down her cheeks. What a freaking mess. Why did her father have to—well, do what he did? If he hadn't gotten in bed with the Russian Mafia, her whole family would be alive today.

Those bastards—especially Dmitry Borenko—needed to pay.

Ani's skin crawled and her heart kept an unsteady beat. "I'm so *stupid*." She rubbed her temples, got up from the floor as she picked up her cell phone. After she pocketed her phone, she slipped into the back room, locked the wooden door between her and the shop. She checked the locks on the big metal door that led to the alley.

When she checked again to see that the doors were secure, she started to pace the length of the room, but then she plopped into a chair by Tammy's ancient rolltop desk. There was one window in the back room and she had to stay away from it. Smells of dust and pine-scented cleaner from the recently mopped floors clogged her nose and made her even more nauseated than she already was.

All she had wanted to do was help that poor child. After being in a burn center herself, she could relate to Jamie, if only in a small way. God. Eighty percent of his little body. She wiped tears from her eyes with the backs of her hands again. She had just wanted to help him.

How could George be any kind of link to the Mob? How could the Russians even know she had called George? Of all the millions of phone calls going on throughout the day, how could her one little call be traced?

Nothing would likely come from it, but still, she had screwed up. Maybe she could have had Tammy call—but then the rather reclusive George Hanover would wonder how she knew of his collection.

But could the Russians have contacted every one of her past clients and friends? Her heart nearly stopped at the thought. Were her old friends and clients in danger? What if they'd been threatened from the time she vanished into the WITSEC program?

The old shoulder wound from the bullet ached and the scar on her back itched. She rubbed her hands up and down her arms as she glanced in the direction of the shop itself, which was on the other side of the locked wooden door. With all the windows the store had, being in that section was like walking out in the open.

The antique shop was a corner building at the end of Main Street. Being the gossipy and busybody type, Tammy liked keeping the fifteen-foot-high windows without blinds so that she could watch everything that went on outside, and so potential customers could see in. The store was directly across from the post office and library, and catty-corner to a small indoor mall. Well, if one could call it a mall.

She stopped rubbing her arms. Oh, jeez. She needed to let Tammy know she wouldn't be back. Ani found a notepad on the antique desk where Tammy preferred to do her paperwork.

Ani felt the weight of her cell phone in the pocket of her slacks, but remembered she wasn't supposed to call anyone. She leaned forward in the chair and started a note, telling her friend and employer she was sorry but she had to leave due to an unexpected family emergency.

Sadness crept over her as she erased "family." Tammy knew Ani had none. Tammy didn't know the true story, just that her mother, father, and sister had died in a fire.

Ani reworded the letter so that it simply said she was leaving due to an unexpected emergency.

For a moment her eyes glazed as she remembered her sister. Her mischievousness, her sense of humor. God, how her heart ached every time she thought of Jenn. They'd fought a lot as they'd grown up—what siblings didn't? But they'd matured, and they became so close that Jenn had been her best friend, and now Ani missed her so badly. Every single day.

Ani shook her head, trying to focus on the present. She fought back more tears, sniffled, then looked around her.

The safe drew her attention. The Harrisons. They had to be taken care of.

With a deep breath, she sketched out a note about the statue, the Harrisons, and their contact information. She also added George Hanover's information.

When she finished the note, she signed it "Ani." She'd really screwed things up now. She'd had a good life this past year, even if it was a small town, so different than what she was used to. After the trial, she would end up in another place with another name, and possibly a different Inspector Marshal if Daniel was mad enough at her.

The fact that Daniel was so upset with her made her gut clench. She gripped the armrests of the chair. The tone of his voice had been cold and professional once she'd told him what she'd done. When he arrived it would be the first time she'd seen him in a year. All the times she'd imagined herself being close to him again, it hadn't been like this.

He'd been in every one of her fantasies. She loved his deep, sexy voice, his soft laughter when they spoke and something amused him. His concern when she'd had a bad day for one reason or another. She even talked with him about her family and how much she missed them. He stayed with her through the tears, calling her "honey" and making her feel like she had someone in her life who really cared for her.

She'd learned a lot about Daniel, too. He told her of his two brothers who were in the military—Aaron was in Special Forces, and Jacob was a Navy SEAL. Their father was a retired U.S. Deputy Marshal. Daniel had told her things about his childhood and about his hobby of creating model airplanes. Sometimes he told her about cases he was working on—nothing classified, of course. After all of their intimate conversations, she almost felt like she knew him heart and soul.

Only now she was going to see him angry. Not smiling that smile that had turned her inside out the times he'd visited her in the burn center in Oregon and escorted her to a safe house there while she went through rehab, and then here to Bisbee, all in the first year. This past year he'd kept in touch with her over the phone. She often wished he'd come and visit her.

Ani wiped her sweaty palms on her black slacks. Even though she'd ended up in jeans-and-T-shirt cowboy country, she still held on to parts of her past she couldn't let go. When she worked she always wore tailored slacks, silk, and high heels.

She closed her eyes. *Please don't let that phone call, that mistake, affect my relationship with Daniel.*

Ani opened her eyes and stared up at the ceiling. What was she thinking? All she had was a phone relationship with the man. He liked to talk to her. So? He probably thought of her as a sister. Or maybe this was part of his job.

That thought depressed her even more.

I'm so stupid!

Ani checked the locks on the heavy metal door again, the handle cool beneath her palm. It wasn't likely anyone could come through that door, but she felt like she had to do *something*.

Damn, she'd forgotten about the window. She started to pass by it to sit in the chair when she caught sight of a man, directly across the street. It was dusk, but she could tell he was staring at the antique shop.

In the fading sunlight, something metal glinted in one of his hands. He was smoking and he flicked ashes onto the sidewalk. The ashes glowed fiery red as they floated from his cigarette.

Ani stumbled back, sat in the chair, and gripped its armrests.

In slow motion, the memory of a glowing red cigarette butt, tumbling end over end, flashed through her mind. It had landed on gasoline-soaked drapes covering Ani's mother's crumpled body.

Ani had tried to scream but the sound wouldn't come from her mouth as she saw her mother's body go up in flames.

Tears spilled down her cheeks as she came back to the present.

Flashback. It was just a flashback, a part of her PTSD from the horrible things she went through when her family got murdered. Post-traumatic stress disorder, the therapists called it.

Screwed up was what *she* called it.

Shuddering, she rubbed the old bullet wound on her shoulder. The images of her mother's burning body wouldn't leave her mind. Her father, her sister . . . The heat, the house going up in flames so fast. So fast.

Ani ground her teeth. She had to make the Mafia pay for what they'd done to her family.

Her throat went dry. What if that man across the street was part of the Russian Mafia?

The back door handle jiggled.

Her heart stilled.

It jiggled again, harder this time.

Ani started shaking so badly her teeth chattered. She looked around the room for something to use as a weapon. As if anything could protect her from a gun if someone *was* after her. There wasn't even a place to hide.

Sirens sounded in the distance, coming closer in a hurry.

The door handle stopped moving.

Ani's heart pounded like crazy.

The police. Thank God.

The screeching of tires and the piercing wail of sirens let her know the cavalry had arrived. The sirens cut out and blue, red, and white lights flashed and illuminated the back room through the single window. To think she'd caused all of this with one phone call.

A knock at the metal door about made her jump out of her skin.

"Police," a deep voice shouted.

She tried to stand, but her legs were shaking so badly she couldn't get to her feet.

"Open the door," came the voice again. "This is the police."

Somehow Ani got her legs to work, made it to the back door, and unlocked it.

"Are you alone?" the officer at the door asked and she nodded. "Step aside."

She did and a couple of officers came into the room, sweeping it first with their guns.

Ani took a few steps back and dropped into the chair. She tried to swallow down her panic, but her eyes were wide and her breathing shallow. She was starting to hyperventilate.

One of the officers made her stand and patted her down for weapons, as if she were a criminal. When the officer finished, he said she could sit, but away from the desk, probably to keep her from going for a gun if she *was* a criminal.

After scouring the back room thoroughly, a pair of officers stayed with her while several others went into the antique shop to check it out.

One officer came up to her. He was a tall man, probably six two, about Daniel's height. She held her breath as he squatted down to face her eye to eye. "Name," he said in an authoritative voice.

At first her mouth wouldn't work. "Ani Carter," she finally got out. To the world, to everyone but

Daniel, Anistana King no longer existed. Until the trial.

The police officer placed his hand on her shoulder, causing her to jump. "Are you okay?"

Ani gave a slow, jerky nod. "I'm fine," she whispered, just before she passed out.

CHAPTER TWO

Yegor Borenko pushed his bulk off his mistress, Mashka, and she groaned. He'd just fucked the hell out of her, taking out his anger on the bitch. She would have bruises on the insides of her thighs and her nipples would hurt as hard as he had bitten them.

Good. She craved the punishment. Masochistic slut.

His men had better find that bitch Anistana King before she testified. The frustration he had taken out on Mashka had done nothing to alleviate the anger he felt.

A knock came at the door of the back room of his office. *"Zahodi,"* he growled. None would dare disturb him but his top in command.

Piterskij came into the room, a stoic expression on his face. He ignored Mashka and addressed Yegor.

"We have a lead on the King woman," Piterskij said as Yegor rolled out of the bed, grabbed his clothing, and started pulling on his Armani slacks.

"Go on." Yegor had heard this far too many times. He fastened his pants below his large belly. Mashka remained on the bed, naked and not covering herself. She knew better. He liked looking at her bruises. He liked showing off her hot, naked body—and his power over it—to anyone who cared to look.

"We believe she is in a small town in Arizona," Piterskij said while Yegor pulled his sleeveless undershirt over his head. "With the trial so close, our intelligence has been almost completely focused on finding the woman. We have people inside the telephone companies, of course, who have the technology to constantly scan phone records of all of Anistana King's known former friends and contacts."

Yegor slid his arms into his starched white shirt and began buttoning it. "Good, good."

"Krutov thought it well to look into this call that came from a cellular phone, as no calls have come from Arizona to any of these contacts. He called the mobile phone and recorded the female voice of the woman who answered. Alkash, who was present when her family was taken out, is certain he recognized her voice. We followed the cell phone's signal and believe it came from a small antique shop in that town."

For the first time in two years, Yegor felt a stirring in his gut. He would like to put a bullet into the head of the bitch himself. She'd identified his son, Dmitry, as her family's killer and put Dmitry behind bars for a day before Yegor had paid the exorbitant bail bond. She was also set to testify with damning evidence that could send his son to prison.

That would never do.

Yegor stepped into his Gucci loafers. "Do we have operatives close enough to get to her?"

"One in Phoenix, four hours from the town where she is hiding." A pleased look came into Piterskij's eyes. "Lev is on his way as we speak."

A good fuck and the good news picked up Yegor's spirits immensely. They would take out this Anistana King before she even testified. Charges dismissed. No one had the depth of information that the woman had.

Anistana King was their final target.

CHAPTER THREE

Daniel Parker ground his teeth and clenched the steering wheel of his black SUV with one fist while he pushed his other hand through his hair.

Goddamnit. Ani *knew* better. After two years she'd screwed up, and just a few days before the trial.

Jesus Christ.

He slammed his palm on the steering wheel as he sped down the I-10 freeway from Phoenix. The darkness was only illuminated by his headlights and the occasional lights of passing cars. The speed limit was seventy-five but his speedometer was pushing ninety.

At least the local cops had Ani. First call he'd made after talking with Ani was to the Bisbee Police Department. Not much later, an officer called back. They'd had three units, a car on each side of the three-sided end building, securing it. The cop said Ani was safe and they were waiting on orders from him. Daniel told the officer to take her to the police department and keep her under tight guard until he arrived.

Daniel had made it through Tucson and was closing in on Benson, but that was still a good fifty miles from where Ani was. An hour away.

The Russian Mafia was loaded with former KGB operatives as well as former Soviet military intelligence, GRU, operatives. They had people employed everywhere, and he had no doubt they had informants at the telephone company.

If Ani's call did get the Russians' attention there was a chance their own contacts in Tucson or Phoenix could get to the scene long before he did. A sniper could've taken her out the moment she walked out of the police cruiser to head into the department headquarters. The Russians wouldn't let any cops surrounding her stand in the way. No, they'd be picked off one by one.

The Russians were absolutely ruthless.

He hadn't told Ani, but the Russians had recently stepped up the search for her by plastering her picture all over the Internet, claiming she was a missing "heiress" and offering an obscene reward for her recovery. The info had passed from person to person by many who forwarded e-mail chain letters.

As soon as the Russians found her, they'd put a bullet in her head.

No way in hell was that going to happen. It went beyond what drove him to protect those he was assigned to.

When he was in the Judicial Security Division of the U.S. Marshals Service, he'd failed a judge whose courtroom he'd been assigned to. If he hadn't been distracted . . . If he'd seen the gun . . . If he could have thrown himself in the way . . .

He hadn't gotten to Judge Moore fast enough—but he wasn't about to let it happen again.

He wouldn't lose Ani.

After Daniel went on a leave of absence, a colleague had recommended Daniel to WITSEC, and he had transferred to the program to be trained as an Inspector, a Deputy Marshal who had the responsibility of keeping in touch with the witnesses he'd been assigned to and making sure they stuck to the rules and didn't break their contracts.

Most of the people in the Witness Security Program were basically thugs. They'd been involved in organized crime, drug trafficking, and other criminal activities, and were now testifying against those higher in the organization, usually to save their own asses.

But Ani . . . she was one of the few innocents forced into the program.

In the two years he'd known Ani, he'd admired her intelligence, her bravery—hell, everything about her. He didn't know when it happened, but something about their relationship had gone far beyond program participant and contact. She was off-limits, but he'd needed to talk to her weekly. Needed to hear her sensual voice.

He could still imagine her flowery scent and picture her full curves and vivid blue eyes. And her lips. He'd escorted her from the burn center, to rehab, then to different safe houses, including the one in Bisbee, where she'd been living up until now.

With the feelings she stirred up inside him, being around her was a bad idea. A real bad idea. He'd have to get another Inspector to take over the case once he got her to New York City to testify.

Without glancing down, Daniel slid his cell phone out of its holster on his belt. As he drove, he flipped the phone open and punched the speed-dial number for Ani without taking his eyes off the road. He'd pushed that button so many times he didn't have to look at his phone to call her.

He brought the phone to his ear as he caught up to a pair of red taillights and switched lanes to pass the vehicle, then moved back into the right lane. In moments he came up on the exit to Benson. If he was going to do any kind of fast driving through the small towns from here to Bisbee, he'd have to use his lights.

A ringing tone started on the other end of the line, but immediately the generic recording came on telling him to leave a message. Looked like she was listening to him in one regard—he'd told her not to talk with anyone.

When he took the exit, he slowed down but switched on his flashing red and blue strobes. He went a bit faster than he should have through the forty-five-, thirty-five-, then twenty-five-mile-an-hour zones. All of the small towns on this stretch of highway were speed traps, and he couldn't waste time being pulled over.

After the three small towns there was a long stretch of highway and a good thirty-minute drive to Bisbee. It felt as if he were driving a boat against a current.

When he finally reached the Mule Pass Tunnel he should have felt some relief, but he remained as tense as a coiled spring.

Ten more minutes and he'd be there.

Agonizing minutes.

Daniel finally reached the police department. He pulled out his credentials, shut off his flashing lights, then stepped from his SUV and headed into the department building.

"U.S. Deputy Marshal," Daniel said to the officer manning the front desk and showed the cop his creds.

After checking them out, the cop motioned him on.

Daniel strode to the back of the building where he'd been directed. In one glance he saw Ani wasn't in the room. Only one woman was there, other than a female police officer. The civilian woman was talking with a paramedic.

What the hell were paramedics doing here?

And where the hell was Ani?

His voice came out in a growl, carrying over the discussions in the room. "Where's Ani Carter?"

"I'm right here, Daniel." The familiar feminine voice came from the left of him—from the woman sitting next to a paramedic.

"Ani?" He narrowed his eyes, taking in the slender woman who looked so unlike the Ani he knew that he hadn't recognized her. But her crystalline blue gaze, her dark brown hair, small nose, and fair complexion were familiar even though her face was much thinner. What clinched it for him were her full lips. Lips he'd wanted to kiss way too many times.

Goddamnit. He had to get those thoughts out of his head and now.

She offered him a nervous-looking smile and he pushed his way past the officers in the room and past the paramedic. He crouched in front of her, wanting to take her in his arms, though he knew he couldn't. "Are you all right?"

"I'm fine." She looked down at her hands in her lap. "I'm so sorry."

He hooked his finger under her chin and forced her to look at him. "Everyone makes mistakes, honey," he said in a low voice that likely couldn't be heard by anyone but her. "But yours could get you killed. You can't take chances with your life."

A tear trickled down her cheek. "I just had to help that boy."

The desire to take her into his arms and hold her was so strong he found it difficult to restrain himself. He dropped his hand away from her face. "We've got to get you out of here."

"All right," she said quietly. "What do I need to do?"

"Wait here for a few moments." He couldn't be mad at her, no matter what had happened. "I'll be right back."

Daniel rose from his crouched position and turned away from her. He talked with a couple of officers before heading out to his SUV, then drove up so that the passenger side door was next to the rear door of the police department. He brought in an extra set of body armor for her to wear for protection. If he could, he'd make her wear a helmet—anything to protect every inch of her.

After she had the Kevlar vest on, over her blouse, he took her by the arm and, with the cover of several police officers, hustled her into the passenger seat of the SUV and slammed the door behind her.

He sucked in a deep breath of relief as he went to the driver's side. They'd gotten her this far. He'd never let anything happen to her.

When he climbed in and shut the door, he paused to look at her. "It's good to see you again, Ani."

She'd been staring at her lap, but her head jerked up when he spoke. "You're not mad?"

"Hell, yes, I'm mad." He reached over and gripped her forearm. "Because I was worried about you."

He shouldn't have touched her. A jolt traveled through him and he removed his hand. Her eyes widened, as if she felt the same electrical feeling he had.

Daniel forced himself to look away from her and turned his keys in the ignition. "Let's get out of here."

The drive back through the small towns and on to Tucson was less hurried, but the tenseness in his muscles wouldn't let go.

They were both quiet for a while, before Daniel said, "I've been looking forward to seeing you for a long time."

"You have?" She sounded so shocked that it surprised him.

"Ani, we've been talking to each other nearly

every week for a year now." He glanced at her. "Don't you think I'd like to see you?" Daniel clenched the wheel tighter. What the hell was he saying?

"I guess," she said as he focused his gaze on the road, and he frowned. "I mean, I feel the same way," she continued, "it's just the circumstances—"

"Are behind us now." He shifted his hold on the steering wheel.

This time when he glanced from the road to look at her she was smiling. She was so beautiful. He'd always thought she was, no matter what she looked like. It might take him some time to get used to this toothpick version of the woman he'd—

Daniel clenched his teeth.

Don't even go there.

After a moment's silence, she asked, "Where are we headed?"

"After we stay the night in Tucson, we'll take a puddle jumper to the Phoenix airport in the morning." Daniel guided the SUV into the passing lane. "We've booked a direct flight out of Sky Harbor to New York. Our plane leaves at noon."

She shuddered. "The trial. It's time."

Daniel gave a slow nod. She stared at his profile that was illuminated by the red dashboard lights. She'd memorized his features down to the shadow of a beard on his jaw. But now her heart was pounding like mad.

"Oh, jeez." She leaned her head against the headrest. "I can't believe it. So much time has gone by that it doesn't seem real now."

"It's real, honey," he said in his deep voice. "We've got to do everything we can to protect you."

Ani's belly did a little nosedive when he called her "honey," the endearment he'd used so many times on the phone. Maybe he said it to all women, but it made her feel special somehow.

"Have you had any more of those bad flashbacks from your PTSD?" he asked quietly. "You sure had me worried the last time."

"Not since then." Ani paused, then remembered that she nearly did this evening. "Well, I almost had one while I was waiting for the cops, but I pulled out of it."

He glanced at her. "Did something trigger this one or did it just come on?"

She shivered before she said, "I saw a man outside the window, watching the store. He dropped his cigarette butt and it reminded me of the fire—how it started."

Daniel's jaw was hard when he looked at her. "That could have been one of Borenko's men. They could already be on to you."

Ani took a deep breath. "The doorknob to the back room jiggled just before I heard police sirens."

Daniel cursed again. She saw him look at the rearview mirror as he said, "It's dark, and with the amount of traffic—it might be hard to see a tail."

"I'm sorry," she said, but this time Daniel didn't answer.

They were quiet most of the trip to Tucson. On the way, Daniel had Ani use his secure cell phone to call the hotel and make a reservation. Her stomach dropped to her toes when he said one room, no smoking, double beds.

Her voice shook as she made the reservation. Daniel and her sleeping in the same room?

That thought drove away her worries about the danger from the Russians.

Daniel. Her.

In the same room.

So that he could protect her, of course. That was it.

After she made the reservations, Ani could hardly think straight the rest of the way to Tucson. She didn't know what to do with her hands, so she clenched them in her lap. Every now and then, Daniel would glance her way, and she felt heat in her belly that traveled downward, and it wasn't to her toes.

When they arrived in Tucson, Daniel drove up and down several streets and said if they did have a tail he hoped they had shaken him off.

At the hotel, Ani walked beside Daniel up to the front counter, her high heels clicking against the stone-tiled floor in the large lobby. It was a nice place with a restaurant and a gift shop.

She had absolutely nothing with her but what she was wearing, which now included a plain navy blue windbreaker she had zipped up over the body armor. Daniel hadn't even let her bring her purse, her cell phone, and definitely not her credit cards. He'd forced her to leave them all at the police station. Now that the location where she worked had been exposed, her identity had been compromised.

Daniel had brought in a duffel bag with him, and

she wondered if he kept one packed in his SUV for emergencies.

Like helping a dumb protected witness who gave away her true identity to someone from her old life.

He'd put on his Stetson before heading into the hotel and that just about made her melt. Between that bod, the tight Wranglers, Stetson, and boots, she'd been a goner from the first time she met him.

Once Ani and Daniel checked in at the front desk, they took the elevator up to their floor. Daniel swiped the key card in its slot to let them into the room. It smelled of new carpeting and starched sheets when they walked in. She blinked in the darkness and Daniel switched on a light.

The first thing she noticed was that there was one king-sized bed in the room. Not double beds.

She could barely breathe and stood still. He tossed the duffel on the bed, laid his hat on a vanity table, and shrugged out of his plain dark blue windbreaker, which he discarded by draping it over a chair.

"I've got to take a shower." Exhaustion was evident in his voice and he rubbed his eyes with his thumb and forefinger. It was well after one in the morning. "Mind if I head into the bathroom first?"

"Uh, Daniel?" She swallowed hard when he turned to face her. "There's only one bed."

He cast a tired glance over his shoulder at the bed. "Yeah, there is," he said just before continuing into the bathroom.

Ani stared at his back and then the bathroom door

as he closed it. She was standing in the same spot when she heard the shower start.

She closed her eyes and imagined water running in rivulets over his hard, naked body. Her breathing elevated and her heart pounded more at the images. She knew his body would be perfection. Picturing his muscled form caused her nipples to harden and she ached between her thighs like she'd never ached before.

Ani opened her eyes and shook her head. In her fantasies she didn't have a scarred back or an equally ugly pit from a large bullet wound in her shoulder. Even if there was a chance of them getting together— a chance in hell—she couldn't handle him seeing the mess her lower back was now.

With a sigh, she kicked off her high heels. When she went to the mirror over the vanity she ran her hand through her thick, brunette hair. She'd lost the clip long ago. Tired, red eyes stared back at her. Mascara smudged one cheek, her makeup pretty much gone from crying. Her black slacks were wrinkled and her white silk shirt limp and clinging to her skin.

This was all she had to wear and she was flying with Daniel to New York tomorrow. She sighed again as the weight of the day settled on her shoulders. She was so, so, tired. She pushed out of the windbreaker Daniel had loaned her, and tossed it on the chair by his.

The door to the bathroom opened, sending wafts of steam into the bedroom along with the clean scent of soap. Suddenly she didn't feel so tired.

Instead, her mouth watered and she could feel the

ache in her nipples as they pressed against her bra. Daniel was rubbing a towel over his head and wearing another towel low around his hips. She'd never seen him in anything but jeans and shirts, and *oh, my God,* did he look delicious.

Fortunately, he didn't seem to notice her panting or her tongue hanging out. Instead he went to his duffel bag, pulled out a T-shirt, and tossed it to her. "Will that do to sleep in?" She caught it and he went back to towel-drying his hair.

A little more and that towel around his waist would just slip off . . .

"The bathroom's all yours if you want it," he said in his smooth drawl.

"Um, yeah." She gripped the T-shirt tight against her chest. "Thanks."

She darted into the bathroom, closed the door, and leaned against it. Crap. Daniel was bound to see how attracted she was to him, and even if he *was* interested in her, they couldn't do anything about it. And she wouldn't want him seeing her—or touching the twisted flesh on her back.

Daniel's body armor was lying on the floor in a heap with the rest of his clothing and boots. She paused to look at the armor. This was what protected him when he was out on the job.

Ani fumbled with the vest Daniel had given her for protection. When she managed to get it off, she put it on top of his. She slipped out of her clothes and folded them on the marble vanity.

She climbed into the shower and let the warm water

ease her tired muscles and relax the tendons at her neck. The hotel's almond-scented shampoo, conditioner, and soap were all relaxing.

Ani felt almost human again when she climbed out of the shower and toweled herself off. The hotel hair dryer was handy, so she used it to get her hair mostly dry. The shirt Daniel had loaned her to sleep in had U.S. MARSHAL emblazoned on the back. When she slipped it on, his masculine scent surrounded her. The shirt was so big on her—or she was just so small now—that it hung to mid-thigh. It was one of the most erotic sensations, to be wearing his T-shirt with no underwear. Nothing had happened, and nothing would, but she always had her imagination.

After hand-washing her bra and panties, she hung them over the shower curtain and picked up her blouse and slacks from where she'd left them on one end of the marble vanity. She slipped into the bedroom, her heart thumping like mad. This was going to be so awkward.

But when she saw Daniel she had to stop and smile. He was passed out cold on one side of the bed, on his back on top of the bedspread. He wore a T-shirt that matched hers and a pair of jogging shorts, and one of his arms was resting across his eyes. She shook her head and went to the closet to hang up the blouse and slacks. She'd just have to iron out the wrinkles in the morning.

Before turning off the light beside the bed she had to study him. He was even better looking than she'd remembered. All those muscles, sinewy forearms, and carved biceps. She was so in lust.

And so in love.

"Nope, nope, nope," she mumbled to herself. "Not happening, not happening, *not happening.*"

She turned off the switch and slipped under the sheets on her side of the bed.

Oh, the sheets felt so good against her skin and the soft pillow . . .

Ani woke to the sensation of being cocooned. Like she was enveloped in a big bear hug.

She blinked to see it was morning, that she was in a hotel room, and Daniel's arm was draped around her waist, his thigh over hers. He was still on top of the covers and she was beneath them, but she was now spooned up against him, her back to his chest. She felt completely and totally safe . . . and loved.

And good Lord, but the man had an early-morning erection that nearly made her moan out loud. She wasn't wearing any panties and the sensation of being naked beneath that shirt made her feel naughty, sexy, and she felt moisture in between her thighs. Nothing but a bedspread separated them now.

To have him inside her . . .

Ani closed her eyes for a moment and pretended that she could wake up every morning like this. With Daniel up against her back and surrounding her with his big body. And then he'd make love to her . . .

"You smell like almonds and woman." His voice was sleep roughened and she groaned when he nuzzled her hair. "So good."

He gave a low rumble and pressed his erection tighter against her back, rocking his hips as if he were taking her. Butterflies flitted in her belly and she ached even more between her thighs. She couldn't hold back a whimper.

Could they?

"Christ!" He drew away from her so suddenly it startled her. "Honey, I'm sorry," he said when she rolled over to look at him and met his coffee-brown eyes. He was already on his feet on the other side of the bed. He ran his fingers through his rumpled brown hair. "I didn't mean—damn."

She didn't know what to say, so she just studied him. What was going through his head?

"I want—I can't—*damn*." He grabbed his duffel bag and strode to the bathroom. "I've got to take a shower," he said, and mumbled under his breath, "A freezing cold one."

Ani didn't think he'd intended for her to hear that last part. If what had just happened meant anything, he had the same intense attraction that she felt for him, or at least partly.

She shouldn't even be going down that path. The main reason being he was a federal agent assigned to protect her, not sleep with her. What she wanted—even if he wanted the same thing—just couldn't happen.

A long, shuddering sigh rose up in her chest. She shouldn't be thinking this way, but she couldn't help it. She wanted Daniel more than she'd wanted anything in her life.

CHAPTER FOUR

Daniel came out of the bathroom with a distracted expression. Ani barely held back a groan of appreciation at how delicious he looked. He was wearing Wranglers, a plain black T-shirt, and blue overshirt. His hair was damp from his shower and his eyes filled with concern.

"Listen, Ani?" He braced one hand against the doorframe to the bathroom and glanced down at his booted feet. He raised his head and his gaze met hers. "I'm sorry about this morning. I don't know how it happened."

"Don't worry about it." Ani's lips trembled as she smiled. She was sitting on the side of the bed and she gripped the sheets in her fists. "It's okay, really."

He raked his hand through his wet hair. "No, it's not okay. I'll need to get another Inspector assigned to your case as soon as possible."

Panic rose like a geyser in her chest. She pushed herself from the bed and walked up to him. "No. Don't leave me, please. You're the only one I trust."

Daniel placed his hands on her shoulders and the heat of his touch went straight through her. She tipped her head back as she looked at him.

He was close enough to kiss. "I shouldn't have called you so much this past year, Ani."

"I needed you," she whispered. "I looked forward to every single call."

A serious expression crossed his face as he rubbed her shoulders. His jaw tightened. "Goddamnit, I can't do my job like this."

She felt him slipping away from her and tears stung the backs of her eyes. "I mean it. Don't leave me, okay? I still need you."

Daniel brought her roughly to him in a tight hug. She wrapped her arms around his waist and rested her cheek against his chest. He smelled of spice and male, just like the T-shirt she still wore. She heard his heartbeat and felt the comfort of his embrace.

He buried his nose in her hair. "I can't do this. I want to, but I can't."

"Just give it some time, please?" She didn't care if she sounded like she was begging. "I don't know if I can go through this without you. Testifying, seeing Dmitry Borenko . . . I'm so scared."

Finally, he said, "I'll take care of you, I promise." Daniel's deep inhale was audible. His voice lowered and he squeezed her tighter. "No way in hell is anything happening to you."

He ran his palms up her arms then drew her away from him. She tilted her head up again and saw him staring at her mouth. He looked hungry and the thrill it sent through her belly made her want to reach up and kiss him.

But no, she didn't want to lose him.

She backed away and he let his arms drop to his sides. "I'd better get ready to go." Ani said. "I, um, need to iron my clothing and get dressed." She was acutely aware of being naked beneath his T-shirt. "We have a plane to catch."

His eyes were dark as he nodded and she scooted to the closet and pulled out the iron and ironing board.

Daniel had never felt such desire for a woman as he did while he watched Ani. Her dark brown hair shielded her eyes and he knew she was avoiding his gaze. It was better that way.

But he couldn't stop staring at her, thinking how adorable she looked wearing his T-shirt. His cock felt as hard as it had this morning when he came to his senses after nearly taking her right in that bed. All he'd had to do was climb under the covers, pull down his gym shorts, yank up that T-shirt, and drive into her. With her underwear hanging over the shower rail, he knew she was wearing nothing under that shirt.

Well, they had been hanging up. They fell into his shower and were now soaking wet. When he'd picked them up he'd held the lace and satin and pictured Ani in them. And then Ani naked beneath his shirt. Then Ani with nothing on at all.

He ground his teeth and clenched one fist as he turned away from her. *Goddamnit*. He had to control his thoughts and his body. His cock was so hard right now his jeans were nearly strangling him.

When she finished ironing, and headed toward the bathroom, he stopped her. "Uh, honey? I accidentally knocked your underwear into the shower. It's soaked."

Ani's jaw dropped. "I can't go without underwear. I'll have to use the blow-dryer."

"Sorry." He did his best to look apologetic. "But we've got to get out of here. They can dry out on the way."

She rolled her eyes. "Oh, sure. We'll just tie them to the back of the SUV and let them flap in the wind."

He laughed at the image and shook his head. "Come on, let's get you dressed."

"I can dress fine by myself." Ani grabbed her freshly ironed slacks and blouse and marched into the bathroom.

Ah . . . He hadn't meant it quite like that, but the idea did have merit.

It only took her a few minutes. When she came out she looked self-conscious—and he could see exactly why. The nipples and areolas of her full breasts could be seen clearly through the white blouse.

She crossed her arms over her breasts. "I can't go anywhere like this."

Daniel tried not to smile. "You have to wear body armor over it anyway. You can use one of my T-shirts over the armor."

"It itches and it's going to rub my—" Her cheeks turned red and this time he had to stifle a laugh.

He picked up the body armor from where he'd set it on the vanity in the bedroom. "I'll help you get it on."

When he approached her, Ani bit her lower lip. He started slipping it on her and his hand brushed her breast. She gasped and he nearly groaned at the feel of her hard nipple and the silk against his knuckles. As he fastened the armor his hands kept brushing her body as if they had a mind of their own. She looked up at him and her lips parted.

Those lips . . .

Christ.

This was killing him.

When he finished helping her with her body armor, Daniel gave Ani one of his plain black T-shirts. She couldn't very well go walking through a hotel with body armor visible. The T-shirt was so big on her she had to tie it on one side. After she slipped on her high heels and pulled on the plain blue windbreaker Daniel had loaned her, he packed his stuff in his duffel.

They headed downstairs to the hotel lobby, and made it out into the morning sunshine. The SUV was parked next to the entrance of the hotel. Out of habit, he scanned the lot. It looked clear.

It was October, but still sunny in Arizona. There was a light chill to the air and he was glad for the windbreaker Ani was wearing to keep her from getting cold. The air smelled crisp and clean and the asphalt was wet from rain that had fallen overnight.

Daniel's stomach rumbled and Ani looked up at him and grinned.

They skirted a puddle of water as he kept an eye on the parking lot. "We'll get something to eat on the way to Phoenix. Maybe Micky D's," he said after they reached the SUV and he started to help her into the passenger seat.

Tires squealed on asphalt.

A shot rang out in the parking lot.

The window by Ani's head shattered.

She screamed.

"Down!" Daniel shouted as he shoved her so that she was half lying on the console.

Another shot exploded behind him.

Pain slammed into his upper back, knocking the wind out of him as he took a direct hit against his Kevlar vest.

His vision darkened and he struggled to catch his breath, but adrenaline kept him going and he dove in after Ani. She gasped and gave a cry as he climbed over her to the driver's side, shutting the passenger door behind him.

Head down, Daniel jammed his keys in the ignition.

The driver's side window shattered as he turned the ignition.

Through the sideview mirror he saw a white Nissan pull up behind them, the shooter leaning out the window.

Daniel revved the SUV's engine, slammed it into reverse.

Tires squealed then metal crunched as he rammed the SUV into the Nissan.

Ani cried out as she hit the dash with her shoulder.

The shooter flew backward from the impact and his next shot went wild.

Daniel spun the SUV through the parking lot. He'd deliberately made sure there was an easy escape route when they'd arrived at the hotel.

The bastards had hidden well, waiting until Daniel and Ani were in the open.

Another shot hit one of his tires specially designed not to go completely flat when punctured. Originally the tires were used for luxury cars, but now law enforcement agencies were experimenting with them. The warning light on his dashboard lit up, showing his right rear tire had been hit.

Daniel tore through the lot trying to keep low at the same time he bolted into the street, nearly sideswiping a catering van. He wove through traffic, the white car flying after them.

Ani stayed down. "Are you hurt?" he shouted as he tried to evade the shooters.

He switched on his lights and siren as he approached an intersection with a red light. He flew through it.

"No," she shouted over the wail of Daniel's siren.

He checked his sideview mirror again. The Nissan was gaining on them.

Daniel ground his teeth, keeping his sirens and lights on as he dodged his way through traffic. He sailed through another light and threw a look over his shoulder just in time to see a Mack truck making a left in front of the speeding Nissan. The crunch of metal slamming against metal was loud enough to hear over the sirens. The Nissan flipped in the air, landed on its top, and spun across the intersection.

Daniel took a deep breath and turned off his sirens and lights. His heart still pounded. "That was too damned close." He glanced in his rearview mirror to see if anyone else was following them. Looked clear.

Wind whipped in through the broken windows. After he checked his rearview and sideview mirrors again, he looked at Ani, who was covered with the shattered safety glass. "Stay down a little longer. Sure you're all right?"

Her face was pressed up against the console. "As well as one can be after getting shot at," she said with a groan. "How about you?"

"Fine." If it wasn't for the body armor he'd be a dead man. His back hurt like hell from the power of the shot, but he was certain the bullet hadn't pierced his armor. He'd just have a bruise the size of a melon.

Daniel continued to drive, putting as much distance between the hotel and the shooters as he could, even though they'd been taken down by a Mack. The men could have jacked another vehicle if either the shooter or the driver survived or were uninjured. But, for now, it didn't look like he and Ani were being followed. Hell, who knew if the men had backup?

"We've got to ditch the SUV and I need to call this incident in," Daniel muttered at the same time his cell phone rang.

He jerked it out of its holster, flipped it open, and brought it to his ear. "Parker."

"You two are hot," came Jameson's voice.

"Tell me something I don't know." Daniel looked

in his rearview mirror again. "We just made it through some serious gunfire."

"Shit." Jameson growled. "Catch that plane and get the hell out of there."

"On it," Daniel said. "Vehicle's pretty shot up. I'm heading to the headquarters on Broadway to make an exchange."

"I'll call ahead," Jameson said, and told Daniel he'd notify the police to arrest the shooters when they reached the scene of the accident.

Daniel snapped his phone shut and reholstered it.

He checked his mirrors yet again. Still looked clear. "You can get up." He cut his attention back to the street then to her.

She sat up and brushed glass from her hair, which was flying around her face in the wind from the shattered windows. She had a cut across one cheek, her face was pale, but other than that she looked fine.

Daniel sucked in a deep breath of relief.

When they reached the U.S. Marshals Tucson headquarters, he turned the vehicle into the lot and parked directly in front of the back door so he could hurry Ani into the station, keeping her exposure to a minimum. Two Deputy Marshals were there to cover her as they took her inside.

Daniel swung the shot-up vehicle into a parking space. After checking the lot around him, he rushed through the door at the back of the building.

One of the Deputies was directing Ani to a chair. "I need to doctor that cut on your face," he was saying.

"We've got to get to the airport." Daniel raked his

fingers through his hair as he spoke to the operations supervisor. "Our flight leaves in an hour."

Atkins shook his head. "Phoenix and Tucson airports are shut down—terrorist threats."

"What the hell?" Daniel stared at the Deputy Marshal.

"Calls to Sky Harbor and Tucson International were made about fifteen minutes ago. Both came from a pay phone in New York City," Atkins said. "Both airports are going nuts. All air traffic in Arizona is grounded. With the exception of the military."

"Borenko." Daniel scrubbed his hand over his face. "Borenko is throwing a net out and reeling us in."

Daniel's cell phone rang. He snatched it from its holster and answered, "Parker."

"Bastards are trying to cage you and your witness," Jameson said.

"Figured that." Daniel pinched the bridge of his nose. "Now what in the hell do we do from here?"

"Head straight to the National Guard in Phoenix." Jameson had a frustrated tone to his voice. "They'll have a plane ready to get your asses to New York."

Daniel snapped the phone shut and looked to Atkins. "I need a vehicle."

"You've got it."

Fifteen minutes later, Daniel had moved all his equipment into a black Ford Explorer and Ani was ushered into the SUV. When he was ready to put it into drive he glanced at her. She looked absolutely miserable.

"Are you okay, honey?" he said.

"All this is my fault." She balled her fist on her thigh. "I really screwed up."

She had, but Daniel didn't blame her. Instead, he found himself wishing he could kiss the wrinkles from her forehead and the frustration from her lips. His gut clenched. He had to stop thinking that way about her. If he turned her over to another Inspector . . .

She'd be taken to Phoenix—

The skin at the back of his neck prickled. If Borenko was calling the shots, the Russians would be waiting exactly for that. There were only two ways to get to Phoenix from Tucson. The drive through Florence would be suicide. Backcountry highway with long stretches of nothing.

Highway I-10 was a possibility, but the long arms of Borenko would likely reach to every possible airport, including the National Guard's. No doubt whatsoever in his mind—they'd be waiting in ambush. That was why the Borenkos had called in the terrorist threats.

He'd bet a year's salary that what they wouldn't expect was for Daniel and Ani to head through Albuquerque or El Paso. Both were around six-plus hours away, with El Paso having a good hundred thousand more residents than Albuquerque.

"Everything will turn out fine," Daniel said as he put the Explorer into gear. "Just hang in there and we'll make it."

A look of determination crossed her features.

"More than anything, I want to put away the man who killed Mom, Dad, and Jenn."

At the mention of Ani's sister's name, Daniel's jaw tensed. He'd always hated the fact he hadn't been allowed to tell her . . . Should he tell Ani now?

Fuck. Not possible. It would put his job on the line and possibly put Ani in more danger. After the trial—then he could tell her before she went back into the program.

He drove the SUV out of the lot.

"Aren't we taking I-10 to Phoenix?" she asked as she glanced at him.

"We're taking I-10," he said, "but we're heading east to El Paso."

When she stared at him, he added, "I think it will be safer this way."

She nodded. "The Russians won't expect that, will they," she said as a statement, not as a question.

Daniel guided the Explorer through traffic and headed for the freeway. "That's what I'm counting on."

It was almost seven at night when they reached El Paso. Daniel was beat, and his back ached between his shoulder blades where his vest had taken a bullet.

Ani looked like she felt as exhausted as he was even though she had dozed off several times on the way. The scratch on her cheek that she'd gotten from broken glass during the shooting was dark against her fair skin.

The entire time he drove toward El Paso, Daniel kept glancing at that scratch.

He couldn't allow another person in his care to die. One mistake was all it had taken back in D.C. to get Judge Moore dead.

The judge had been receiving death threats and the Marshals Service took threats to judiciary officials more than seriously. Daniel had been assigned to guard Judge Moore within the courtroom and had kept constant surveillance on those assembled inside, and he thought, at the time, that he was doing a damned good job.

But he didn't see it coming.

That one mistake.

Heat burned in Daniel's gut at the memory. Somehow the killer had procured a visitor's pass and had a functioning plastic gun strapped to his ankle. And he'd had someone on the inside who smuggled in a couple of bullets.

That was all the sonofabitch had needed.

Daniel clenched his hands around the steering wheel.

After declaring a recess, Judge Moore had stood at her bench, prepared to step down. Daniel had turned to look behind him at two men who were arguing.

He took his attention off his principal for just a brief moment.

Then a movement had caught his eye. The moment Daniel spotted the gun, he'd shouted and dove to take the bullet—

But the bullet got to Judge Moore first.

Blood had splattered through her robe. She fell back, her eyes wide and sightless.

Daniel pinched the bridge of his nose with his thumb and forefinger.

If only he'd been more vigilant. If only he hadn't let the two men arguing behind the barrier distract him even for a second. If only he'd spotted that gun, the judge would still be alive.

He glanced over at Ani, at the scratch on her face. *No more mistakes.*

As they drove, Daniel had constantly stayed alert for anybody following them, but he was positive they weren't being tailed.

He'd called his regional office and explained what they were doing. Jameson didn't sound pleased, but Daniel figured it was because Jameson hadn't thought of it first. The man liked to make the plans and have them followed to the letter.

One of the administrative support staff was arranging a flight out of Fort Bliss for the following morning. They'd have one of the U.S. Marshals private jets fly in from Dallas, and then head straight for a hangar in New Jersey.

Daniel and Ani would have to hole up in a hotel for another night. The assistant made reservations for them at a decent hotel—with room service as Daniel insisted. They didn't need to take the chance of being seen while going out to eat. The way Ani's picture had been plastered on the Internet, she might be recognized despite the fact she was thinner.

It was dark by the time they reached the hotel in El

Paso and he was starving. They'd made a stop for food and a couple of bathroom breaks along the way, but Daniel was ready for a good meal.

The fact that he'd be sharing a room with Ani again set him on edge. He'd make sure they'd have double beds this time.

After they checked in, they headed up to their room. They were standing in the elevator when Ani clapped her hand over her mouth.

He raised an eyebrow. "What?"

Ani dropped her hand away her mouth. "I left my underwear at the hotel."

Daniel went hard in a hurry at the thought of Ani being naked beneath her slacks and body armor. He shifted his duffel bag to hide his erection, which made his jeans so tight he ground his teeth.

Bad idea, Parker. Should have had another Inspector take her to New York.

Was it just an excuse that he didn't trust her safety to anyone but himself?

When they went into the hotel room, shut the door behind them, and flipped on the lights, both relief and disappointment flooded Daniel as he saw there were two beds this time, just like he'd requested.

The way he'd felt waking up with her in his arms this morning—it had been heaven.

Trying to get his mind off being in bed with Ani, he tossed his duffel and Stetson on one of the beds and searched for a room service menu.

"I've got to get out of this thing." Ani pulled the T-shirt over her head, revealing the body armor.

His muscles tensed as he looked at her. He remembered the silk shirt she wore under the armor—with no bra. His cock hardened even more but he tried to ignore the pressure against his jeans.

"Let me help," he found himself saying and moving closer to her.

Ani looked up at him and audibly caught her breath.

Those lips . . . he wanted to kiss her more than anything.

He forced himself to act impartial as he helped her take off the body armor. She stood so still, like she was afraid to move.

"Is there something wrong?" he asked as he finished unfastening the Velcro on one side.

She licked her lips and continued to look up at him. "Nothing," she whispered.

As he removed her armor, he brushed one of her silk-covered nipples with his knuckles.

Ani gasped. Her lips parted and her beautiful eyes widened. He tossed the armor aside and heard its soft thump on the carpet. Mesmerized, his gaze landed on her full breasts. Her dark nipples and areolas showed clearly through the white silk. Her nipples were hard and raising the soft fabric.

Daniel tried to breathe, but it was nearly impossible.

His muscles strained, wanting to touch her, taste her. His cock was primed to be inside her.

He raised his gaze to meet hers and saw the same desire reflected in her eyes.

The muscles of his throat worked as he stared at

her, unable to break the connection. It seemed like everything around them, the world, life, had come to a grinding halt.

Goddamnit. He was a U.S. Deputy Marshal assigned to protect Ani. Not have sex with her.

It was the hardest thing he'd ever done, but Daniel clenched his fists and turned away.

CHAPTER FIVE

Yegor narrowed his eyes as Piterskij approached him. His second in command's footsteps made no sound as he walked across the lush burgundy carpeting of Yegor's office.

Piterskij cleared his throat as he reached the enormous mahogany desk. "Our associates were unsuccessful in eliminating Anistana King in Arizona."

"Urody!" Yegor roared as he pushed his considerable bulk from his leather chair. The chair flew back and hit the wall behind him with a muted thump. He braced his palms on the papers scattered across his desk.

"Lev was unable to take out the target before the police arrived." Piterskij's features were hard and cold. "Lev followed the target with her police escort to the police department. The King woman was then taken to Tucson by a man he believes to be a U.S. Deputy Marshal."

Piterskij's body was clearly tense but he remained

still, his hands behind his back, as he continued. "Lev and another associate staked out the hotel. This morning they tried to take out the woman, but failed again. Our associates attempted to follow the target, but were impeded by an auto accident."

Yegor picked up a brass bull paperweight and considered heaving it at Piterskij. "Tell me, what about the terrorist threats on Arizona air traffic? What happened to our stakeouts of every possible avenue to Phoenix and every military base?" He clenched the paperweight tighter. "Tell me!"

Piterskij's Adam's apple bobbed as he spoke, but he exhibited no fear. "The target and her escort never showed. We believe they may have headed in the opposite direction. Perhaps El Paso or Albuquerque, the next two towns with large airports. El Paso has Fort Bliss."

The bull weighed heavier in Yegor's hand and a vein pulsed at his forehead as he let out a string of curses. Putting his weight behind the throw, he flung the bull across the room. With a loud crack the bull buried its head in the wall and hung there.

Piterskij flinched.

Yegor's breathing grew heavy and he placed both palms on his desk again. His arms shook with the force of his anger. "What do you intend to do now to rectify this situation?"

"We will find associates to stake out the airports in both cities and as near as possible to the military base." Piterskij extended one hand from behind his back, holding out a photograph. "Lev hired a photographer to witness the executions and provide the evidence to you. Before the attempts were made, the photographer captured the target and the Deputy Marshal with his camera."

Yegor reached for the photograph, which was clear enough to see her features. "This is the bitch? I remember her as quite fat."

"Lev is certain it is her," Piterskij said. "Apparently her appearance has changed considerably."

"Get this picture on the news and in the papers in Albuquerque and El Paso." Yegor thrust the photograph back at Piterskij. "Find our 'missing heiress' and offer a million-dollar reward for her return to her 'family.' The moment she is brought to the meeting place, kill her. No ties to *our* family."

Piterskij bowed. "As you wish," he said, before turning and striding out the door.

As Piterskij walked out, two little girls ran in, giggling. The five-year-old twins had their blond hair in ringlets, wore matching pink dresses and shiny black patent leather shoes, and each carried her favorite doll. *"Dedushka!"* they shouted, calling him grandfather in Russian.

Everything else evaporated for the moment as he laughed, crouched, and hugged his granddaughters. Dmitry followed the girls into the room, and Yegor spared his son a glance.

A moment of blackness clouded Yegor's mind at the thought that the girls' father, Dmitry, could be put behind bars because of that King bitch.

Still giggling, the girls released him and he stood

to stroke their silky curls. His beautiful girls, Natasha and Alyona, were the pride of Yegor's life.

He would take care of business so that his grand-daughters would never be separated from their father.

CHAPTER SIX

When Daniel turned away, Ani's heart clenched. He wanted her—that much was obvious. Currents of electricity still crackled in the air around them.

With his back to her, he gripped the doorframe to the bathroom to either side of him. His knuckles were white, his shoulders tensed, and his voice hoarse when he said, "I don't know if I can do this, Ani."

She couldn't get a word out to save her life. All she could do was look at the man she wanted more than anything, knowing that he was right, they couldn't take their relationship any further than they already had.

Daniel slammed one of his fists against the wall, startling her into taking a step back. Without looking at her, he leaned over and grabbed his duffel bag from off the floor, headed into the bathroom, and shut the door behind him. Hard enough to rattle the lamp on the desk.

The hurt burning in Ani's chest didn't make any sense as she sank onto the bed. She stared at the console where the TV perched, not really seeing it. "If we go any further I'll lose him," she whispered aloud.

She shook her head. No. she wasn't about to lose Daniel. She'd do her best not to get too close to him, to keep her distance. It was better for them both.

While the shower ran, she kicked off her high heels and peeled off the clothes she'd been wearing for two days now. They felt sticky and dirty, and her feet hurt from wearing those damned heels for so long. She'd wash her clothing as best as she could with shampoo and use the hair dryer to get most of the wetness out, then let them hang dry. At least she wouldn't forget her blouse and pants like she did her underwear.

By the time Daniel came out of the bathroom, she was in one of the hotel robes that she'd put on until it was her turn to shower. He was wearing jogging shorts and a T-shirt, and looked so good she couldn't hold back a sigh. There was so much raw power in the way he moved.

"I'll order room service." Daniel avoided her gaze for a moment as he picked up the menu by the telephone on the table next to the TV. He looked up and met her eyes. "What are you hungry for?"

The first thing that popped into her mind was "you," and she almost slapped herself upside the head. She gave him a strained smile. "Medium-well cheeseburger with fries. A Pepsi would be great, too."

With a nod, he turned away as soon as she gave him the order and picked up the phone. Ani put on the façade that she'd always worn when she'd lived in the kind of elite circles where faking her true feelings was the norm, and she walked into the bathroom.

Daniel's grip on the telephone receiver was so hard it was a wonder he didn't crush it in his fist. He gave the order to whoever was on the other end of the room service line then slammed down the receiver.

He raked his fingers through his wet hair. What the hell was he going to do? Ani was like a drug. He was addicted to her, and he didn't want to let her out of his sight. Didn't trust anyone else with her life even though he knew there were damn fine agents in the service.

It occurred to him that Ani didn't have any personal items with her and they hadn't had a second to take a breath and get anything. He called down to the hotel gift shop and they sent up a toothbrush, toothpaste, and deodorant within a few minutes. He'd answered the door with his gun in his hand, behind his back, ready for anything.

After a good half hour, Ani reappeared from the bathroom at the same time another knock came at the door. No doubt room service. Again, unwilling to take a chance with her life, he drew his Glock and held it behind his back with his right hand as he checked the peephole. "Get in the bathroom just to be safe," he said, and she obeyed immediately.

A man with a round tray stacked with silver-domed items stood in the hallway. Daniel kept his gun behind his back as he unlocked the door.

The waiter started to come into the room, but Daniel stopped him by stepping in front of him. "Just set it on the floor," he said, still holding his Glock behind him.

After the waiter left with a puzzled expression Daniel shut the door. The delicious smells of hamburgers and fries made his stomach growl as he set his gun where he could easily reach it.

Daniel didn't expect anything to happen at this hotel, but the bastards had caught him by surprise in Tucson. He and Ani must have been followed from Bisbee. No other explanation made sense.

He picked up the tray and carried it to a table on the far side of the room. "It's clear, honey," he said, and immediately tensed. He had to stop calling her that. It was too intimate.

Ani slipped out of the bathroom and took the chair opposite him. They were quiet at first as they dug into their food.

"This is so good." Ani closed her eyes. "Orgasmic." Her eyes flew open and her face turned several shades of red when her gaze met his.

He couldn't stop the grin that crept across his face. She was so cute when she was embarrassed.

The tension between them seemed to evaporate and she smiled, too. They started talking again like they always had over the telephone. Comfortable, easy camaraderie. Only this time he got to watch her instead of just hearing her over the phone. She talked with her hands and had to keep putting her cheeseburger down when she spoke.

"How are your brothers doing?" Ani asked as she toyed with a French fry on her plate, rolling the end in ketchup.

Daniel shrugged. "Jacob's on leave for a couple of weeks, staying with Dad up in Montana, and I don't know where the hell Aaron is." Jacob was a Navy SEAL while Aaron served in Special Forces, and most of the time Daniel didn't know where either of them were.

Ani propped her elbow on the table, her chin in her palm. "Did the three of you get along very well when you were growing up?"

Daniel bit into his hamburger and chewed as he thought a moment, then answered. "We're so close in age that all we did was fight most of the time. We about drove Mom insane." A familiar pang twinged his heart as it always did when he thought about their mom. "She put up with a lot when we were kids. And with Dad out in the field so much, she had her hands full with us."

Ani's voice softened. "You told me once—you were twelve when she passed away?"

"Yeah." Daniel ate a fry then took a drink of his soda. "I'm the oldest, so I ended up having to grow up pretty fast to help out with my brothers who were eleven and ten."

"What happened to her?" Ani asked, her pretty blue eyes meeting his.

"An aneurism." It had been damn near twenty years ago, but it still sent a sharp ache through his chest. "We were outside and she was watching my brothers and me race our bikes around the ranch. One moment she was standing. The next, she was on the ground."

Ani's expression held sadness for his loss. "I miss my mom so much, too. But at least I got to know her a while longer."

Daniel wiped his mouth with his napkin. "It was a long time ago."

"I'm sorry." Ani reached over and squeezed his hand. "She must have been in her thirties at most."

Having Ani ask him such personal questions didn't bother him. She'd told him a lot about her childhood over the past year, but he'd been pretty vague about his own. Now, though . . . Now their relationship went a little more beyond professional, even if they had to rein in their attraction to one another.

She seemed to catch herself and removed her hand from his, her cheeks a little pink. "One time you said your mother got you started on your hobby of collecting and building model airplanes."

He couldn't help a smile. "She said when she was young that it was the tomboy in her—that she had always loved the hobby, and Granddad encouraged her. I still have most of her collection."

"Tell me about it," she said as she toyed with another fry.

"You need to eat." He pointed to her partially eaten cheeseburger. "Instead of talking so much."

Ani smiled and picked up her cheeseburger. As he spoke, she appeared fascinated as he told her a little about his hobby, and he enjoyed talking with her about it.

When he'd finished his food, she said she was done. She'd only eaten half of her cheeseburger, so he finished that half as well as some of her fries.

The smell of the apple pie called to him, and when they ate it, he practically inhaled his piece. Apples, cinnamon, soft crust. "My mom made the best apple pies," Daniel said after he took his last bite. "This is good, but nothing compares to hers."

Ani smiled back but he could see exhaustion catching up with her from the droopiness in her eyelids to her slack posture.

He stood and automatically held his hand out. "Let's get you to bed."

They both went still, but after a pause Ani took his hand and he helped her up from the chair. The warmth of her touch went straight to his cock and he hoped she didn't notice the tent in his jogging shorts from his instant hard-on.

"I got you some toothpaste and a toothbrush." He gestured to an end table. "Over there."

She looked up at him with an expression of relief. "Thank you."

He smiled and waited for her to brush her teeth and return to the bedroom.

When she was finished, Daniel followed her to one of the beds and she turned to look up at him with her crystalline blue eyes.

"Thank you for watching over me, Daniel," she said softly.

He brushed his knuckles across her cheek and she closed her eyes. Those lips. Just one kiss—

And he'd never be able to stop.

Instead he placed a light kiss on her forehead and drew away. The scent of mint from the hotel's shampoo and the warm smell of her skin flooded his system.

Ani opened her eyes and tilted her head back.

He swallowed and took a step back. "Good night."

" 'Night," she said, then drew back the covers on her bed and crawled under them. She faced away from his bed as if knowing they needed to keep every bit of distance they could.

Daniel turned to his own bed and wondered how he was going to make it through the next few days.

Her clothes were still damp from washing them last night. With a groan, Ani stood in the bathroom and dried her silk blouse the best she could with the hotel blow-dryer. Her slacks would just have to stay damp.

When she was done with her blouse she slipped into it, then the body armor. Over it she pulled one of Daniel's plain black T-shirts and tied it off to the side. She needed to cover her armor to make sure she didn't stand out in public. This time she made sure she was out of his sight when she put on her clothing. They needed to fight this incredible attraction before they took it too far.

Maybe after the trial was over . . . would he be interested in pursuing a relationship with her then? Could he? She bit her lower lip. She'd likely have to stay in WITSEC and there would be no way she and

Daniel could manage any kind of personal ties. She'd likely have to move to another state, which would probably mean a new Inspector Marshal.

She needed to put things in perspective and acknowledge the fact that she had to stop this infatuation and keep her distance.

It didn't take them long to get ready. After she slipped on her high heels, they headed down in the elevator to the lobby. It was a busy day in the hotel—looked like a whole crowd had come in for a convention. The lines in front of the registration desk were long enough to reach across the lobby.

To avoid the throng, Daniel and Ani walked around the crowd to the sports lounge. They had to go down three or four steps into the sunken lounge. She waved cigarette and cigar smoke out of her face and wrinkled her nose.

She glanced around the lounge, which was full of big, beefy men—some muscular and some who could stand to lose a few pounds—or fifty. Maybe some kind of professional wrestling competition was in town. The heavy smell of testosterone from that many men in one crowded place was nearly as bad as the lounge's cigarette and beer stench. Maybe worse.

Ani came to a complete halt.

Her mouth fell open.

A picture. On one of the lounge's big-screen TVs. Of her. And Daniel.

Fire raced across her skin and she thought she was going to throw up. A quick glance and she saw that on every TV in the sports lounge was a clear photograph of her and Daniel walking out of the Tucson hotel just yesterday morning.

"According to police reports," the newscaster was saying, "the missing heiress is suspected to have been taken right here in El Paso. A million-dollar reward has been offered for information leading to the return of the heiress to her family." The newscaster went on to add that the man in the photograph may have abducted her and gave out the number of a hotline to call if she was spotted.

Ani hugged her belly with both arms. Chills racked her body.

"Christ." Daniel grabbed her hand and said in a low voice, "Let's go."

She kept her head down as she and Daniel rushed through the bar.

Someone shouted behind them, "That's her! The missing woman!"

Ani's heart raced faster as she and Daniel picked up their pace.

A man moved in front of them, directly below the steps they needed to climb out of the sunken lounge.

A big man who smelled of beer and sweat, who wore a T-shirt too small for him that exposed a couple of inches of his flabby belly.

Daniel and Ani came to an abrupt halt, inches from him.

"Move the hell out of the way," Daniel said, in a low, controlled voice.

"The broad." The man jerked his head toward Ani. He grinned and her heart pounded in her throat. "She stays while I make a little phone call. A cool million sounds good to me."

Daniel didn't hesitate. He drew back his arm, fisted his hand, and clocked the man, hitting him at just the right location on his jaw to take him down and out.

Another man grabbed Ani's arm from behind. Heart racing, she whirled around and jammed her high heel onto the large man's foot as hard as she could. He shouted in obvious pain, and loosened his grip on her arm. She jerked away and grabbed Daniel's hand. He'd been right there ready to deck the man who'd grasped her arm, but she'd taken care of him first.

Ani stumbled over the big man Daniel had taken out, and lost one of her heels. She kicked the other one off and they bolted up the short flight of steps and rushed hand in hand through the hotel at a dead run.

Fury roared through Daniel like wildfire as they had to push past people in the long lines in front of the reservations desk. *Sonofabitch.* He and Ani both bumped into several hotel guests, hard, as they tried to put distance between themselves and the men following.

Behind them came shouts and he could almost feel the hot breath of the men chasing them.

Daniel shoved past the bellhop. He kept one hand near his Glock and searched the parking lot with his gaze for any sign of Borenko's men as they burst out into a rainy El Paso morning. It would have been impossible for any number of hit men to stake out every hotel, but he wasn't taking any chances.

Ani's face flushed with heat as she forced herself to run faster as rain poured down on them. Daniel practically dragged her through the parking lot. Gravel and small stones bit into her bare feet and she splashed through water puddles as her clothing stuck to her body from the rain.

At the same time he brought her to the driver's side of the Explorer he unlocked the door with the remote. He yanked open the door and shoved her inside. He landed in the seat, almost on top of her feet as she scrambled over the console and jammed her knee.

A man reached in to grab at Daniel. He slammed the door, catching the man's arm and causing him to shriek. Daniel opened the door just enough to release him, then pulled it shut and locked the doors.

Blood roared in Ani's ears as she sat up in time to see several of the huge men from the bar rush the SUV while Daniel turned the ignition. He threw the vehicle into reverse, barely missing one of the men as he backed up. With a squeal of his tires on the wet asphalt, he thrust the SUV into first and charged forward. Three men had to jump aside or Daniel might have flattened them.

Head pounding with fury, Daniel growled and hit the heel of his palm against the steering wheel's grip as they drove away from the hotel. "This means the Russians figured out what we did and have a good idea exactly where we're heading. The airport or Fort Bliss. The road to the military base won't be safe. They're likely waiting to ambush us."

Think, he told himself. *Think!* He thumped the steering wheel again.

Rain continued to fall steadily and he had to use the wipers to see clearly. They made a thump and squeaking sound as they traveled back and forth across the window. Both he and Ani had gotten drenched when they'd run through the hotel's parking lot. He glanced at her and she pushed a strand of her damp hair behind her ear. A few droplets were on her face and she wiped them away with her fingers.

With one hand on the wheel, he guided the Explorer through traffic, dodging the slower vehicles and gunning it in the open areas. He checked his rearview mirror to see if one of the local yokels had managed to tail him. Looked clear.

He jerked his cell phone out of its holster with his free hand, flipped it open, and pressed the speed-dial number for the Phoenix main office. He talked to Bob, the operations supervisor on duty, and apprised him of the situation.

"I'm going to head out on U.S. 180." Daniel stopped at a red light, checked for traffic, and hung a right. "Have a helicopter from Bliss pick us up. Call me back with an exit number and we'll meet them there."

"Watch your asses," Bob said in a tight voice.

"Damn straight." Daniel shut the phone and reholstered it as he drove through El Paso, taking the necessary roads to hit 180.

"A helicopter?" Ani said, and he glanced at her to see her color had returned, but she had a troubled expression. "I've never been on one."

He did his best to give her a smile to set her at ease. "You'll like it."

When he cut his gaze to her again, she had an eyebrow raised. "Uh-huh. Sure."

This time his smile was genuine. He heard the familiar feistiness in her voice. "Just hang on for the ride," he said as he took another turn to get them out of town.

Fifteen minutes later, Daniel's cell vibrated. Bob gave him the exit number and instructions on what they needed to do. A soldier would be sent along who would drive the Explorer to the military outpost.

It was another good twenty minutes before they reached the exit. The rain had stopped, but there were large puddles and potholes on the road.

Daniel followed the instructions they'd been given, parked behind an isolated gas station, and told Ani they needed to stay in the Explorer for protection until the helicopter showed up.

A few minutes later the whir of chopper blades cut through the air, followed by a Black Hawk that took only moments to settle a fair distance from the Explorer. The whoosh of the blades caused grass to stir and flatten and the sound was deafening.

Daniel motioned Ani to get out of the SUV. The ground was damp from the rain and the air smelled of wet dirt and rain-washed sky. When Ani walked around the Explorer to stand beside him, he noticed her bare feet were a little muddy.

Ani's heart pounded. After everything that had happened she felt like she was in a spy movie. It all seemed surreal. Everything was a blur.

After Daniel grabbed his duffel, he took her hand and they ducked as they ran toward the helicopter. Her damp hair whipped across her face and her clothing pressed and flapped against her skin. She could hear nothing but the whir of the helicopter's blades.

A soldier climbed down, held his hand out, and Daniel handed him the keys to the Explorer. The soldier gave a thumbs-up and headed for the SUV.

Two other soldiers helped her into the helicopter. She could feel the vibrations through her bare feet and was almost deafened by the noise.

Daniel helped strap her in and then placed a set of earphones over her head that a soldier handed him.

As soon as they were buckled in, the helicopter rose off the ground.

Ani's belly dropped as it climbed higher, then set off in a smooth path. Still, it caused her to feel a little lightheaded and gave her motion sickness.

With the headphones on, she couldn't hear the roar of the air, but she could feel the *whump-whump-whump* of the rotors in every joint in her body.

At the same time she was amazed at how responsive the helicopter was to the controls. In some ways she was scared out of her mind, and in others she was fascinated. She hoped the fascination would outweigh the fear and soon.

Over the headset came Daniel's deep, soothing drawl. Whenever he spoke, it made her blood stir. "How are you?" he asked.

She looked at him and spoke into the microphone attached to the headset. "Scared out of my mind."

"You're doing great."

Ani's chest rose and fell as she took a deep breath, but she looked at Daniel and smiled. He gave her a smile in return. He glanced around the interior of the helicopter, back to her, and said, "We're in a US-60L Black Hawk. I made a model of this helicopter."

Daniel proceeded to tell her some details about the copter that helped to get her mind off the flight itself. There wasn't much to see outside and it made her dizzy to look out of the helicopter.

It didn't take long before they landed and disembarked. Daniel and another soldier helped Ani step out of the Black Hawk. She wasn't sure that was an experience she wanted to try again very soon. She'd never been a good flyer to begin with.

Daniel spoke with someone and relayed to her that the private jet that would take them to New Jersey hadn't arrived yet. Regardless, he said he'd take her to the PX, post exchange, so that she could get new clothing and whatever else she might need. Like underwear.

She gave a relieved sigh. She couldn't wait to get out of these sticky, dirty clothes.

After thanking the soldiers and pilot of the Black Hawk, Daniel checked in with his operations supervisor as he and Ani were escorted to the PX.

At the PX, Daniel purchased clothing and other items for her. Ani was able to change out of her old clothing into the new. She felt so much better once she was in jeans, two T-shirts—one under and a larger one over the body armor. Having underwear on felt almost strange after spending the last couple of days without.

When she'd finished putting her hair into a ponytail, she crammed her hair beneath a NY Mets baseball cap that Daniel had picked out for her. He'd also chosen a pair of aviator glasses and a black leather blazer. Once she was dressed all the way to the sunglasses, she had to admit she looked a lot different. She stuffed her dirty clothing into a backpack that he'd also bought her, along with the other essentials.

When she left the dressing room, she almost didn't recognize Daniel. He'd purchased a plain black ball cap for himself, along with aviator glasses, a black leather bomber jacket, Levi's, and jogging shoes, changing his appearance, too.

She was going to miss that Stetson, those Wranglers, and his boots. He was one sexy cowboy. But then he was sexy wearing anything. Or nothing.

That thought caused heat to rush to her cheeks. She hadn't actually seen him naked. She'd seen him wearing only a towel, and her imagination had filled in the rest.

"Plane's waiting," Daniel said when she reached him, and he led her out of the PX.

She slung the backpack over her shoulder and kept her gaze focused ahead as her cheeks cooled. "Do you think we're in the clear now?"

He was quiet for a moment and she looked up at him. She couldn't see his eyes because of the glasses.

"We can't take any chances. They've anticipated our moves so far. No doubt they're going to be expecting us in New York or New Jersey at one airport or another, and the Russians will be sure to know we wouldn't take a commercial flight. So they'll be watching all the smaller hangars."

She took a deep breath. "Man, I really know how to screw things up."

"All we can do is go forward." He stared ahead as they drew closer to a small white jet like those she'd seen in the movies. He glanced down at her. "The goal is to keep you safe, Ani, and that's exactly what we're going to do."

CHAPTER SEVEN

Ani was keenly aware of Daniel on the flight to Newark. He was seated beside her and she could feel heat emanating from him. His musky scent and the smell of the leather seats and their jackets filled her senses.

He looked down and gave her one of his smiles that made her heart beat faster. She shifted in her seat, trying to squelch the ache he caused within her.

She was actually getting used to wearing the Kevlar vest. The body armor wasn't too heavy, just different, and sometimes it chafed.

Two other Deputy Marshals were on the plane, a woman and a man. They talked with Daniel, mostly about football, a subject she had no desire to discuss. She never could quite get the point of men chasing a ball down a field and beating each other up to keep the other team from getting it.

Now basketball, *that* was a sport. Pure athleticism.

Ani liked watching Daniel laugh and joke with the

other Deputies. She enjoyed his quick grin and even quicker wit. He acted so relaxed as they chatted. The tenseness from all they'd been through seemed to slip away from him as he enjoyed the easy camaraderie with his colleagues.

Ani turned to look out the window at the squares of fields and oval lakes so far below. She'd never been on a small jet before, and she felt a little more vulnerable than in a commercial airliner. But it was definitely better than the ride on the helicopter. This was a piece of cake in comparison.

After a while, the captain announced over the intercom to prepare for landing in Newark. Ani took a deep breath as the plane began to descend. She clenched the armrests tight, wondering how smooth a private jet was when it landed. This was always the hard part— the sensations of the plane dropping in altitude and then landing.

Actually, the hardest part would be stepping out of the plane and wondering whether a bullet would hit her right between the eyes. The vest wouldn't do much good in that scenario.

The thought caused her stomach to take a nosedive and a light sweat to break out on her skin. An image of being shot dead like her father came to her mind, but she shoved it away as hard as she could. No, she couldn't think about that right now.

A few minutes later she discovered that touching down in a small jet wasn't too bad. The captain guided the plane to a smooth landing and approached an empty hangar. The huge, empty hangar looked like it was made of corrugated metal and was open on one side, large enough to house several private jets.

It wasn't long until they came to an easy stop within the hangar and deplaned inside the building rather than outside. She slung her backpack over one shoulder and Daniel carried his duffel. It was nearing dusk, but still light enough to see around them.

When they reached the foot of the metal staircase that they'd used to climb down from the plane, she was surprised to find two couples waiting for them. The women were about her height, dressed very similarly, and the men were close to Daniel's size, each with black jackets and jeans. The men and women had aviator glasses and caps, too, despite the fact it was dusk.

Ani looked up at Daniel. "Decoys," he said. "I called ahead and arranged it. When we leave the terminal, we'll all go in separate directions to confuse anyone who might be watching."

Would she ever get used to all this covert stuff? She rubbed her arms, trying to warm away the chill that had overcome her from feeling so vulnerable . . . and scared.

"Don't glance around," Daniel said as they walked away from their plane, toward a door that obviously led into another part of the hangar. "Just look straight at the cars. Stay close."

The sheer professionalism and caution in his voice made her pulse jump. The look on Daniel's face increased her panic. It was like watching a suspense movie, only she was the star. Or more accurately, the

victim all the bad guys wanted to slaughter. Once
again, that sense of unreality descended on her, and
she started to shake.

Ani swallowed down more rising panic that caused
her chest to ache. Her breath strangled in her throat
and she had to stop walking.

I don't want to die. I don't want to die.

Images filled her mind.

Men were talking to her father in his den, their
voices raised. She slowed her approach and came in
line directly with his open door. It smelled of cherry
pipe tobacco, like it always did, but this time mixed
with the scents of cologne from the three men in the
den with her father. Two stood, one to either side of a
man casually seated in a chair in front of the desk.

Ani had been headed to the den to confront her father about the damning evidence she'd discovered on
his computer. Anger had been simmering inside her
all day the more she'd gone over it in her mind.

But all thoughts of confronting him at that moment
fled her mind when she saw him and the other men.

Her father was standing, his face red and flushed.
"I want out, Dmitry," he said to the seated man.

The voice of the man called Dmitry was too calm.
Deadly calm. "Our family doesn't tolerate deserters,
Henry," he said in a thick Russian accent.

Her father's face went from red to purple. "Killing
the mayor wasn't part of the bargain."

Dmitry shrugged. "We do what we must."

"I'm out." Her father thumped his hand on the mahogany desk. "Tell Yegor Borenko I'm retiring. Zoning

the Blue Meadow project as commercial to build your money-laundering businesses was enough. I'm done, I'm out, and that's *final*."

"Then this discussion has ended." Dmitry adjusted his suit jacket as he stood. He casually drew a handgun from an inside pocket. He aimed it at her father. The sound of a gun discharging blasted through the room.

A small, round hole appeared on her father's forehead and a single drop of blood rolled from the wound.

"Problem eliminated," Dmitry said with a smirk.

Ani screamed as her father's body collapsed into his overstuffed chair.

Dmitry turned, and with cold calculation in his eyes, he shot her.

She cried out as pain exploded on her left side. In her shoulder, just above her heart. Her body crumpled and she landed in a heap on her back, her legs curled under her. She couldn't breathe, couldn't scream. Dmitry pointed the gun at her again, but her mother came rushing into the room, followed by Jenn. Dmitry turned his gun on her mother and sister and with two shots dropped them.

Horror flooded Ani in waves as her mother landed near her. Jenn just behind.

OhGodohGodohGod.

Dmitry spoke to the two men. "Torch it," he said before casually walking out the door.

Ani tried to move but couldn't make her muscles work as one of the men followed Dmitry outside. Her breath rasped in her throat when the man came back with a can. The smell of gasoline filtered through her shrieking senses. The man yanked down the drapes, flung them on her mother, and started soaking the heavy cloth with the gasoline.

Ani's breathing came in short, harsh gasps and she coughed from the stench of the gasoline. The pain racking her body was outweighed by the horror of her family being shot. Her father dead.

She screamed.

Someone was shaking her. God, the pain in her chest. Was she bleeding to death? Her head jerked back and forth.

"Come back," came a voice. "Ani, what day is it?"

"Mother!" Ani shouted. "Get up!"

The grip on her shoulders tightened and the pain in her bullet wound was almost unbearable. "Ani, come back. You're okay. Tell me today's date."

Tears poured down her cheeks. "August nineteenth." She took a pained breath and gave the year next.

"It's October fifth." Someone shook her by the shoulders again. "Two years later. Tell me the date again."

Her sight shifted. Airplanes. Metal building. Fire. Father with bullet hole in his head. Airplanes. Daniel. *Daniel.*

"What day is it?" Daniel asked again as he came into focus and everything else began to fade away. "Ani, come back to me. Tell me what day it is."

Her whole body shook and she could barely speak. Daniel stroked her hair. "Come on, honey," he said softly. "Tell me."

"October fifth." She took a deep breath as reality came into focus. This time she gave the correct year.

"That's right." He began to smooth his hands down her shoulders. "What's my name?"

She swallowed. "Daniel Parker."

"Good job." He gestured to the people behind him. "Who are they?"

She looked at the concerned faces behind Daniel. "Decoys. They're Deputy Marshals, too."

When Ani looked back to him, he gave her a gentle smile.

"Post-traumatic stress disorder. PTSD." He looked over his shoulder at the other Deputies. "She'll be all right." His gaze turned back to her.

"I'm okay." Her breathing was harsh and she realized she was holding her palm to her old wound. It throbbed and hurt as bad as it did the day she was shot. The burn scars on her back felt like they were on fire. "Sorry."

He gave her another gentle smile. "Nothing to be sorry about. Are you ready to leave? Or do you need to rest?"

"Just give me a minute." Her heart still thundered. "Can I sit?"

"Sure." Daniel took her by the arm and led her through a doorway inside the hangar to a tiled hallway that led past several offices to a large sitting area. It was different than any hangar she'd seen on TV. This one was a business. The waiting room was huge, with planters, a butter-soft black leather couch, and a couple of matching overstuffed chairs. The floor was tiled in a checkerboard pattern with black-and-white marble tiles.

Ani sat heavily on the couch, still holding her palm to her shoulder. She stared straight ahead at a pair of metal doors with windows too high for her to see out of from where she was seated.

She leaned her head back and tried to relax against the leather and concentrate on the present. They were going to go to the hotel. She wasn't going to get shot. None of them were going to die today.

A man came out of a hallway and shook hands with Daniel.

"I'm Richardson, the general manager," the man said.

Daniel nodded with an impatient look on his face. He didn't give her name to the GM, she noticed.

Ani offered the GM a weak smile. It was time she got up anyway. She pushed herself from the couch to her feet. She noticed Daniel taking a protective stance as she shook Richardson's hand. "A pleasure to meet you," she said, feeling trite but not up to anything more original than, "Nice place."

"Yes, it is." His hand was limp as he shook hers. You could always tell the caliber of a man by his handshake. Firm and strong, or weak like a wet fish.

A man dressed in a chauffeur's outfit pushed the doors open and from her side view she saw Daniel had immediately moved his hand near his gun. He visibly relaxed when the man came through the doors.

"All cars have been checked for explosives, Inspector," the man said. "They're clean."

Daniel nodded and put his hand on Ani's elbow. "We're set."

The GM walked out the doors as Ani, Daniel, and the two pairs of decoys went out. The pilot and the other two Deputies who had been onboard the jet had stayed behind in the hangar, apparently planning on leaving with the jet.

The seven of them approached three identical black cars with dark tinted windows. It was an Indian summer, as Daniel had called it, and early October sunshine warmed her face. It was bright enough to cause her to squint until her eyes adjusted to the light.

A chain-link fence surrounded the parking lot and in the distance she could see two hotels in what seemed like the middle of nowhere.

Ani and Daniel climbed into the back seat of the rear car while the decoy couples slipped into the other vehicles. He let her in first, then scooted in after her mimicking exactly what the couples in front of them did.

"Let's take a tour of the city," Daniel told the man in the front seat who was also dressed like a chauffeur but had the same cautious gaze as Daniel.

"You got it," the man said.

The man reached forward, grabbed the keys, started to crank the engine—

Ani heard a strange whistling sound.

Something exploded.

She cried out as the force rocked their car.

A fireball roiled up to lick the clouds.

Shrapnel hit the front window of their car, cracking it.

"Out!" Daniel shouted as he opened the car door and grabbed her hand.

Another whizzing sound. Another explosion rocked the world.

A car. One of the cars in front of them!

Ani froze, realizing people had just died to protect her. That she was about to die.

Daniel dragged her out of their car. She landed hard on the pavement, scraping her hands and her knees through her jeans.

They're dead. I'm dead.

The memory of her mother's body, her father with the bullet hole in the center of his head, her burned and bleeding sister flashed through her mind.

Daniel jerked her to her feet, shielding her from the car with his body. They bolted for the doors.

Their car exploded before they made it to cover.

The force of the explosion flung Ani, twisting her in the air so that she slammed side first against the doors, her cheek and head hitting the metal along with her shoulder, hip, and thigh. Pieces of glass and metal from the cars buried themselves in the flesh of her legs.

Pain racked her body and her mind spun as she fell and landed on her ass on the concrete.

She held her hand to her head as she willed the spinning and ringing in her ears to stop.

The sound of popping and hissing, the crackle of flames echoed in her ears and the smell of smoke and burning metal filled her nostrils.

Frantically, she looked around for Daniel.

The body of the general manager was the first person she saw. He was sprawled out on the sidewalk. A piece of metal stuck up from between his brows and his eyes were wide and sightless.

Ani's head swam and her heart felt like it was going to explode like the cars had.

She squinted. Tried to focus. She didn't see any other bodies.

No one else had made it out of those cars.

Daniel? "Oh, God, Daniel." She scrambled to her feet and almost fell.

And then she saw him.

He was lying facedown on the concrete sidewalk.

And he wasn't moving.

"Daniel!" she screamed and bolted to his side. "Get up, get up, get up!" Tears poured down her face as she dropped to her knees and touched him. Still warm. He was still warm. He had to be alive. "You're okay. You've got to be okay."

Ani touched her fingers to his neck and felt his strong pulse. Both relief and terror balled up inside her.

Smoke and flames shrouded the air and the heat burned her face. She glanced around for help but saw no one. She'd been right. None of the other Deputy Marshals or drivers had made it.

Billows of smoke from the three burning cars likely hid the entrance, along with her and Daniel, from the sight of anyone who might be watching. But she had to get him inside the building in case they were seen and shot at.

Terror screaming through her mind and body, she grabbed one of Daniel's hands and tugged, trying to pull him toward the doors. He was so big and heavy that at first she couldn't move his body. A surge of adrenaline rushed through her and gave her the strength to haul him to the doors. She put her back to the swinging doors, pushing them open. With another burst of strength that surprised even herself, she hauled him inside the waiting room of the hangar. The doors swung shut behind them. He was still facedown.

The roar of fire thrummed, the sound loud even through the closed doors. Another explosion almost made her fall and her heart rate notched up.

Probably a gas tank. Not another bomb. Not a bomb. Please, no more bombs.

Sirens blared from everywhere at once. Near. Far. Inside. Outside.

Her ears rang from the explosions and sounds seemed muffled as she had a chance to look Daniel over.

A large piece of shrapnel stuck out of his back and Ani almost screamed.

His body armor. Please let his armor have protected him.

Heart pounding like it was going to burst from her chest, she felt around the place where the metal was sticking out. No blood that she could feel in that area. As she pressed, the piece of metal fell to the side and tumbled onto the floor of the waiting room. Through the tear in his T-shirt she saw that the shrapnel hadn't punctured his armor.

She brushed off the other small fragments on his back then looked at his legs. His jeans were bloody and torn in a couple of places, but she didn't see any big pieces of metal or glass. Wait, there was a good-sized one in one of his ass cheeks.

Should she turn him onto his side so she could see if he was injured anywhere else? Hadn't she heard that you're not supposed to move a wounded victim? But she had already dragged him into the building. She'd just push him up a little so that she could see how bad his injuries were.

Outside, emergency vehicles pulled up to the hangar, lights flashing through the small waiting room windows and illuminating the walls.

Ani pushed Daniel onto his side and her gaze raked over him from head to toe. It looked like the back of his body had taken the brunt of it. Except his temple. A bump was beginning to form. He must have struck his head on the concrete when they were propelled in the air by the force of the explosion.

Two police officers shoved open the doors and entered the waiting room. Through the open doors she heard shouts and glanced up to see water shooting from hoses as firemen started putting out the flames. Emergency vehicles with red and blue flashing lights were everywhere.

Immediately one of the cops who came through the door knelt beside Daniel and checked his pulse. The other cop shouted for paramedics.

"He's a federal agent." Ani tried to breathe as she

spoke to the cop checking Daniel's pulse. "We've got to get him to a hospital."

The cop looked at her. "Fed?"

"U.S. Marshal."

A pair of paramedics rushed in with a gurney that rattled as it came across the threshold. The man and woman immediately came to them. One started checking Ani out and another looked over Daniel.

The paramedic put an oxygen mask over Daniel's face. "Lacerations on the back of his legs," she said as she examined Daniel. She pushed open his eyelids and flashed light in his eyes with a small flashlight. "Pulse steady, respiration normal, pupils equal and responsive."

"Body armor?" the other paramedic said, sounding surprised as he began examining Ani's back.

She jerked in surprise. She hadn't been paying attention to him. When she looked over her shoulder, she saw a large piece of metal sticking out of her own armor.

"It saved his life, too," Ani said when her gaze darted from the cop to the medics. She was vaguely aware of the pain on her face, her shoulder, and hip from slamming into the metal door.

The paramedics continued to examine both her and Daniel. They tried to put an oxygen mask on her, but she pushed it away. "I don't need it."

The police officer spoke to two cops at the doors as she gestured to Daniel and Ani. "Get them out of here."

After lowering the gurney, the paramedics and cop

heaved Daniel onto the stretcher on his side because of the shrapnel sticking out of his backside.

Before they could strap him down, Daniel gave a low groan behind the air mask and Ani pulled away from the paramedic who'd been examining her and was at Daniel's side in a second.

"You're going to be okay," she said as she swiped hair from his brow. Somewhere along the way he'd lost his ball cap, and they'd both lost their aviator glasses.

His eyes opened and he narrowed his brows as if trying to remember something. His gaze met hers and immediately he yanked the mask off, pushed himself to a sitting position and shouted, "Fuck!" just before he reached behind him and jerked out the piece of shrapnel that had been buried in his ass. He got to his feet and wobbled.

Blood started to soak his jeans. "That wasn't a good idea," one of the paramedics said with a scowl.

Daniel's mind and vision swam, and his ass hurt like a motherfucker. "Goddamnit," he said as he reached behind him and pressed his palm to his ass cheek. His hand came away covered in blood.

"Turn around," the paramedic in front of him said.

After Daniel wiped the blood from his palm onto his jeans, he glanced to his side so that he could still see Ani. He wasn't about to let her out of his sight. The paramedic crouched beside him and sliced a hole in his jeans where the shrapnel had been. She poured antiseptic on a thick piece of gauze, then applied the bandage to the wound. It stung like hell when she taped it in place. He looked over his shoulder. Blood spotted the center of the thick bandage, but not much.

"Get back on the stretcher," came Ani's voice and he focused on her face.

He held his hand to his temple and touched the huge egg growing there. The pain felt like it was splitting his head in two and the shrieking of sirens and flashing red and blue lights made it worse. "We've got to get her out of here," he managed to say through gritted teeth. He jerked his credentials from his pocket and flashed them to the cop. "Her life depends on it," he said.

"Understood." The cop nodded, and said, "Get back on that stretcher and we'll take you both out to one of the ambulances."

"No. Back an unmarked unit up to the doors." Daniel looked to the cop. "Full protection around her on the way out of here."

The police officer spoke into her radio and in seconds two other cops were there. Quickly, the officer explained as much as she knew. The other officers headed off to make the arrangements.

The paramedics backed off when Daniel barked at them that he was okay. "I'm walking on my own steam." He looked to Ani. "You're sure you're okay?"

"Just a little banged up." She pushed up her cap and he could see her face more easily.

Ani had another scratch on her face, in addition to the one she'd received yesterday morning when they were ambushed in the Tucson hotel parking lot. This one was on her forehead. But what was worse was the side of her face—it was bright red and looked like it was starting to turn purple.

What the hell had happened? Two Deputies had checked the vehicles and said they were clean.

But that whistling sound before each explosion—

No, it wasn't bombs that had destroyed the cars. Fuckers had to have used some kind of long-range rocket-propelled grenade launcher.

By silent agreement, the cops moved to the front door with Daniel and Ani. Daniel kept his hand near his right hip, under his overshirt, close to his Glock.

Until they reached the hotel and got to their room, he didn't feel that Ani was one damn bit safe.

By the time they walked out of the building, dusk had turned to darkness. The flashing red and blue lights reflected off each of the cars in the lot. They were escorted to a black car similar to the one they had been in before all hell broke loose.

"Watch for a tail," Daniel said to the cops in the front seats as he pulled out his cell phone. He had to adjust so that his weight was on one hip and off his ass cheek.

The cop at the wheel looked over his shoulder. "On it." He eased the car from the hangar and kept the emergency lights off.

When he called headquarters, Daniel quickly apprised them of the situation. He was assured Deputy Marshals would be at the hotel whenever they arrived, and would of course be undercover.

After he put his phone back in its holster, Daniel studied Ani. She looked pale, other than the growing bruise on one side of her face, and he was afraid she was going to go into shock. He wrapped his arm around her shoulders and pulled her up against him so that her head rested on his chest. She was shaking hard enough that he felt it.

"This is insane," she mumbled against his shirt. "So many people . . . and all because of me."

"Shhh, honey." Daniel had to keep himself from looking any less professional by kissing the top of her head. "Stop blaming yourself. It's the Russians who are doing this. Even before you made that call, they were likely planning on using any means of technology they have to track you down."

She sighed. "Yes, but—"

"No buts about it." He rubbed her shoulder with his palm and she winced. "They're going down with your testimony, and they know it. The Russian Mafia is brutal, and they don't care who they take out, including law enforcement officers. If we were dealing with the Italian Mafia, we'd have a different set of problems. The Italians avoid killing cops because they know it will bring more trouble down on them. The Russians don't live by the same set of rules."

"How did they manage to get bombs on all three of those cars?"

Daniel tensed. "I think they used RPGs, not bombs."

She looked up at him, her face dirt streaked, her eyes rimmed with red. "What are RPGs?"

"Rocket-propelled grenade launchers."

Ani looked puzzled. "How?"

"I'm guessing they had someone posted at one of those hotels across the way. Possibly from one of the balconies."

She buried her face against his chest again. "This is a nightmare. I keep hoping to wake up and find it's all a dream."

He looked out the window as they sped out of the terminal. "Unfortunately this little nightmare isn't going to end anytime soon."

Daniel instructed the cops to take them to a large hospital in Manhattan after driving around a bit to make sure they weren't being followed. The farther they were from the airport, the better off they were. And the larger the hospital, the harder it would be to locate them. Not that he had any intention of registering Ani under her real name or her other identity.

"How do you feel?" she asked. "Really."

"Hurt like hell." He shook his head. "How about you?"

"I think I made out a little better than you did," she said with a hint of humor in her voice. "At least I don't have a hole in my ass and an egg on my head."

He smiled and squeezed her to him. Fact was, he did hurt like a sonofabitch, his body aching like he'd been in a heavyweight fight and knocked out for the count.

When they reached the hospital, they were taken to the emergency entrance. They both limped as they made it into the room. Daniel's muscles had stiffened during the ride and he imagined Ani's had, too.

The cops arranged for them to be treated without registering. "We aren't here," Daniel told the nurse in charge as he showed her his credentials. "We were never here."

She glanced from his creds to the cops behind him. "This way, Mr. and Mrs. No-name."

Despite incoming casualties from a four-car accident, it wasn't long before Daniel and Ani were patched up, but he sure felt like shit.

The nurses had used the medical version of Super Glue to seal wounds on both of them since the wounds weren't too deep. The liquid bandages were waterproof and would eventually dissolve on their own once the wounds healed. Daniel had been treated in two places on the backs of his legs and on one side of his ass. He and Ani both had liquid bandages in several other areas from minor lacerations.

"Raggedy Ann and Andy," Ani said as they limped out of the hospital with the two Deputy Marshals who had arrived and replaced the cops. It was already close to midnight. "We're like a couple of patched-up rag dolls."

Daniel managed a smile. "I don't think I've ever looked so forward to a nice clean hotel bed in my life."

"I'm falling facefirst into bed." She glanced up at him and then to his ass, and he gave a soft chuckle when she added, "Looks like you'll be doing the same."

Before they left the hospital the Deputy Marshals checked out the immediate vicinity. When they were sure it was clear, the Deputies drove a black unmarked SUV up to the ER entrance, then guided the vehicle from the hospital parking lot.

Ani hadn't realized how homesick she'd been until they passed through Times Square. The place was lit up and alive with flashing signs, the huge Trinitron, and people still out and about as if it were midday. What a difference it was from the little town of Bisbee that she'd been living in for the past year, where everything closed at five or six in the evening.

New York City was alive twenty-four hours a day. Skyscrapers dominated the landscape, but as she passed them it was the small places, like her favorite deli and the pastry shop she loved that made her feel like she was home. She used to purchase her fitted jackets and skirts in a dress shop they drove by. A few doors down was her favorite place to buy shoes.

From the time she was a little girl, she'd been to so many Broadway and Off Broadway shows, she couldn't begin to count them.

She swallowed and her heart sank down to her belly. This had been home. A part of her everyday life before the Russians took everything away from her.

At that thought, fury seared her veins. The bastards. She would do all she could to make sure the Russian Mafia paid for what they'd done to her family and what they'd done to all of the Deputy Marshals they'd killed at the airport tonight.

Daniel must have sensed the way she was feeling, because he looked at her and squeezed her hand. "How are you holding up?"

His hand was so warm over hers, and she wanted to turn her palm over so that she could interlock her fingers with his.

Instead she tried a halfhearted smile. "Good, considering we've been shot at, chased, evacuated, and almost blown up. All in a day's work for you?"

He gave her a cockeyed smile. "Something like that." She wished she could see his brown eyes in the darkness. He had a way of looking at her that made her feel like everything would be okay.

The Deputies took them to the Hotel Martinique on Broadway, a block from the Empire State Building. Ani was familiar with the area.

In another life, another time.

At that thought, she remembered Jamie, the boy who needed money for burn treatment. Hopefully Tammy had been able to get a hold of George Hanover. Her heart clenched at the thought of that boy with burns covering all but twenty percent of his little body.

Before Daniel would let her out of the SUV, he and the two Deputies got out. Daniel scanned the street then held out his hand and helped her out of the vehicle. They no longer had his duffel or her backpack, both items casualties of the bombings.

Tension cramped her shoulders as one of the Deputies handed them a key card. "Only one room was available," the Deputy said. "Hotel is overbooked. We've registered you as Mr. and Mrs. Johansen."

"Thanks, Dobson," Daniel said in a low voice, and the other man gave a nod in response.

As they walked away, Ani looked over her shoulder to see the Deputy was gone. Like he'd never been there at all.

This was the third hotel in as many days, and Ani was beyond exhausted from everything that had happened. A creepy sensation still crawled along her spine, like they were being watched. Part of her felt like no matter what they did, they'd never escape the Russian Mafia.

When they entered the elevator, two men followed them. Both had casual expressions on their faces, but Ani sensed they were anything but casual.

For some reason her adrenaline spiked even though she was so exhausted it was almost all she could do to hold herself up as they rode the elevator to their floor. The men followed them out of the elevator and she looked up at Daniel. He didn't seem concerned, just tired.

By the time they reached their door, Ani was shaking double time. The men came to a stop beside them and Ani's heart beat like crazy when she looked from them to Daniel with wide eyes.

"Oh shit." Daniel dragged his hand through his hair and gestured to the pair in the hallway with his free hand. "I'm sorry. Forgot to introduce you to our door guards." He gestured to the first man. "Deputy Thompson." Then to the next man. "Deputy Baldwin."

Relief flooded through her. "Er, hi," Ani said as Daniel opened the door. Both Deputies nodded, but didn't say anything.

Daniel guided her through the now open door. Ani stumbled and would have fallen if he hadn't had such a good grip on her arm.

"I'd climb right into that shower, if I wasn't so wiped out." She kicked off her jogging shoes, not paying attention to where they landed, then peeled off her socks. "Right now, I have to say I don't give a damn."

He held on to the edge of the television cabinet and toed off his shoes before taking off his own socks. "Nothing to sleep in but what we've got on."

"I don't know about you," she said as she pulled off the filthy shirt covering the body armor. "I'm sleeping in my underwear."

"Sounds like a good idea to me." Exhaustion was heavy in his voice. He drew the bed covering and sheets back on his bed, then slid his handgun under his pillow.

Not caring about anything but sleep, Ani slipped out of the body armor, tugged down her jeans and took off the undershirt so that she was only in her bra and panties. Her body ached, her head ached, her eyes ached. She went into the bathroom to at least wash her face, and winced when she ran the washcloth over the scratches on her cheek and forehead, and the bruise on one side of her face. Boy, was that going to look good in the morning. Not.

When she came back out of the bathroom, Daniel was already in his bed, lying on his belly with his face turned to the side on the pillow. His eyes were shut and it looked like he'd conked out.

It wasn't until then that she realized she had stripped down to her underwear and hadn't even thought about her burn scar or what Daniel might think about it.

Right now it didn't matter. They were alive.

CHAPTER EIGHT

Natasha jumped up and down and clapped her little hands as she watched the model yacht races on Conservatory Water in Central Park. Yegor smiled at his granddaughter's delight, warmth spreading throughout his chest.

Alyona sat on a grassy spot nearby, playing with the new porcelain doll he had purchased for her from F.A.O. Schwarz. Natasha's matching doll lay near the Alice in Wonderland statue.

Early morning sunshine threw a soft glow on the girls' blond ringlets. The scents of grass, trees, and water washed by him in a chill breeze.

The chirp of Yegor's cell phone drew his attention away from the girls. He withdrew the phone from his inside suit pocket and answered it with a short, clipped, *"Chto?"*

"It is done." Piterskij's voice held no inflection. "Last night the King woman was eliminated."

For the first time in two years, the weight he'd carried began to lift from Yegor's shoulders. "Are you certain?"

"Our operatives 'convinced' a man named Richardson to give us the required information. He provided the jet's scheduled time of arrival and the number of cars that would be waiting to escort the woman and the Marshals from the hangar," Piterskij said. "One of our associates used an RPG to take out the three cars. However, he was captured by the Port Authority police."

Yegor glanced from one granddaughter to the next to reassure himself they were both safe.

His thoughts immediately turned back to Piterskij's statement. "Ensure the associate will never have the opportunity to speak to anyone about this matter."

"As you command," Piterskij said without hesitation.

"Now tell me of the King woman's death."

"We believe," Piterskij said, "that none could have survived the explosions."

The pulse at Yegor's temple throbbed as he shouted into the phone, "You believe? You believe? I want proof!"

"Nothing remained of the vehicles or those inside them." Piterskij's voice sounded tense. "As I said, none could have survived."

"How do you know this?" Yegor shouted.

He had to force himself to calm down as Natasha looked from where she was now sliding on the mushroom on the Alice in Wonderland statue. He offered her a smile and circled his fingers in the air, in a gesture that told her to continue.

Yegor ground his teeth and lowered his tone. "How can you be so certain that no one escaped the vehicles?"

Piterskij cleared his throat. "Richardson was to serve as witness, but he did not remain inside the building as he should have. According to the police, he was killed from shrapnel from the explosions and his was the only body recovered."

Yegor's hands trembled and Alyona looked up at him and smiled. It was harder to return her smile but he did then turned his back to the girls.

"If there were no witnesses to ensure they did not escape the car, then how can you be so certain?" he growled.

"The blasts—"

"Until the trial we will continue to treat this as if the woman is still alive!" Even though it was early morning, Yegor pulled his handkerchief from his suit pocket and mopped his brow. The vein at his forehead pulsed. "You will ensure that every measure is taken to locate her."

"I will start on the task immediately," Piterskij said. "Do you have any further instructions?"

"Continue to monitor phone records of her friends and acquaintances," Yegor said as he glanced at his granddaughters again to keep an eye on them. "Have our operatives call every hospital in Manhattan with her description. Post constant surveillance around Federal Plaza where she is likely to be taken for witness preparation."

It was getting harder and harder for Yegor to keep

his voice down. "Do not be negligent in your attempts at obtaining the names of persons on that jury."

"Security on this matter has been tighter than we've ever encountered," Piterskij said, but rushed to add, "However, we will take care of it."

"See that you do." Yegor looked at his granddaughters to make sure they were far enough away that they would not overhear him. "Until we see her dead body or a piece of her, until we have absolute proof, do not stop looking for the bitch."

CHAPTER NINE

The cigarette tumbled through the air, landing on the gas-soaked drapes covering her mother.

Flames encased her body in a whoosh of yellow and red.

Ani screamed then coughed from smoke and the acrid smell of gasoline filling her lungs as the man walked away and closed the door behind him.

Fire spread like a living entity coming to consume her and her whole family. More flames erupted and fire licked the walls, spreading to the ceiling, engulfing the family room. It moved so fast!

Pain racked Ani's body as she pushed herself to her feet. She pressed her hand over the bullet wound on her left shoulder. Blood coated her fingers and heat caused sweat to roll down her face. Despite the heat, she felt a flash of cold inside her that made her body shake. For a moment her vision wavered and she had to steady herself. She listed to the side and stumbled, almost tripping in her high heels.

She heard a moan and turned to find her sister squirming on the floor. Jenn was alive! But so much blood was on one side of her face. Heart pounding, Ani took her bloody palm from her shoulder and caught one of Jenn's hands in hers.

Ani shot her gaze to the front door. It was on fire now, as was everything in their path.

Fire was all around them.

When she looked at the doorway to her father's den, she saw that the fire hadn't reached it yet. She choked and coughed from smoke, and her muscles strained as she dragged her sister into her father's den.

She tugged Jenn toward the window at the far side of the room, trying not to look at her father but failing. The bullet hole in his forehead . . . his sightless eyes . . . the expression of shock frozen on his features.

Ani forced back the desire to throw up, scream, and cry as she reached the window and released her grip on her sister.

Jenn slumped to the floor and groaned. So much blood covered her face. And was that a bullet hole? Had she been shot in the head?

Ani forced panicked thoughts from her mind, ignored the screaming pain in her shoulder, and focused on the window. When she tried to grab the metal window grip, she jerked her hand back from the heat. Her palm burned from where she had touched it to the metal.

Her mind raced and panic speared through her. What could she use to protect her palm when she opened the window? She and her sister would be cut by the glass if she broke the window and dragged them both through it, but she'd have to do whatever it took.

She had to get them out of here.

Continual coughing from the smoke racked her body as her gaze traveled her father's den with a quick sweep of her eyes.

The heat. The smoke. *The heat*. Flames were closing in on her, closing in on the window. She couldn't stop coughing and her eyes watered continuously. She could barely breathe. Her sight kept blurring and her knees threatened to buckle. Was the roaring from the fire or inside her head?

Her mind snapped into action again and a fresh rush of adrenaline pumped through her. She had to ignore everything and get them out of the house.

Ani started to grab a heavy glass paperweight from her father's desk when she remembered her father always had a handkerchief in his suit pocket.

She turned, avoiding looking at his face, and snatched the handkerchief from his pocket as fast as she could. Holding the cloth, she flipped the hot metal of the window lock and in seconds she had the window open.

Ani grabbed Jenn under her arms and strained to lift her sister's dead weight. She started to raise Jenn to the window—

A flaming beam swung down from the ceiling.

It slammed them both to the floor. The power of the impact knocked the breath from Ani's lungs.

The beam landed on her lower back and on her sister's legs. Burning wood melted Ani's suit into her flesh.

She screamed.

The pain. The agony was almost unbearable, matching the gunshot wound at her shoulder.

But what was worse was seeing her sister's pants catch fire. Ani's fear for Jenn, and panic to get them both out of the house, gave Ani the strength she needed. She choked on fumes and smoke, her body racking even harder with the power of her coughs.

Giving it everything she had, she climbed out from beneath the beam and with her shoe shoved the beam off her sister. Tears rolled down Ani's face as flames licked the lower half of Jenn's body and burned Ani's own back.

Adrenaline continued to pump through her body, helping to make her strong enough to raise Jenn and shove her flaming body out the window. Ani's heart stuttered when Jenn made no sound as she landed on the hedge and flipped onto the grass. Ani used the handkerchief to grasp the lower part of the window frame. She toppled through the window, over the hedge, nearly landing on her sister.

Someone grabbed Jenn and started putting out the flames on her legs.

Screaming and holding her hand to her bleeding shoulder, Ani rolled onto her back on the grass, trying to smother the flames burning her back through her suit.

Vaguely, she heard the sounds of sirens and felt

someone grasp her under her arms and drag her farther from the burning house.

"Jenn!" she cried out and fought to get away.

The voice of the person helping her barely registered. A neighbor. Which one? "Someone else has her," the voice said.

"I don't think Jennifer is going to make it," came a frantic voice that Ani recognized as another of her family's neighbors. The sound of sirens cut through the night and the screech of tires sounded in front of their home as the person shouted, "Jennifer's shot in the head and over half of her body is burned."

Ani screamed, "Jenn!" again as tears poured down her cheeks. Another person applied pressure to her gunshot wound, but she hardly felt it. No matter how hard she tried to fight the person holding her to get to her sister, she couldn't move.

In her mind, all she could see was her sister's bloody face and flaming clothing, her mother's body encased in a cocoon of fire, and the bullet hole in her father's forehead.

Ani woke, sobbing, her head aching and her eyes burning from crying, her whole body shaking. Gradually she became aware of a soothing voice speaking low, caring words. Someone stroking her hair from her face.

"Just a dream, honey." Daniel's voice came from behind her. "You were having a nightmare."

Images wouldn't stop racing through her mind.

She hiccupped and sniffled as she gradually became aware of what was around her, but trembled for a long time. Daniel continued to sit beside her murmuring that she was okay.

When she stopped shaking so hard, she rolled onto her back to look up at Daniel and blinked from the light pouring through the sheer curtains into the hotel room.

It hadn't mattered that she'd gotten her sister through that window. The shot to Jenn's head had skimmed the side of her skull, not entering her brain. But still her brain had swollen and her body had been too badly burned. She'd died on the operating room table.

That had been the last thing Ani had been told about her sister before she signed the contract to go into WITSEC.

Ani couldn't hold back another sob.

"Are you with me, Ani?" Daniel was sitting on the side of her bed and he gently caressed her damp cheek. "Are you all right?"

Ani took a deep, shuddering breath. "I dreamt of the fire. My family." Her throat closed off and she couldn't talk anymore. She squeezed her eyes shut.

"The bastards who did it are going to pay." The inflection in his voice went from gentle to angry. "We'll make sure of it."

She opened her eyes and brought her hand to his, where he was caressing her face. She linked their fingers. "Thank you," she whispered, clinging to the warmth of his hand.

His eyes were dark and filled with confidence in what he'd said. He meant every word. As she gradually became more aware of him, she saw that his hair was damp, his face clean of dirt and smoke, but exhaustion was evident in his slightly reddened eyes. The bump on his head was deep red, turning purple.

As things came more clearly into focus, she noticed he was wearing only a towel around his waist and smelled of soap and man. She wished he'd take her in his arms and just hold her. All she wanted right now was to be held.

Now that she was becoming more alert, her aches and pains started yelling at her to pay attention. The cuts on the backs of her legs stung. The side of her face hurt, along with her shoulder and hip from where she'd slammed into that door.

"Your injury." She looked to where he was sitting as the memory of his wounds came back to her. "You shouldn't be putting pressure on it."

"I'm sitting on the half that doesn't burn like a sonofabitch." Daniel smiled and squeezed her fingers with his. He brought their hands to his mouth and kissed her knuckles.

She glanced down. "Looks like you're not going to be doing a whole lot of sitting for a while."

The corner of his mouth turned up in a grin. "Don't underestimate me." His smile faded a little. "I can handle anything that comes my way."

"Anything?" Her words came out soft, husky.

Daniel lowered his head until his face was close to hers. "Anything."

Butterflies filled Ani's belly and her heart started to race again. He was going to kiss her. His breath was warm against her face as his mouth came close to hers.

"So many times I could have lost you, Ani." His eyes were dark as he gazed at her. "I don't ever want to lose you."

His lips hovered over hers for a long moment. She waited, barely able to breathe. The brown of his eyes was so dark, drawing her closer to him. She moved her lips closer to his.

Daniel paused a heartbeat then moved his mouth to her forehead. He kissed her there before drawing away.

Disappointment rushed through her. A little whimper slipped from her that immediately caused her cheeks to warm from embarrassment.

His chest rose with his harsh intake of breath. He tipped his head back and closed his eyes, his hands balled into fists on his legs. For a long moment he stayed that way and she just watched him, unable to move.

There he was, perfect, every cut, every bruise, making him seem more real. She wanted to reach out and touch him, feel his strength.

When he looked at her again, his features were composed, showing no true expression, and her heart sank.

"Daniel—"

He put his thumb over her lips, stopping her. "What do you want for breakfast?" He glanced at the clock. "Lunch, I mean."

His thumb slid across her cheek as she turned her head to see the illuminated green numbers on the clock perched on the nightstand. "Wow." She looked back up at him. "It's already noon?"

"We both more than needed the rest." He stroked her hair from her face one more time before he eased to his feet. "I'll order room service."

The sheet fell to her waist when she pushed herself to a sitting position. She snatched it back up to cover her chest when she realized all she was wearing was her bra and panties. Warmth heated her cheeks again, overcoming the aches and pains she felt at that moment.

He visibly swallowed. "How does a club sandwich sound?"

"Fine."

"Fries or chips?"

"Barbecue chips and a Pepsi."

"You've got it."

Their exchange was stilted, like two strangers instead of two friends—who meant even more to one another.

She'd have to be made of stone to not realize that Daniel wanted her, too, and that he cared about her. How much, she didn't know, but they had some kind of connection. Even more so after the past few days.

"I'm dying for a shower," she said. All the dirt, smoke, blood, and grime made her feel sticky and gross. She'd been so captivated by Daniel she hadn't even noticed until this moment.

"I'll have one of the Deputies outside order lunch and bring it up." He pulled his cell phone out of its holster. "It should be here by the time you're done."

Ani swallowed as she looked as his muscled form. Those broad shoulders and powerful chest tapering down to taut abs. Once again a towel hung low around his lean hips.

When she glanced up she saw Daniel watching her. Was his hand trembling as he held the cell phone? His knuckles were white. He turned from her and began talking into the phone, speaking to one of the other Deputy Marshals and giving their order.

Heart pounding, she tugged the sheet loose, then wrapped it around her body as she eased from the bed. She tried not to look at Daniel but couldn't help darting a glance at him over her shoulder as she walked to the bathroom. He was staring after her and didn't avert his gaze. She took a deep breath and forced herself to face forward, slip into the bathroom, and shut the door behind her.

The moment she saw herself in the mirror she didn't know whether to laugh or cry. Daniel had wanted to kiss *that* woman?

Her dark hair was tangled and wild around her face, which was bruised completely down one side. The bruise was warm to her touch when she lightly ran her fingertips along it. She winced.

Jeez, that hurts.

She had a new scratch on her face to join the one she'd received when they were shot at in Tucson, when the car window had been blown out. A dark smudge crossed one cheek and her eyes were much redder than Daniel's.

She let the sheet drop to the tiled floor and peeled off her bra and panties. When she examined her body, she shook her head at the bruises on her shoulder and hip that were on the same side as her face. Then she turned to look at her legs at the scrapes and cuts. Lord, she did feel like Raggedy Ann. Make that Raggedy Ani.

She climbed into the shower and let the warm spray soothe her aching body and tried not to think about Daniel and how much she wanted him.

Daniel's throat was so dry it hurt as he watched Ani disappear into the bathroom, the door shutting tight behind her. He'd come so close to losing it and kissing her, taking her, bruises and stitches be damned. Being with her was driving him out of his everlovin' mind.

But he couldn't *not* be with her. He couldn't let her out of his sight. He couldn't trust her safety to anyone else.

He should, but he couldn't.

He wouldn't.

Daniel clenched his fists and ground his teeth.

Get a grip, Parker.

Before Ani had woken from her nightmare, he'd been up a while. He'd used his cell phone to call one of the Deputies who was on duty downstairs and ask to have someone purchase clothing and supplies for the two of them. The only clothing they had was torn and bloody. He'd checked her pants and shirt for her size and gave the information to the Deputy.

In the meantime . . . Things were looking a little dangerous between them. Way dangerous.

He scrubbed his hand through his damp hair. *Christ.*

While Ani took her shower, his friend and fellow Inspector Marshal, Gary McNeal, had brought up their meal. After tugging on his bloodied jeans and drawing his Glock, Daniel had answered the door. He let his friend in, tucked the Glock in the back of his jeans, and took the tray of food to set on the room's table.

When Daniel had taken a leave after Judge Moore had been murdered, McNeal had paid him a visit. Daniel had known McNeal from their training days at FLETC, the Federal Law Enforcement Training Center in Brunswick, Georgia, and considered him a good friend.

McNeal had been the one who'd recommended Daniel to WITSEC. He had forced Daniel to mentally step through everything that happened in that courtroom. To face up to the fact that there was nothing he could have done to save the judge.

Still, Daniel couldn't quite let go.

McNeal was gone by the time Ani came out of the bathroom, steam rolling out in her wake. Her hair was wet, hanging to her shoulders, and her face fresh and clean.

A burst of anger shot through him again at the

sight of the cuts and bruises on Ani's tender skin. They seemed to stand out even more now than they had before.

His gaze dropped from her face. She was wearing only a towel.

Things were just getting better and better.

"Looks good." Ani avoided his gaze and held her towel tight to her as she slipped into a chair on one side of the table. He adjusted his jeans as he sat. He was so hard he felt like his cock would shatter.

While they ate their sandwiches, the tension between them climbed so high that neither one of them spoke.

Except when their gazes met. Her blue eyes were large and expressive, telling him exactly what he didn't need to know right now.

She wanted him. She'd let him take her. Now.

His cock got harder by the moment. His balls ached and his body vibrated with need for Ani.

When she finished, Ani wiped her lips with her napkin, but she'd left a little mustard at one corner of her mouth.

"You missed some." He leaned forward and wiped the mustard from her mouth with his index finger. But he couldn't stop there. He traced her lower lip, gently brushing it as their eyes locked and held.

She parted her lips and took his finger into her mouth and lightly sucked, her eyes still focused on his. A wildfire sensation went straight to his groin. He imagined those beautiful lips surrounding his cock as he slowly pumped in and out of her mouth.

If he didn't cool off in a hurry, he wasn't going to be able to hold back any longer

Ani sucked harder.

He jerked his finger from her mouth and got to his feet in a rush. Her gaze lowered to his waist and he looked down to see his erection outlined against his jeans.

Well, hell, there was no hiding how much he wanted her.

Ani pushed back her chair, stood, and came toward him, her gaze never leaving his.

He couldn't move if his life depended on it.

When she was just inches from him, she paused. Tilted her chin.

And let her towel fall away from her body, leaving her naked.

Christ.

She's beautiful.

All other thoughts fled. Nothing mattered but Ani.

He found his hands moving toward her breasts in slow motion until his palms covered both of them. Perfect handfuls. As he massaged them, he barely heard her soft moans. She gripped his biceps in her hands, drawing him closer.

Such perfect breasts. He had to taste them. He lowered his head and cupped one breast so that it was raised, and he flicked his tongue over the hard nipple. A rumble rose in his chest as he nipped and sucked and licked. Ani's moans grew louder and she shuddered as he adjusted his hand to cup the other breast and began to pay the same close attention to it. Every time he gently bit her then sucked, she moaned.

He was on another planet, another plane of existence. She smelled so good. Of the clean smell of shampoo and soap, and the scent of woman that he'd been aware of ever since she'd walked back into his life. A scent he remembered so clearly from a year ago, the last time he'd seen her. It had nearly driven him out of his mind with need for her even then.

Daniel raised his head from suckling on her nipples. His gaze landed on her mouth. How many times had he wanted to kiss those lips? He'd lost count. All he could think of was how badly he wanted to kiss her right now.

He lowered his head and he gently brushed his lips over hers. She moaned into his mouth, her lips parted and ready for his kiss.

He was a Deputy U.S. Marshal. An Inspector. Her bodyguard.

This was wrong.

No, this was right.

So right.

He slipped his fingers into her damp hair and grabbed her ass with his other hand. With his lips still a breath away from hers, he ground his jean-clad cock against her much softer skin. She felt so good against him. He had to be inside her.

"Daniel," she whispered, before she pressed her lips firmly against his.

He groaned and slid his tongue into her mouth. As her tongue moved with his, he closed his eyes. He savored her unique flavor mixed with the taste of the soda she'd been drinking.

God, how he needed her. He gripped her hair in his hand and brought her tighter to him. Their kiss became more urgent, more needy. He thrust his tongue in her mouth and imagined his cock pounding in and out of her pussy as he took her.

He was lost.

There was no turning back.

CHAPTER TEN

Ani could barely breathe as Daniel kissed her, and her heart thrummed hard enough her chest ached. She'd wanted him so badly for so long, while at the same not wanting him to see or touch the burn scars on her back.

What had possessed her to drop her towel—she didn't know. It had been wrong of her to push things this far, but she needed him too badly. And she was sure he needed her, too.

After coming so close to death yesterday, it was as if they needed to grasp onto the life that they had. That they could have lost. That they might never have known together. One day. One precious moment.

This kiss . . . God, could the man kiss. She found herself lost and wanted to stay lost with him forever.

Her knuckles ached from how tight she was holding on to his biceps. She loosened her grip, moved her palms up his chest, and slipped her arms around his neck so she could cling to him. It was all she could do to keep herself standing, her knees were so weak. His hair was slightly damp against her fingers and the clean scents of soap and shampoo surrounded her.

Daniel groaned and moved his moist lips from her mouth to her jawline. He kissed her all the way to her ear where he nipped at her earlobe and darted his tongue inside her ear.

Sounds she'd never heard herself make before rose up within her and spilled out of her lips in a soft, low moan. He held her tight to him, one of his hands still in her hair, his other gripping her ass. His cock rubbed her belly through his jeans, her breasts snug against his chest. She imagined him inside of her and that place between her thighs went on overdrive. She hadn't had sex for two years, since before the fire, and need made her even crazier for him.

Daniel drew away and slipped his fingers from her hair to brush the side of her face that was bruised. "How do you feel?"

"I've never, ever felt better than I do right here, with you, at this very moment." She reached up and caressed his forehead, below the big egg on his temple. "Maybe the question should be, how do *you* feel?"

He took her hand from where she was touching his temple and brought it down to his cock. A rush of electricity caused her to tingle from head to toe as she squeezed it through his jeans. "Does that answer your question?" he asked.

She bit her lower lip and released him as he

stepped away, unfastened his torn jeans, and let them drop to the floor. He left them behind as he came back to her and she wrapped her fingers around his erection.

His cock felt satin-soft over its hard core. Ani rubbed her thumb over the thick head and felt the slickness of his precome. Just touching him made her jittery with excitement.

He groaned and grasped her hand, and brought it back up so that her arms were around his neck again. "Maybe touching me isn't too good of an idea right now."

Was he stopping them? She swallowed. "Why not?"

"How long do you want me to last?" he asked as his lips hovered over hers.

A sigh of relief and pleasure rose up within her. "All day. Maybe all night, too."

"Hell, woman." He bumped his nose against hers. "You're going to wear me out."

"I'm going to try." She drew away and looked up into his eyes as her stomach pitched at her next thought. "Just one thing."

Daniel caught her chin in one of his hands. "What's that?"

"I . . ." She took a deep breath, her chest rising and falling. "I don't want you to touch or see my burn scars. They're horrible."

He gripped her chin tight and his gaze was intense. "You have nothing to be embarrassed or self-conscious about."

Tears were building up in her eyes. "Yeah. I do."

"No. You don't." He kissed a tear that tracked her cheek, tasting the salt of it. "Everything about you is special to me. Got that?"

Did he mean it? She trusted him so much, why shouldn't she trust him in this? "Okay," she said.

He smiled and brushed his knuckles across a second tear. "I won't look until you're ready."

She nodded, warmth traveling through her. Maybe he'd seen them when she'd gone to bed last night, maybe he hadn't. But she didn't want him to *really* look at her burn scars.

Daniel grasped her face in both hands and kissed her hard. She opened up to him, allowing him to slide his tongue in before she lightly sucked it. He tasted so wonderful.

He moved his lips from hers and kissed his way along the side of her neck to the hollow of her throat. "You taste so good," he said, echoing her thoughts.

Ani's belly flipped at the husky sound of his voice. She shuddered as he trailed his lips downward. She went completely still when his lips brushed the scar from the gunshot wound, but he didn't seem to notice as he gently kissed it.

He continued working his way to her breasts. A groan rose up from his chest and Ani matched him when he latched on to one of her nipples with his warm mouth.

The feel of his tongue on her bare nipples was indescribable. "Daniel," she whispered, and slipped her fingers into his hair.

"Mmmmm . . ." he murmured as he licked and sucked each of her nipples.

After a few moments, when she felt like she was completely on fire, Daniel rose up and looked at her. He massaged her shoulders with his palms. They felt work-roughened against her skin.

"You are the most special woman to me, Ani." He lowered his head and brushed his lips over hers. "You're beautiful. You've always been beautiful to me."

More heat flushed through her and she bit her lower lip, but he teased her mouth open again with his tongue. She moaned and leaned into him as he kissed her.

Before she knew what he was doing, he picked her up by cupping her ass. He took her to one of the beds and sat her on the edge of it.

"Lie back," he said.

Ani sucked in her breath, her heart pounding. As she lay on her back, he hooked her legs over his shoulders.

He paused. "Does that hurt? Your cuts?"

She shook her head. "Nothing hurts right now. Except for how badly I need you."

He smiled and slid his hands under her ass again. She stilled for a moment—his fingers were so close to her scars.

But then she couldn't think and nothing seemed to matter. Her thighs quivered as he kissed the inside of one of them. He licked small circles along her skin, moving in closer to her folds.

When he reached her mound, he took an audible

breath. "You smell so good. I've been wanting to taste you for so long."

She whimpered and squirmed. They were actually doing this. In her fantasies and wet dreams she'd pictured him with his head between her thighs, but now it was real. It wasn't her imagination anymore.

Daniel dragged his tongue along her slit and she arched off the bed with a cry. His tongue. Her folds. She couldn't begin to describe the feelings rushing through her. His hands were still under her ass and he pressed his mouth tighter against her sex.

Ani's mind whirled and she gripped the bedcovering to either side of her. If she didn't she just might spin right off the bed. She'd thought her body was on fire before—now it was a blazing inferno. A powerful orgasm coiled within her but he paused and she almost screamed.

"Do you like that, honey?" He gave her clit another swipe with his tongue, then kissed her mound.

"Are you nuts?" She squirmed some more, wanting his mouth back on her. "Of course I like it."

He gave a soft laugh and withdrew one of his hands from beneath her ass cheek. He slipped two fingers into her core and began pumping them in and out, his knuckles hitting her folds, and she groaned.

"How about that?" he said in a teasing voice.

Ani gave him her best glare. "I'm going to kill you, Daniel, if you don't finish what you started."

This time he snorted back a laugh and lowered his mouth to her folds. His stubble chafed the inside of her legs and she clenched her thighs tighter around his head. The feel of his tongue and mouth on her clit while he thrust his fingers in and out made her eyes roll back in her head.

Heaven, sheer heaven.

A moan started to rise up in her throat.

"Not too loud, baby," he murmured against her slick folds, "we don't want to be heard."

Oh—the Deputies outside the door.

Thoughts of them vanished in a hurry.

Sensations combined to put her on overload. Perspiration coated her body. Fire licked at her veins. Heat burned beneath her skin.

Her orgasm began building and building. She could barely breathe as she felt the power of the oncoming firestorm.

She had to bite her lip to hold back the cry that tried to escape her as her climax slammed into her. Shaking, her hips bucking against Daniel's face, she gripped the bedcovering tighter. She held back another cry and whimpered instead as wave after wave of heat rolled through her.

He took long swipes with his tongue, from the soft spot below her folds all the way up to her clit.

"Okay, okay." Her breathing was hard and fast. "You can live now."

Daniel chuckled and slipped her knees from his shoulders. Ani didn't think she would be able to move on her own. Her mind spun as he took her by her hands and brought her to a sitting position.

Still on his knees, he carefully cupped her injured face in his hands and brought his mouth to hers in a

fierce and completely dominating kiss. She was so
sated she felt like she was melting in his grasp. The
taste of herself on his tongue was different to her.
She'd never had a man go down on her, and again she
thought of heaven, reliving in her mind the finest details, what Daniel had just done to her body with his
mouth and fingers.

He took both her hands and drew her to her feet as
he stood. She sank against him, her knees wobbly and
her body limp. She still felt the convulsions in her
core and the prickling of heat on her scalp. If this was
what it was like to have him bring her to orgasm with
his mouth, she could just imagine what it would be
like to have him inside her.

Ani ran her hands over his chest, her heart pounding
as she felt his skin beneath her palms. A light sprin-
kling of dark hair was soft beneath her hands. It
pleased her as he groaned while she explored his body
by touch. When she laved his flat nipples with her
tongue, she was rewarded with the tiny nubs tightening
beneath her touch and hearing him suck in his breath.

While she explored his body, he rubbed his hand
up and down her shoulder that wasn't bruised. She
liked the feel of his biceps beneath her palms. He was
so strong, so virile, all man. His abdomen tightened
beneath her fingertips as her hands neared his groin.

She could be just as much a tease as he'd been. She
smiled and twisted her fingers in the curls around his
cock. She heard him catch his breath. Rather than
touching his erection, she moved her palms back up
his chest until she wrapped her arms around his neck.

His breathing sounded more labored as he held her close. "You feel so good in my arms, Ani."

She gave a soft little moan as her hard nipples brushed his chest and his erection rubbed her belly. She snuggled against him, her face against his warm skin, letting his delicious scent fill her senses. "It feels so good to be right here with you," she said with her eyes closed.

"I can't tell you how much I've wanted this." His voice was husky and she heard the stark honesty in his words. "How long I've wanted you."

Butterflies went crazy in her belly at his words. She opened her eyes, tipped her head back, and looked into his gaze. "I've imagined a moment like this with you, so many times. To be here with you—it's amazing."

The expression on his face was one of carnal need, and something else she couldn't discern. He took her mouth in a hard, fast kiss that literally took her breath away.

When Daniel drew back from the kiss, his heart twisted at the look in Ani's eyes. He could read so much in them—how much she desired him and how much she cared for him. But did it go beyond that?

Before he knew what she was doing, Ani slipped out of his arms. She ran her palms down his chest and abs and knelt in front of him.

She brought her mouth directly in front of the head of his cock. He stilled. Almost tentatively, she reached up and wrapped her fingers around his erection. He closed his eyes, lost in the sensation of her hand slowly moving up and down his length. Her other hand cupped his balls and he groaned.

But when he felt her hot, wet mouth slide over the head, he just about lost it. If this was how her mouth felt, how would it be to have his cock buried deep inside of her?

Every ache and throb in his body vanished as he just let himself feel Ani and what she was doing to him.

Daniel opened his eyes to look down and meet her gaze as she slipped him in and out of her mouth. He bunched his hands in her hair as she began to bob her head, moving one of her hands in time with her mouth. With her other palm she cupped and lightly massaged his balls. She licked and sucked him as she worked magic with her hands.

Heat suffused his cock and balls as she continued licking and sucking him, and she kept her gaze focused on him. The world was centered in his groin and he started to shake. That world was beginning to tilt on its axis.

"Ani." He tried to stop her but she kept on giving him the best head of his life. "I'm going to come if you don't stop. Now."

Damned if she didn't smile around his cock.

All sensation exploded in his groin as his semen squirted into her mouth. He had to bite the inside of his cheek to hold back a shout. She didn't stop and he saw her throat work as she swallowed.

His vision blurred as she continued to work him, drawing out every bit of come. He felt like the floor was going to collapse beneath him.

When he couldn't take any more, he drew Ani up, brought her against him, and gripped her tight. That climax had about knocked the wind out of him and he took a few moments to catch his breath.

"You are so beautiful." Daniel caressed the back of her uninjured cheek with his knuckles and smiled. "Everything about you. From the first time I met you I knew I was in trouble." He released her face and took one of her hands in his.

Ani gripped him tight and let him lead her to one of the beds. She eased onto it with her back against the bedspread. For a moment he just looked down at her. She was gorgeous. Her dark hair was a wild mass down to her shoulders, her lips were swollen from his kisses, her body pink wherever he'd touched her. Her nipples were large and extended from his attention. Even with all the bruises and scratches, he'd never seen anything, anyone, so beautiful in his life.

"Daniel?" she said, nervousness in her eyes.

"I'm just looking at the gorgeous woman I'm going to make love to." He knelt on the bed and eased between her thighs, spreading them apart so that he could clearly see her pussy and the dark triangle of hair on her mound. He wanted to lick her clit again and bring her to another orgasm, but he had to be inside her, he had to take her until she cried his name.

Ani couldn't believe how hard Daniel was again after just having climaxed. She could still taste him and she swept her tongue along her bottom lip.

The bed sank under his weight and the springs creaked as he moved up between her thighs. She caught her breath, waiting for the moment she'd feel him deep inside.

Instead he braced his hands to either side of her chest and lowered his mouth to hers. A groan rose up within her as he teased her lips open and slipped in his tongue to mingle with hers. She just couldn't get over how good he tasted, how good he smelled, how good it felt with his body against hers.

It was almost like she was in a dream. Daniel was hers. At least for today.

He moved the head of his cock to the opening of her core, and she held her breath.

"Finally," she whispered, not meaning to let the word slip out.

His sexy grin added to the wild sensations already coursing through her body. "Yeah. Finally."

Daniel thrust his cock in so hard and fast that Ani cried out in surprise. He slowly rocked in and out of her as she got used to the length and girth of him.

So good. So incredibly good.

Low moans rose up in her throat as she felt him so deep it was like his cock touched her belly button. He thrust a little slower as she looked down and saw his erection moving in and out of her core and her tummy flipped.

His voice sounded like a growl when he said, "You feel like heaven, woman."

That word again. Heaven, yes. It was like heaven having him inside of her.

Perspiration coated her skin and his, and their bodies were slick against one another. She felt hot. Burning hot. Even more than she had when he gave her that spectacular orgasm. She thought she might burn up just from watching him pump in and out of her.

"That's it, honey." He continued thrusting. "Now look into my eyes."

Ani obeyed, her gaze meeting his. "I dreamed about this every time we talked on the phone," he murmured. "I've wanted you forever."

"Me, too." As soon as she admitted to it, he brought his mouth to hers and kissed her in rhythm with his hips as he moved in and out of her.

Sweat dripped down the side of her face and between her breasts from the heat of their lovemaking. His chest rubbed her nipples and she couldn't hold back the small whimpers that slipped from her with every thrust of his cock.

Her orgasm came charging toward her from out of nowhere. First her mind spun and her body felt like it wasn't even her own. She felt outside herself, as if she was a part of Daniel. Somehow they'd fused their minds and bodies and, in her case, her heart. She'd fallen for him long ago, and she'd take anything he'd give her. Anything at all.

The climax barreling down on her had her whole body shaking. She clamped her thighs around his hips to ground herself. But nothing could hold her down.

She writhed beneath him and he raised his head. "Come for me."

It was as if his words were magic, tearing a low cry from her lips. "Daniel," she moaned as her body bucked and she scratched her fingernails down his back.

"I love it when you say my name." He continued to pound in and out of her. "Especially when you come."

His words made even more spasms erupt in her core and her channel squeezed down on his cock.

He shouted, "Goddamnit!" and stilled.

Ani's core still clenched and unclenched around his cock. He looked like he was in so much pain that she wondered if he'd injured himself. Maybe the liquid bandage holding the cut together on his ass had come apart.

She ran her hands up and down his back, caressing him. "What?"

"No condom."

Goose bumps prickled her skin, but she didn't want him to lose what they'd just shared. "Finish, Daniel. Pull out when you come."

His jaw was tense as he pumped in and out a few times. With a fierce expression, like he was holding back a shout, he jerked his cock out of her core and grasped it as his semen spurted onto her belly. His big body shook and his eyes were intense as he focused on her.

With a groan, Daniel rolled onto his side and brought her with him so that she was facing him. He took a corner of the rumpled sheet and wiped the come off her belly.

When he'd cleaned her off, he eased her into the curve of his arm. She snuggled into his embrace, her head close to his muscular chest. The scent of sex and sweat relaxed her even more.

She sighed, feeling more contented than she'd ever felt in her life. Her heart pounded like crazy and it wasn't just from the sex.

So this was what it was like to be thoroughly, completely in love.

CHAPTER ELEVEN

The contentment of holding Ani in his arms pushed aside some of the guilt Daniel felt at taking their relationship a step away from his position as an Inspector Marshal.

A monumental step.

He held her tightly to him, reveling in the softness of her body against his, her breasts to his chest, her arm draped over his waist.

Ani snuggled closer. Bruises spotted her left side from her face to her shoulder and arm to her hip. He brushed his hand gently along the curve of her waist to the large purple bruise on her hip.

The feelings of pleasure slipped away as the bruises reminded him of what had happened to her.

Trying to get his anger under control, Daniel took a deep breath. It was nearly impossible to calm the fiery rage that nearly consumed him at the thought of those Russian bastards who'd been trying to kill her. He'd almost lost her too many times.

Everything seemed to crystallize for him in that moment. Even after the trial, when Ani returned to WITSEC, he intended to keep her in his life.

But, shit. She'd be under the jurisdiction of another Inspector. Ethically, he couldn't continue to serve in that capacity. Hell, ethically he shouldn't be in bed with her right now.

Fuck.

Frustration stabbed at his mind over and over like an ice pick through his skull. But he tried to keep his expression neutral as Ani snuggled closer.

He had to get another Deputy Marshal assigned to her now. But he wanted, *needed,* to be there for her. He couldn't give up control of her fate to anyone else, no matter how qualified any other Deputy Marshal on this case was.

Daniel closed his eyes. An image seared his mind. Judge Moore with blood pouring from her chest as she lay crumpled behind the judges' bench.

He opened his eyes and forced the image of the dead judge away, but the determination to not lose another person under his care was stronger than ever.

The initial question rounded on him again. What about after the trial?

He'd find a way to make it work between them. He'd make it happen.

If she wasn't too pissed to even speak to him once she found out what he'd been holding back.

A stronger feeling of guilt twisted like a knife in his gut. From the beginning, he'd believed she needed to know the truth about her sister, but his hands had been tied. He would tell Ani, but legally he couldn't until after the trial. She'd signed the contract before going into WITSEC, leaving him with no choices.

Ani brought him back to the present as she ran one fingernail down the center of his chest, moving lower and lower until she neared his cock.

He groaned and placed his hand over hers, catching her fingers before they touched his growing erection. "You're playing with fire, honey."

She gave him the cutest grin that made him smile in response. "Good ride, cowboy. Too bad we don't have any condoms or I'd climb on for another go-around."

This time Daniel's groan was louder. "Woman, are you trying to drive me crazy on purpose?"

This time her grin was wicked. "Is it working?"

"Hell, yes." He took her mouth in a hard kiss. He released her hand and cupped her pussy before slipping one of his fingers into her wet folds.

Ani gasped and moved against his hand as he slowly slid his finger in and out of her slit. She wrapped her hand around his cock and started gently pumping it in her fist at the same time he stroked her clit. She licked her lips and he dove down for another kiss.

This past year he'd had sex with a couple of women, but no one had satisfied him physically or mentally. Come to think of it, none of his past relationships truly had. He'd never had the feelings for any woman that Ani stirred within him.

Once he started talking with Ani regularly she'd been the one on his mind, no matter how much he'd tried to deny it. Ani's sensual voice, soft laughter, and everything else about her had made him want her. Only her.

And despite the situation they were in, she was his. Only his.

Ani increased the pace of her hand on his cock and he rubbed her clit harder as they continued to kiss, their hands, mouths, and bodies moving more frantically as they each neared orgasm. Daniel knew she was close by the way her body quivered against his hand. She made soft moans that became louder as he circled her clit with his finger and stroked her faster.

She cried into his mouth as her body shook. She faltered in her strokes on his cock, but resumed her pace.

It was hard as hell, but he withdrew his fingers from her folds and took her hand from his cock. "Let's save this for later." He needed to conserve his strength for all the time he intended to keep her in bed.

What the hell am I thinking?

She looked up at him. "Are you sure?"

"No." He brought his fingers to his mouth and licked her juices from them. "For now I'll just have to take a real cold shower. Later I'll get some condoms."

"Make sure you get a big box," she murmured before she kissed him. A knock at the door startled them both and they drew apart. "Who could that be?" she asked.

"Probably one of the Deputies returning with the clothing and personal items I asked for," he said as he slipped out from Ani's embrace. She made a sated sound of disappointment as he eased from the bed. "You need to get up, honey. We can't get caught like this."

She sat up in a hurry. "I need something to put on."

"Here." He scooped up a towel from the floor and tossed it to her. "Get in the bathroom."

A knock came at the door again and Daniel called out, "Hold on."

As Ani slipped into the bathroom and shut the door behind her, he grabbed his torn and bloodied jeans and jerked them on again, then yanked on the shirt he'd been wearing under the vest.

He picked up his Glock from the nightstand beside his bed and eased toward the door. He was expecting one of the Deputies, but he wasn't taking any chances. He prayed like hell that the Deputy who brought the items wouldn't catch the scent of sex in the room or on him.

Daniel peeked through the peephole. Good, it was McNeal again. He was holding several plastic bags from clothing stores. In the hallway, guarding their hotel room door, were two other Deputy Marshals whom Daniel was familiar with.

Still cautious, Daniel opened the door, keeping his Glock in his hand. "Thanks, McNeal," he said. "Just toss them on the floor and I'll take care of them."

McNeal set the packages down. "This and lunch is going to cost you more than one drink." The extremely fit man, who was Daniel's height, looked up and down Daniel's form when they were face-to-face again. "You look like shit."

"Feel like it, too." Daniel started to close the door when McNeal said, "Need someone to relieve you?"

Daniel paused for a moment. "I do need to make a run, so I'd like someone in here with her as well as the guard in the hall. I'll call after I shower."

"Will do, buddy." McNeal slapped Daniel on the shoulder, before turning and heading toward the elevators.

Daniel nodded to the other Deputies before he shut and locked the door and looked at all the packages. Apparently someone had outdone themselves while shopping.

The sound of the shower caught his attention and he stepped over one of the bags and headed to the bathroom. The door wasn't locked, so he let himself into the steam-filled room. After he peeled off his clothing, he pushed aside the shower curtain and climbed into the shower with Ani. Good thing they didn't have to worry about stitches getting wet since they had liquid bandages.

She was rubbing a soapy washcloth over her body and she smiled when he joined her. Water hit him full in the face as he leaned down to kiss her. She gave a soft little whimper and he growled against her lips, clasped his hands around her waist, and drew her up tight against him.

She stilled, and immediately he knew why. His fingers were touching the bumpy, twisted flesh of her burn scars.

He wasn't about to let her pull away from him or

let her think that her scars mattered one bit. He kissed her harder, held her tighter.

Water pounded down on both of them as she gradually relaxed against him and accepted him as he deepened the kiss. When he finally raised his head, he smiled, took the soapy washcloth from her, and began rubbing her body with it. He was careful to avoid her bruises and cuts as he gently cleansed her.

"How do you feel?" she asked. "That egg on your head has got to ache. And your butt—that must have hurt like crazy when we, when we . . ."

He smiled. "Being with you makes everything else go away."

Ani returned his smile and let him continue to soap her body.

She felt so good beneath his hands and he found it hard to find any words to speak. Right now he'd like to turn her around, brace her hands against the porcelain shower wall, and drive his cock into her slick core. The fact that they still didn't have any condoms shot that idea down in a hurry.

He tried to turn her around just to wash her back, but she shook her head and braced her hands on his biceps as she looked up at him. "I'll wash my own back, okay?"

Daniel had a hard time smiling. He didn't want anything to be between them. "We have clothes now." He forced his thoughts to washing her shoulders, leaving a trail of suds wherever he touched her. "Hopefully some toothpaste and a few other goodies."

"Wonderful." She moaned as he soaped the wash-cloth and began working on her breasts and belly. "I hope they didn't forget the underwear."

He grinned, remembering that first day when she'd forgotten her underwear at the hotel in Tucson. His grin faded at the thought of all they'd been through. It seemed like it was weeks ago that they were in Tucson instead of a couple of days.

"I can't believe I didn't think about a condom," Daniel said, grumbling under his breath. "I lost my mind with you."

"It's okay." She smiled. "No regrets, right?"

"Not one." He pushed her wet hair from her face. "I just worry about you getting pregnant. It could still have happened, even though I pulled out."

She caught his hands in hers. "I know. Let's just worry about one thing at a time." She gave a wry smile. "Like living through the next few days."

He sobered. "I'll protect you, honey. With everything I have."

Ani reached up and brushed her lips over his. "I know you will."

He took her in his arms, pressed her head against his chest and simply held her as the water pounded down on them.

After they climbed out of the shower, Daniel noticed Ani made sure he didn't see her back by wrapping a towel around herself. He wished she hadn't. He wanted to see all of her.

She headed straight out of the bathroom for the bags of clothing and essentials. Instead of getting to see her naked again, he settled for watching her go through the bags. She dumped everything out then began to hang shirts, jeans, and other clothes in the closet. He pitched in and helped her.

She bent over to draw more clothing from the pile and the towel barely stayed on over her breasts. His mouth watered at the sight of her cleavage.

"Wow, even a couple of suits." She held up a black two-piece woman's outfit. "For the trial, right?"

"Guess so." He leaned over beside her and picked up a white button-up shirt, a pair of men's black dress trousers, and a matching blazer. "Looks like they expect me to appear civilized."

Ani gave him a sexy little grin that turned his heart inside out. "I rather like you uncivilized."

He leaned closer and kissed her. "I intend to be as uncivilized as possible when I'm alone with you."

"Good," she said softly, before standing and hanging up her suit. She had to tug her towel firmly around herself again to keep it from falling.

Come on, baby, let it drop.

After they'd sorted everything out, he was pleased to see a pair of toothbrushes among other things. All that was missing was a box of condoms.

Like Ani said, a big box.

He'd have to remedy that with a trip to a pharmacy.

A great little Korean bakery was just down the street from the hotel, several doors before the pharmacy. He'd just make a run to purchase sweet red bean and white bean buns and other bakery items and hit the pharmacy, too.

Ani selected a pair of blue jeans and a blue blouse, along with panties and a bra. Facing him, she dropped the towel and started dressing. She gave him a sultry smile, watching him as she dressed, knowing exactly what she was doing to him. His cock ached so badly. If he had a condom he'd take her right now.

Daniel's mouth watered at the sight of the curls of her mound and her hard nipples that were covered all too quickly to suit him when she yanked on her underwear.

"How'd they know my size?" she said as she slid into the jeans.

His mind had stalled and he had to snap his attention from her breasts to her face. She wore an amused expression.

"A little detective work," he mumbled as he headed for the bathroom. "I need a drink of water."

Once he was standing in front of the sink, he braced his hands on the countertop and looked in the mirror. "Get a grip, Parker," he growled at himself. He couldn't protect her if his mind was always on being inside her sweet body.

He clenched his hands and ground his teeth before running the tap and grabbing one of the covered glasses on the countertop. He filled it to the brim and drank three glasses straight before he had calmed down enough to go back into the bedroom and dress.

He didn't say anything as he jerked his clothes on.

The jeans were a little snug, especially the way his cock was straining against the zipper. Just being around Ani alone gave him a hard-on. Nothing like being in constant pain.

After he'd put on his belt with his gun and other equipment, he pulled on an overshirt then called Mc-Neal on his cell. "Come on up."

"Be right there," McNeal said before punching off.

"I'm heading out for quick run," he said to Ani as he raked his fingers through his damp hair.

"It's been so long since I've been in the city." She glanced toward the window that was shaded by gauzy curtains before her gaze returned to his. "I've really missed it."

Despite herself, she felt the backs of her eyes sting. "This was my city. I loved everything about this place, and I've been forced to stay away from it for over *two years,*" she said, as Daniel moved closer. She reached up and gripped his T-shirt in both hands, her eyes moist and her throat hurting. "I want to feel it. Taste it. Experience it."

He moved his palm up to the side of her face that wasn't bruised and she leaned into it. "I'm sorry, honey. I don't think it will ever be safe for you here. Even after the trial."

She closed her eyes. Maybe she shouldn't be hurting so bad about it, but it was just one more thing taken away from her.

Daniel's soft lips brushed first one of her eyelids, then the other. When she opened her eyes, he was looking at her with an expression that told her how much he cared.

"Stay far away from the window." His warm brown eyes focused on hers. "I didn't close the heavy drapes so you could have some sunlight, but you can't go near the window, just in case you're seen. Understand?"

She nodded and reached up to touch the large bruised bump on his forehead from the attack yesterday. That and her own bruises and cuts were a good reminder she was in danger, which meant he was in danger, too.

A knock came at the door.

"Hold on." Daniel ducked into the bathroom and came out with a can of the hairspray that had been brought up with the other essentials. He sprayed it over the beds and in the air.

She didn't even have to ask why. He was trying to mask the scent of their sex.

He handed her the can of spray and placed a soft kiss on her lips. She set it on the end table as he walked away from her.

The sight of him moving slowly to the door as he drew his gun made her shiver. After checking through the peephole, he opened the door just wide enough that she could see three men, but he still held the gun. Whatever the men were saying she couldn't hear because they spoke in such low tones.

Then Daniel introduced her to the Deputies, Gary McNeal, Tyrone Jacobs, and George Harper. After she shook hands with them, Gary McNeal entered the room to stay with her. An odd feeling curled in the pit of her stomach to have someone other than Daniel with her.

Daniel gave her a single nod before shutting the door behind him.

While Daniel was gone, Gary kicked back and watched a baseball game as Ani used her nervous energy to straighten up the beds. She hoped like crazy the hairspray masked the scent of sex, and that Gary didn't wonder why the room smelled like hairspray when her hair was still wet.

Feeling rather depressed about being stuck in the hotel and not able to be out in her city, she started ironing the wrinkles in the clothes that had been brought for them. Gary seemed friendly enough, but she didn't attempt to get into any kind of conversation with him the couple of times they spoke. The silence between them was actually kind of comfortable.

Less than an hour had gone by when a knock sounded at the door. Gary drew his gun like Daniel always did, and gripped it as he checked the peephole, then holstered it again after letting Daniel in.

Daniel stepped inside with a nod to Gary, who stayed in the room, and let the heavy door slam shut behind him. He was carrying a white paper bag, a white plastic bag, and two Styrofoam cups with steam wafting through the plastic covers. Something in one of the packages he was carrying smelled *really* good and her mouth watered. Something sweet, along with the scent of ginger.

"Mmmmm . . ." She pushed herself up from the chair she'd been sitting in and went to him. "I hope whatever it is tastes as good as it smells."

"Like Korean sweet bean rolls?"

Ani almost clapped her hands in excitement. "Lord, it's been so long since I've had one. Gimme, gimme."

Daniel snorted a laugh and set the packages down on the vanity table in front of the mirror. He handed her one of the steaming cups. "Ginger tea from the Korean bakery, with piñon nuts in the tea."

She snatched the cup from him. "I know exactly what bakery you went to." She sipped at the very hot tea that tasted of ginger with a hint of piñon. "This is sooooo good."

"None for me, Parker?" Gary said with a touch of humor in his voice.

"Hell, no." Ani looked at him. "Mine," she said, then grinned. "You can have some if you want."

"No, thanks." Gary shook his head and smiled. "Ate my fill a little while ago," he added as he walked to the door, then let himself out of the room, shutting it securely behind him.

Daniel handed her a sweet bean roll and she bit into it with relish. Her favorite—white bean. The roll was so soft and the sweet bean paste had just the right texture and flavor.

"Perfect." While she devoured her roll, she set the cup down and peeked inside the plastic bag. She looked up at him from beneath her lashes when she saw the box of condoms. A *huge* box. When her gaze met his, she swallowed down her last bite of roll and said, "Big plans for the week?"

He gave her a grin and a wink, and heat flooded her body. Her fresh pair of panties were totally damp now.

She turned her attention back to the pastry bag. "Got any more?"

"Knock yourself out," he said, just as his cell phone rang.

Ani dug into the bag and pulled out a huge almond cookie and another bean roll. Too perfect.

Daniel tensed when "unknown" came up on his cell caller ID. He flipped the phone open and answered, "Parker."

"John Singleton," came the man's voice on the other end of the line. "We've talked before. I'm the AUSA for the Borenko case," the assistant United States attorney continued without pause. "We need to take care of witness prep with Anistana King. She'll probably be on the stand day after tomorrow—Friday. I'd like you to bring her to the U.S. attorney's office at nine tomorrow morning."

Daniel clenched his jaw and pinched the bridge of his nose with his thumb and forefinger. *Damn.* The last thing he wanted to do was move Ani.

"We need to run her through her testimony and make sure there are no surprises," Singleton was saying.

Daniel raked his hand through his hair. "We'll be there," he said before the prosecutor dropped the connection.

"What's wrong?" Ani watched him as he raked his hand through his hair again.

He jammed the phone into the holster on his belt. "We have to be at the U.S. attorney's office tomorrow morning to go over your testimony."

"Okay." She straightened her shoulders and raised her chin. "I'm ready."

"Are you?" He went to her and took her by her arms and couldn't help the harshness in his tone. "I'm not. I'm not ready to take the chance of you being in public and being a target for any reason. Hell, just taking you to the trial is going to be bad enough."

"Hey." Ani tugged on his overshirt with both of her hands. "Everything will be fine. We'll get through this." She gave him a little smile. "We've made it this far, haven't we?"

Not without several near misses, Daniel thought as he crushed her to him and held her tight. The thought of putting her at risk scared the shit out of him. She wrapped her arms around his waist and settled her face against his chest.

"I'll be fine, Daniel," she murmured. "With you, I'll be okay."

CHAPTER TWELVE

As he and the other Deputy Marshals escorted Ani through the lobby of the Martinique, Daniel's gut ached.

Five Deputies surrounded her, counting Daniel. One in front, another behind her, and one on the opposite side from Daniel. One additional Deputy walked ahead of them. As was the norm, all the Deputies were dressed in civilian clothing, ensuring they blended with the crowd.

With such a tight guard, Daniel should have felt some confidence, but as badly as the Borenkos wanted Ani, he didn't believe she was safe enough.

The fact that other Deputies had lost their lives doing their job grated at him. Every loss of life was another slam to his chest.

Last night Daniel and Ani had made love two more times and this morning he'd woken with her in his arms. It had felt perfect. She was perfect.

He couldn't get his fill of her. Every time he saw

her, touched her, scented her—it stirred desire in him, primal and deep. It all magnified his need to protect her, keep her from harm of any kind. Especially from the Borenkos.

Even if she were merely a program participant and he just her contact, he'd protect her with all he had. Failure of any kind wasn't an option.

He felt that ache in his gut, an ache that became more intense whenever she was in potential danger.

And his personal feelings for her grew stronger every minute that passed. Damned if he knew what to do about it.

This morning, Ani wore black jeans and a black T-shirt, along with a black ball cap she'd tucked her hair under, and of course she wore her body armor under a T-shirt. Earlier this morning he'd gone out and purchased some of that beige makeup crap from the pharmacy. She'd smoothed the makeup over the bruise while he'd watched, and she'd winced when she'd touched the purpled skin. It seemed to help tone the bruise down so that it didn't show as badly. But it didn't lessen the fury in his heart.

While they headed through the hotel, she kept her face lowered, just as he'd instructed her to.

Four blacked-out SUVs were parked in front of the Martinique. Before Daniel would allow Ani out of the hotel, he and another Deputy spoke with two more Deputy Marshals who had been watching the street.

Another Deputy had been running constant counter-surveillance around the block and two others had swept the vehicles for explosives.

None of the Deputy Marshals had spotted anyone loitering or sitting in any of the parked cars. Deputies had been on duty from the time Ani had arrived at the hotel, keeping an eye on the street. They rotated out so that they were on duty for eight hours before being relieved.

Even though Daniel and the other Deputies didn't see anything or anyone suspicious, his jaw still tightened when they brought Ani out of the hotel. They rushed her into one of the waiting SUVs, the one immediately behind the lead vehicle. He and two of the Deputies who had been surrounding Ani climbed into one of the vehicles with her. Two pairs took the rear SUVs, and another pair of Deputies were already in the front vehicle.

From the time they'd left the hotel room, until they were seated in the vehicle, everyone had remained quiet.

Once they were driving along Fifth Avenue, Ani tilted her head back and let out a long breath. "This is too much, Daniel." She looked at him and her features were strained. "The closer we come to the trial, the more scared I get."

He could have echoed the same sentiment—that he was scared shitless for her—but he chose to reassure her instead. "Everything will be fine. After your testimony tomorrow it'll all be over with."

"Will it?" Ani's belly churned at the thought that it was almost time to face something she'd known was ahead of her for over two years. "I'll be in hiding for the rest of my life."

Daniel looked at her like he wanted to take her into his arms to reassure her and make her feel better, but of course he couldn't. Not with all of the other Deputies in the SUV.

Ani settled for occupying herself by taking in the sights of her city. She drank it all in, wishing again she could feel some excitement at being in New York City—taste it, smell it, live it. But knowing she'd never truly experience it all again put a damper on her mood. Not that it could really get any darker considering she was a murder target.

Sometimes she was so angry at her father that she wanted to scream. God, she missed him. But if it wasn't for his being involved with the Russian Mafia to begin with, none of this would ever have happened. He had been bought. And they all had paid.

New York City couldn't possibly be more different than the places in Oregon and Arizona that she'd lived in after leaving the city. Towering buildings crammed one up against another; streets packed with people of every nationality, creed, and color; cars nearly outnumbering mustard-yellow taxis; stores selling every possible thing a person could wish to purchase; and vendors hawking everything from tourist items to fresh fruit and vegetables.

Ani caught a whiff of roasted chestnuts and peanuts through the SUV's air vents as they drove. She could almost taste hot dogs and her mouth watered at the thought of eating one with the works. Or with a load of sauerkraut, plain yellow mustard, and ketchup. Nothing compared to New York's hot dogs or pizza.

The city was so bright, so vivid, so colorful.

That was, if one ignored the aged walls dirtied from pollution, scaffolding on too many buildings to count, and the cracked sidewalks marred with gum and other sticky substances blackened and trod on by countless people.

But that had never mattered when she'd lived here. She'd just loved it.

Her thoughts turned for a moment to that tiny town in Arizona where she'd lived for the last year. What a difference. People in the small town would smile and say hi when she passed them on the sidewalk. If a person did that in New York, they were likely to get mugged.

Along the way to Federal Plaza, they passed Madison Square Park, Union Square, and SoHo boutiques. As they skirted Chinatown, Ani wished she could go back to her favorite dim sum restaurant and have her fill of fried potstickers, along with steamed dumplings crammed with pork, shrimp, and other delicacies. Not to mention the baked pork buns and hot jasmine tea.

She sighed again as countless memories assailed her. Just breathing in the city's air brought to mind things she'd nearly forgotten.

Much too quickly, it seemed, they reached Federal Plaza, which was south of Canal Street. When the four SUVs arrived, the Deputies in the first vehicle stopped at a Marshal checkpoint. Then all four SUVs drove down a side street to an alleyway next to a dark red brick building. The vehicles stopped in front of a metal plate that slanted about three feet upward. The plate lowered so the SUVs could pass through. They drove up to a corrugated metal door beneath the building that slowly rose, allowing them entrance to a dark parking garage. Daniel told her Deputy Marshals escorted other witnesses and prisoners into the building this way.

She sure felt like a prisoner right now. And all because of the Russian Mafia.

After everyone climbed out of the SUVs, Daniel and the other Deputies escorted her from the underground parking lot, which smelled of oil and dirt. They left the garage by way of an elevator, then navigated through a series of hallways to another elevator.

The building's cafeteria must have been nearby, because she caught a whiff of something like broccoli-cheese casserole. Finally, they reached a conference room where two men were waiting.

Daniel accompanied her into the windowless conference room with its wooden oval table and chairs. The carpets looked dirty, the table worn, and the room had a musty odor.

The other Deputies stayed outside the door to the room. Ani pulled off her ball cap and her dark hair tumbled from beneath it to her shoulders.

She held the cap as one of the men stood, smiled, and approached her. "You must be Anistana King," he said as he extended his hand. "John Singleton, from the U.S. attorney's office. I'm prosecuting this case."

Ani wasn't sure what she thought of him, but the

prosecutor had a firm grip when he shook her hand. His aftershave was light and spicy, and his dark hair cut short and professional-looking—like he'd just stepped out of a TV law show. He had brown eyes that reflected the intelligence and arrogance of a man who knew his job and knew he was good at it.

"What does AUSA stand for?" Ani couldn't think of anything else to say.

"Assistant United States attorney," Singleton said. He then reintroduced the FBI case agent, who also shook hands with Ani.

She vaguely remembered Special Agent Michaels from two years ago, a short period of time that was a blur in her mind after the murders and fire. He'd been the agent who'd debriefed her—to whom she told everything—before she'd been whisked away.

Ani settled into a chair the prosecutor pulled out for her. He seated her close to him at the long, dark conference table.

Daniel shook both men's hands then retreated and hitched his shoulder up against the doorframe, his arms crossed over his chest.

Singleton focused on Ani. She noticed his gaze went to the bruise down the side of her face before he looked directly at her.

"I want to let you know how much I appreciate and commiserate with what I understand you've been through over the last couple of days," he said as he adjusted a thick file folder in front of him.

Ani still had no idea what to say to this man, so she just nodded and clenched the ball cap in her fists.

"Before you go into the courtroom tomorrow," Singleton said as he gestured with his head to the FBI case agent, "Special Agent Michaels will be on the witness stand. He'll testify regarding evidence the FBI has garnered that corroborates your testimony.

"Other witnesses have been testifying up until this point," he continued. "The neighbors who helped you when you first got out of the house. Emergency personnel, as to what they saw when they arrived—you and your sister and the condition you were in when they reached you. Today the doctors are testifying about your and your sister's medical conditions when you were treated."

He paused and her stomach sickened, somehow knowing what was coming next. "Also the coroner will testify about your parents and what killed them—burns, what caliber bullet—"

Daniel cleared his throat and Ani held back tears. She hadn't even been able to attend her parents' or her sister's funerals.

"And about Jenn, too," she whispered. "The coroner will talk about how she died."

Singleton looked away from her and down at the file folder in front of him without answering. She frowned. Something felt off, but she couldn't pinpoint what it was.

When he looked up at her again, he gave her an all-business smile. "Your statement is what we need to pull all the pieces together."

Ani bit the inside of her cheek and nodded again.

"It's time to get started." Singleton opened the file

folder. "I'll give you a general outline of how my questions will proceed, then I'll go into possible cross-examination by the defense. Don't get flustered. Focus on telling the truth as you know it. Don't elaborate with your answers, but answer truthfully. And try to remember everything you can right now. I don't want any surprises in that courtroom."

The thought of having to look her family's killer in the face again made her so nauseated she couldn't speak. As much as she wanted to put him away, a rockhard feeling of fear settled in her belly—she could still picture Dmitry Borenko's deadly ice-blue eyes and feel the horror as he shot her father and turned his gun on her. The memories alone caused her shoulder wound to ache and her burn scars to itch.

Singleton folded his hands on top of the open file folder. He looked up at Daniel then back to Ani. "After we're finished here, we'll arrange for you to walk through the courtroom and get a feel for it so that you'll be more comfortable with everything. How does that sound?"

"Fine," Ani managed to get out. "I'm ready."

But the churning in her stomach made her wonder if that was remotely close to the truth.

"I'm going to start by asking you some basic questions about yourself, so the jury can get to know you," Singleton continued. "Then, I'll ask you to explain the sequence of events leading up to your father's involvement with the defendant, your knowledge of the money-laundering, racketeering, wire fraud, and so forth. We'll finish with your family's murder."

Singleton didn't waste any time beginning her witness prep. After he asked questions about her past two years in WITSEC and prompted her on what to share with the court, he said, "Start from the beginning, Ms. King. Explain to the jury how you came to obtain the documents you read that relate to the defendant."

Ani's heart clenched and she thought she was going to be sick as her mind went back to the day she had discovered the damning information on her father's computer.

She took a deep breath before she started. "On August eighteenth, two years ago, I went to visit my mother and my sister, Jenn. She'd been home for the summer and was getting ready to return to San Francisco State University to work on her bachelor's degree in education. My mother, Jenn, and I spent some time gardening in the backyard in my parents' Brooklyn home."

"Go on," Singleton said with an encouraging nod.

"I decided to take a break and check my e-mail on my father's computer." Ani started wringing the ball cap in her hands and Singleton glanced down and shook his head in the negative, telling her not to fidget by the look in his eyes.

She straightened her spine and forced herself to still her hands. "I was waiting for an important e-mail regarding a transaction for a priceless work of art the museum was interested in. The museum where I worked as a curator.

"My father, Henry King," she continued, "was away for a couple of days, but he had given me the password to his computer. He let me check my e-mail whenever I needed to when I was visiting."

Singleton leaned closer, his gaze never wavering from hers. "What did your father do for a living?"

"He was a security consultant." Instead of the pride she'd once felt for her father, cold betrayal washed through her. "He was elected to the city council in our district and served for three years before he was murdered."

"Don't use the word 'murdered,' Ani," Singleton said. "Defense will object to it as a question for the jury to decide."

Even though Borenko *was* a murdering bastard, Ani nodded.

Singleton's gaze was almost unnerving as he studied her. "Where was Mr. King the day you used his computer?"

"In Boston. He was scheduled to come home the following day."

"What happened when you logged on to Mr. King's computer?"

The cold wouldn't leave her body and goose bumps broke out on her arms. "Before I opened up the Web browser, I noticed my father's e-mail program was up and one of the e-mails was open."

"Did you make a habit of reading your father's e-mail?"

Ani shook her head. "Never. But just as I was about to log on to the Internet, a short sentence jumped out at me."

"And that sentence was . . . ?"

Heat suffused her cheeks and she looked down at the cap in her hands before looking at Singleton. "It said . . ." She paused to clear her throat. " 'No fuck-ups this time, King.' "

His face was expressionless. "Continue, please."

"It was a short e-mail," she said. "The subject line was 'Blue Meadow Arrangement.' " She could picture that e-mail as if she had just viewed it. "The text read, 'Problem eliminated. Proceed with transaction and funds will be transferred as arranged.' " She fiddled with the cap. "It ended with that line about no fu—that line I just said. The whole thing sounded off to me, not quite right. And the implied threat, well, it scared me."

"What did you do then, Ms. King?"

"I was worried. I knew something had to be wrong. I began going through more of my father's e-mails." Just thinking about them made her entire body tense. What her father had become—how would she ever get over it? "Several of the e-mails referred to 'deals' and funds having been transferred. A few more said 'problem eliminated.' All were on different dates."

Singleton was the picture of professionalism as he asked the questions. "Was that all you read on your father's computer?"

"No." Ani shook her head. "I knew I was invading my father's privacy, but I felt compelled to look for any documents that might explain some of what I'd read in the e-mails. The whole thing made me feel like my father was into something deep and dangerous."

As cold and nauseated as she felt at that moment, she wasn't sure how she continued to speak. "When I went through one of his computer file folders, a document with the name Blue Meadow Project caught my eye because of the correlation to the heading on a few of the e-mails I'd read. The Blue Meadow Project had been a touchy subject, and my father had been on that zoning committee."

Ani brushed a lock of hair out of her face and tucked it behind her ear. "I just assumed that my father had been against it because changing the zoning would allow the area to be used commercially. A developer could tear down the existing apartment complex, displacing elderly residents. Despite protests, the commercial zoning won out."

The apartment buildings had been torn down several months before she'd read the document, and businesses in Blue Meadow had already begun to sprout. The businesses included a nightclub, a Russian restaurant, an arcade, and a coin-operated Laundromat. At that time there'd been a few other spaces left for more businesses.

"What information did the document contain?" Singleton prompted her again.

Ani's heart had begun to thump like it was going to burst through her chest just as it had when she had pored over the notes. "My father was extremely obsessive, and had always kept intricately detailed journals."

But that one . . . it had made her sick enough she'd wanted to throw up the moment she'd read it. How could he have done what he had? The man who'd fathered her, whom she had loved so much, had trusted implicitly . . . how could such a good man stoop to such horrible actions?

She took a deep breath. "The journal mentioned specific council members who were bought off in order to zone Blue Meadow as commercial so the Russian Mafia could build businesses they would use to launder funds. It specifically mentioned Dmitry Borenko and his 'family.' "

A dead weight lay in Ani's belly and her nausea grew. "My father had apparently documented all he'd been involved with. Every meeting, every conversation, every e-mail, and every wire transfer, along with the corresponding bank accounts."

Tears bit at the back of her eyes. "It mentioned people who'd been 'eliminated,' who had stood in the Mafia's way. Names and the dates that these people were found murdered. They corresponded with the e-mails about elimination."

Ani was almost certain she was going to throw up. She remembered looking around her after reading the document, her eyes glazed as she stared at the finely appointed den. She'd thought about all the expensive things her father had been able to provide for his family and the beautiful house they had owned in Brooklyn. Not to mention the cruises, trips to Australia, Europe, and Asia.

Her father had been bought out by the Russian Mafia.

"What then, Ms. King?" Singleton asked, interrupting her tortured thoughts.

"When I couldn't take any more," Ani said, "I

closed the document and sought out my mother and sister to tell them I didn't feel well and that I was going home."

It hadn't been far from the truth.

She hadn't been able to stop thinking about what she'd read. All the details had continued to churn over and over in her mind and she'd been unable to fight back tears. After tossing and turning most of the night, she'd come to the conclusion that she had to confront her father.

"The following evening," Ani finally continued, "after I left work at the museum, I went straight to my parents' home. I was going to use my own key to get in, but the door was unlocked. I didn't want to talk to my mother or sister until I'd confronted my father, so I went directly to my father's den.

"When I reached it, I stopped just outside the doorway because he had three guests in his office. Two men stood to either side of a man who was sitting in a chair between them.

"My father was seated behind his desk. They didn't seem to notice me and I was planning to leave the den until the men were gone.

"But Father called the seated man Dmitry, which caught my attention immediately because Dmitry was the one member of the Russian Mafia who was mentioned most frequently in the document I read.

"I was too stunned to move." Ani clenched her fists and her jaws. "They were there. The Mafia was there. Right in my family's home."

Singleton leaned forward. "Tell us about their conversation."

She squeezed the ball cap in her hands hard enough that her knuckles hurt. "Dmitry told my father the 'family' needed more help from him to take care of the mayor—that he had become a 'problem' for some other reason than the Blue Meadow project. He didn't specify. Dmitry said he needed my father to procure a visitor's pass to get someone inside City Hall. Someone to 'eliminate the problem.' The bastard had used the phrase in such a casual way, like he really enjoyed saying it."

The closer she came to the events that had destroyed her life, Ani's throat wanted to close off. "My father stood. 'I want out, Dmitry,' he said. Dmitry replied, 'Our family doesn't tolerate deserters, Henry.'

"Father looked so angry. 'Killing the mayor wasn't part of any bargain,' he said." Ani tried hard to swallow. "Dmitry just shrugged and said, 'We do what we must.'

"My father went on about how he'd gone through enough trouble convincing other council members to vote in favor of zoning Blue Meadow commercial so that the Borenkos could build businesses to launder their funds. He said he'd performed every other function the Borenkos had requested of him."

Singleton's gaze was steady, unemotional. "He specifically mentioned the Borenkos?"

"Absolutely." Ani nodded. "He said he'd decided he wanted out. He refused to have anything more to do with the Russian Mafia. He was done."

Ani's vision blurred and her voice shook. " 'Then this discussion has ended,' Dmitry said. He got up from his seat, reached beneath his jacket, and drew out a gun. Faster than I had time to process what was happening, a shot rang out and a hole appeared in my father's forehead." Tears rolled freely down Ani's face. "He—he collapsed into his chair."

She didn't bother to wipe the tears from her eyes. "Dmitry said, 'Problem eliminated,' just before I screamed."

The memories of the disbelief and the horror of the moment made Ani feel as if she'd been broadsided. "Dmitry—he casually looked over his shoulder and saw me standing outside the doorway, and raised his gun.

"I started to turn to run, but pain slammed into my left shoulder, above my heart, and I fell." Ani reached up and rubbed the wound that now ached as if she'd just been shot.

She could still hear her own screams from the pain, could feel the agony. She'd pressed her hand against the wound, and remembered the feel of blood leaking through her fingers. She'd had a hard time focusing, so overcome with pain and horror at watching Dmitry murder her father.

"My mother and sister ran into the room. I tried to shout at them, to tell them to get out, but nothing would come out of my mouth." Ani held her arms tight around herself and rocked back and forth as she cried. "But Dmitry shot my mother then my sister. Jenn screamed before she hit the floor, then she was silent," Ani whispered. "Our mother never made a sound."

They hadn't moved. They'd been so completely still. Ani's breath had come in short, harsh gasps as the unreality of it all had swept through her.

Singleton's firm gaze kept her in the here and now as she looked at him. "Please continue," he said.

Continue, continue, continue . . .

Ani cleared her throat. "Dmitry ordered the other two men to torch the house before he walked out." She clenched her arms around herself tighter. "The two men followed him, then one came back and returned with a can—and I smelled gasoline. The man tore a drape from the curtain rod and threw it over my mother's body. He soaked her and the drape with gas, then dropped his cigarette."

It had tumbled through the air, end over end, its glowing red tip almost mesmerizing.

It landed on the drape.

Flames whooshed over her body.

Ani screamed for her mother.

The man tossed more gas on the furniture and in front of the door before he let himself out and shut the door behind him.

By the time Ani finished her story her whole body was ice-cold and she could feel herself slipping into that place where reality no longer existed. Her eyes began to glaze over and she started to feel fire licking at her body.

No. She fought to regain control. She couldn't let the PTSD take over and push her back into that place again. And definitely not in court. She had to have complete control over herself. She took the hem of the shirt she was wearing over her body armor and wiped her face with it before straightening in her seat and meeting Singleton's gaze. She felt Daniel's presence behind her, and wished he could take her in his arms and just hold her.

"Are you all right?" Singleton asked, but in a calm, professional tone.

No, she wanted to scream. She wasn't all right. She would never be all right again.

But she took a deep breath and exhaled before saying, "Yes," in a voice so quiet she could barely hear herself.

Singleton nodded and began grilling her mercilessly. He fired question after question after question, tearing apart every bit of her story.

"The defense will be brutal in their cross-examination, Ms. King," Singleton said, his voice hard. "It won't matter to the defense attorney that you lost your family to that bastard. What they're going to do is rip you up one side and down the other. By the time they get through with you, you'll feel like you've been through a meat shredder."

His expression and his tone gentled as he leaned back in his chair. "You did well today, Ani. Tomorrow your testimony will help us put Dmitry Borenko behind bars for a very long time."

Her eyes stung and she had to fight more tears. She was exhausted from the constant questions he'd thrown at her and emotionally drained from crying and going through what had happened to her family. Tomorrow she would experience this again and likely it would be worse. She only hoped she could keep from completely losing her composure like she had today.

The prosecutor got up from his seat and shook hands with her again. "You're going to do all right." Singleton released her hand and patted her shoulder before walking out the door.

Special Agent Michaels, the FBI case agent, stayed behind to coordinate plans for her actual arrival for the testimony. Ani remained quiet as Michaels and Daniel discussed the plans.

After the case agent left and the door had closed behind him, Ani sniffled and took a shaky breath as she pushed back her chair. Daniel was at her side and held out his hand to help her stand.

To her surprise he enveloped her in a tight hug. His clean male scent calmed her and she wished they could stand right where they were and hold on to each other. She needed his strength so much.

He drew back and took both of her hands in his. He had such big, strong hands. "You okay?"

The air in the conference room was stale and she felt like she couldn't breathe. She stared up at Daniel's handsome face that was marred only by the purple bump on his forehead. He looked so concerned, so caring.

"Get me out of here. Please."

Daniel released her hands. "Sure you don't need a minute?"

Ani brought the shirt up and wiped her face again, almost dropping the ball cap. The makeup she'd been wearing was now a beige smear on the black shirt.

When she straightened, he put his hand on her elbow and they walked out into the hallway where the other Deputies waited. There were about ten Deputies accompanying her, she realized. It hadn't quite hit her before. So many—to protect just her.

Daniel dropped his hand. "We'll take you on that tour now so you can get accustomed to a similar courtroom before tomorrow."

"Sure." Her chest ached with the knowledge that tomorrow this would all be very real. If today had been bad, what was tomorrow going to be like?

She met Daniel's gaze. "He's here, now, isn't he?"

Daniel nodded. "Borenko is testifying, but on another floor, in another courtroom than the one we're taking you to. We'll be far enough away that no one will even know we're here."

Ani looked at all the men and women surrounding her. Yeah, right. Like she didn't stick out with a mob of people around her, even if they were dressed like civilians.

With the other Deputies following, Daniel guided her along a hallway and down a series of steps until they reached a barren passageway with a steel door at one end.

"This underground hallway was finished only recently," Daniel said as he escorted her into it. "There's no way in hell I'd take you outside to walk from the U.S. attorney's building to one of the federal courthouses. There are two courthouses—the old one and a newer, more modern one, where the trial will be held. Before this hallway was built, only the old courthouse was connected."

The hallway smelled of freshly painted walls. It was a simple concrete rectangular tube that seemed to go on forever, with only lights to break it up along the way. Ani found herself breathing a little faster, feeling almost claustrophobic. Her heart beat hard, as if Dmitry would be waiting for her at the end of the tunnel.

A little over two years ago Ani had given her statement to the cops and the federal agents when they debriefed her. They had secreted her away while the case agent worked with the AUSA to get an indictment against Dmitry for all the violations, including murder. An arrest warrant was issued and Dmitry was locked up.

However, because he could afford a good attorney, he made bail, after his long-standing ties to the community had been established ensuring he wasn't a flight risk. The bail had been extraordinarily large, but his family hadn't had a problem making it.

Ani and the Deputy Marshals finally reached another steel door, and they entered a different building. More hallways, more steps, and then an elevator.

After they got into the elevator, a man tried to join them, but the Deputies blocked the door with their bodies and told him to take the next car.

The elevator opened to an enormous hallway. The floor tile was mottled black-and-white marble and their footsteps echoed as they walked.

When they entered the courtroom, her eyes widened at the sheer size of the place. It was so much bigger than any courtroom she'd seen on TV. She'd never been selected for jury duty, so everything was new to her. Right now she wished she had been chosen to serve on a jury just so she'd have more experience to draw from.

Daniel directed her down the aisle between the rows of wooden benches, to the dark mahogany barrier between the spectators and the floor of the courtroom. He opened the swinging gate for her and she stepped through. The other Deputies followed behind them.

On the right were risers contained within the jury box where the jurors would sit. She remembered from a TV program that the prosecution table was always closest to the jury. The defense table was on the left side of the gates. A large desk sat in front of the raised judge's bench. The smaller table was close to the witness box for the court transcriber. The American flag stood on the left side of the Court of the United States seal positioned behind the judge's bench.

Daniel gestured to the witness box. "Why don't you try it out?"

Ani rubbed her arms from the chill. Either the air-conditioning was up high, or she was really nervous. She voted for nervous.

After she took a step up into the witness box, she sat and looked out into the courtroom. Two of the Deputies guarded either side of the door they'd just come through.

Another chill caused her to shiver as she stared at the defense table. All she could think about was facing her family's murderer. She'd never forget his face, the casual way he'd shot her father and then turned the gun on her.

"In some ways I don't want to be forced to look at the man who murdered my family." She felt Daniel's warmth behind her as she spoke. "In other ways I want to stare him down. I want him to see the person who's going to send him to prison."

Daniel rested his hand on her shoulder and squeezed. "Do you realize what an incredible woman you are?" he whispered.

She turned in the chair to face him, and kept her voice low. "I don't feel incredible. I feel scared and angry and it's all balled up inside of me so tight I think I'm going to lose it. I want to scream and cry. But right now I'm just drained. I'm totally out of energy."

"Come on." He took her hand to help her to her feet. "Let's get back to the hotel."

After she tucked her hair up under her cap again, Daniel and the Deputy Marshals took her back the way she'd entered the building, and out into the dirty underground garage where the four SUVs were waiting.

CHAPTER THIRTEEN

After they left Federal Plaza, the four SUVs snaked through traffic, McNeal driving the vehicle Ani and Daniel occupied, Hernandez riding shotgun.

Daniel ground his teeth the moment they hit congestion.

Deputy Jacobs's voice came over the radio, "There's a suspicious van trying to edge in behind you. They look nervous as hell and we're pretty sure we saw the passenger holding a handgun. Kramer and I can divert the van away from you, but it will leave your ass open."

"Shit." Daniel looked over his shoulder. "Do it," he shouted into his handheld radio. The two rear SUVs of their motorcade edged off a blue van.

In front of them, gridlock.

McNeal practically rode the bumper of the lead SUV, not allowing more than a foot between the vehicles.

Then McNeal stepped on the brakes, hard, as the SUV in front of them came to an abrupt halt. Their vehicle bounced off the lead's bumper and Daniel's body jerked forward against his seat belt, then back in his seat.

Just as they started moving again, Daniel glanced over his shoulder to see a green sedan slide in behind them.

McNeal grabbed the radio microphone and spoke into it, asking Jacobs if he'd run the tags on the van behind Kramer and Jacobs.

Ani sat beside Daniel, looking from him to the men in the front, her mouth pressed into a thin line.

"Done," came Jacob's voice over the speaker. "It's registered to a Matvei Suhov. We've got the son-ofabitch pinned in traffic."

McNeal slammed on his brakes again, causing everyone to jerk forward and back in their seats. "Accident ahead. Total fucking gridlock."

The lead vehicle came to a hard stop again.

Daniel looked over his shoulder. One of the men in the sedan leaned his forearm on the vehicle's window frame, his right hand out of sight. The other man started opening his door.

"Get out, McNeal," Daniel braced his hands on their seats. "You and Hernandez take care of the bastards behind us and I'll get Ani the hell out of here."

"You got it." McNeal drew his gun just before he pushed open his door and Hernandez stepped out from the passenger side, Glock in hand.

As soon as the Deputies were out of the SUV and had slammed the doors shut, Daniel climbed into the driver's seat. "Stay in the back," Daniel told Ani. "You'll be safer there."

Daniel looked at the lead vehicle. Totally jammed in traffic. He glanced to his right and saw an opening on the sidewalk.

He glanced over his shoulder and noticed her face looked pale. "How are we going to get out of this mess?" she asked.

"A little creative driving." Daniel whipped the wheel to the right, climbing over a sidewalk, barely missing a fire hydrant and an elderly woman. People jumped out of his way as he hit the siren.

In his side view mirror, Daniel spotted the green sedan. It turned out of traffic, almost running over McNeal and Hernandez, and followed their SUV over the sidewalk. "Hold on, honey."

"We've picked up a tail," he said as he radioed the Deputies in the other SUVs.

The accident ahead looked serious and must have just happened. Only one cop car had reached it. Sirens and horns of the FDNY and the NYPD blasted through the air as the emergency vehicles attempted to shove their way to the accident site. The lights and sirens of the Marshal SUVs just blended in.

As he drove on the sidewalk, siren blaring, lights flashing, Daniel considered heading toward the accident where cops and emergency vehicles would converge. He tensed so tight his whole body ached.

No, he couldn't take the chance of making Ani a sitting target.

She gasped as he continued to drive the SUV on

the sidewalks, dodging people and delivery trucks but scraping the sides of the SUV on a couple of mailboxes and a fire hydrant. The SUV rattled as he nicked several parking meters. He slowed down as people flattened themselves against the buildings to let him by.

The lights and siren didn't deter the sedan from hanging on to their asses and gaining on them.

Getting through all the pedestrians on the sidewalk was so slow that Daniel thought his head would explode from frustration. Anger rose in him like heat from a furnace.

The sedan battered its way through pedestrians, getting closer.

Within shooting distance.

A man leaned out of the passenger side window and pointed a handgun at them.

"Get down!" he shouted to Ani just as a bullet slammed into the rear window's bulletproof glass. He glanced in his rearview mirror for a split second. Ani was down like he'd told her. The glass had spider-webbed where the bullet had struck.

Two more shots hit the back of the SUV.

"Goddamnit!" Daniel tried to push the vehicle faster without running over any pedestrians.

Ani cried out as another bullet smashed the rear window, near the first one. The glass was weakening. Another hit like that and he might be taking a bullet in the head.

Daniel saw the light of day. They were almost past the gridlock.

A few more moments and he guided the SUV back onto the street where traffic was actually moving. He revved the engine and jerked the steering wheel as he wove his way in and out of the traffic. Even with his lights and sirens on, horns blared as he narrowly missed sideswiping several cars.

Sweat had broken out on his forehead and his heart thundered. The green sedan still clung to their asses.

"I can't shake the tail," Daniel said over the radio.

Deputy Zaharis's voice came from the former lead vehicle's radio. "Get the witness someplace safe and we'll try to keep these assholes off you."

Ani climbed into the front seat, her head nearly striking the passenger door window when he swerved.

"I told you to stay in the back," he growled as she snapped her belt buckle on.

"Take a left ahead," Ani said in a tense voice, and he glanced at her. "I grew up here, remember?"

At the next intersection, Daniel spun through the light and headed in the opposite direction, away from the Martinique. The SUV's tires squealed as he whipped the vehicle around a corner. He smelled burning rubber.

A double-decker tourist bus came at them head-on, horn blaring.

Daniel jerked the wheel. Avoided the bus.

The sedan fell back as the bus continued through the intersection.

In moments, the tail was on their asses again.

Following Ani's breathless directions, Daniel took a quick right onto another street, then shot into the left-hand lane, cutting in front of several vehicles.

As it made the turn, the car skidded behind them.

A small Honda shot in front of the sedan. The vehicle sideswiped it. Tires screeching against asphalt and the crunch of metal reached Daniel's ears over the sound of the siren.

The minor accident only slowed the bastards following them. They fled the scene and continued after Daniel and Ani.

The vehicle managed to evade the rest of the traffic until a produce truck swung in front of the sedan. The truck nearly ripped off the car's door when the sedan slid into the truck. Melons and vegetables went flying from the truck, splattering on cars. Horns blared, tires screeched.

The sedan shoved its way through the mess, but had fallen far enough back that Daniel figured there was a good chance of losing them.

When their SUV reached streets with traffic that wasn't nearly as heavy as it had been downtown, Daniel flipped off the lights and sirens so they wouldn't stick out as much. Their tail was farther back, but their pursuers were relentless.

Ani told Daniel what side streets he could take and he gunned the SUV as fast as he could, given whatever amount of traffic was on the road. The streets were narrow and it was a wonder he didn't hit any pedestrians as he sped the vehicle along.

Finally the car chasing them fell back far enough Daniel was confident they could lose the bastards.

Ani gave him another street to turn down. "It splits off two ways when we near the end." She sounded as if she was having a hard time speaking. "If we can get there fast enough, they might not be able to tell which way we've gone."

Daniel took the corner hard and fast, almost skidding into an oncoming car. He raced down the side street, dodging a garbage truck and a bicycle messenger. He looked in his rearview mirror. With the garbage truck blocking the way, the sedan was out of sight.

"Here," Ani said. "Take a right, then a fast left, then a real quick right."

He pushed the SUV faster, made the right, and booked down the street and made a left that was closer than he'd expected. Same for the next right. They drove for a ways down that street, past businesses and restaurants. No sign of the men following them.

"There's a parking garage up here on the left. The garage has a back entrance," Ani said. When he spotted it and started to turn, she said, "I don't see anyone behind us."

He monitored the street behind them as he lowered the window and punched the red button for a parking voucher.

"Where's the other entrance?" he asked as they waited for the wooden lever arm to rise, then drove through the fairly dim parking garage.

She gestured to the left. "Around that corner."

Daniel followed her instruction, then turned right as he watched the signs until the lever arm of the other entrance was in sight. Instead of exiting, he kept going until he came to an empty parking spot. He backed up into it and turned off the engine, but left the keys in the ignition.

His heart still pounded and he took a deep breath. The injuries on his ass and thighs ached from being so tense, tightening his wounds. The area between his shoulder blades throbbed where he'd taken the bullet to the back of his body armor the other day and blood pounded through the bump on his head.

"Hopefully we'll be safe and out of sight here," he said, and reached over to take Ani's hand.

She looked as wrung out as he felt. "It was a wonder we weren't killed a few times. Especially when we almost got nailed by that tourist bus."

He managed a wry smile. "Had my heart racing a bit, too."

"A bit?" Ani shook her head. "I thought mine was going to explode."

Daniel radioed in their situation to the other Deputies, saying they were going to stay put until he was sure he had the witness out of danger, but didn't give specifics. "We'll head to a safe house once we're sure we're in the clear," he said before signing off.

"Now that there's the possibility our location's been compromised," Daniel said as he fisted his free hand on his thigh, "we're going to have to switch to a safe house."

"What about all of our things?" Ani frowned. "We have some very personal items in that room."

Yeah, they sure as hell did. Daniel pushed his hand through his hair. "I'll take care of it."

The sound of a car driving through the garage echoed against the concrete walls.

"Down!" Daniel ducked and caught Ani by the back of the neck and drew her low with him. He pulled out his Glock. He hoped to hell it wasn't those assholes in the sedan. The way their SUV was shot up, it wouldn't be hard to recognize.

The unseen vehicle's motor purred as it passed. Daniel raised his head just high enough to see a family of four in a BMW heading toward the exit. After the car was gone, he let Ani sit up.

For the next fifteen minutes or so they sat, tense silence between them. He gripped the Glock tight where he held it on his thigh.

A good long while later, when he felt they were definitely in the clear, he holstered his weapon and looked at Ani.

He released her hand, raised his own, and caressed the bruise on her face with his knuckles. Bruises or not, she was so beautiful in every way. Her big blue eyes, that cute nose, her full lips, the curve of her face, her delicate hands. From the moment he'd met Ani, he'd known something was special about her. Because she was so thin now, she looked different, which was taking him sometime to get used to. But she was just as beautiful now as she had been when they'd first met.

At least half an hour had passed since they'd entered the garage. He leaned over the console and tugged her hand. "Come here." His voice was a husky command.

Ani wet her lips again and moved toward him, and he caught the scent of mint and woman. When their faces were close enough, he brushed his mouth over hers. She gave a soft sigh and a little moan against his lips.

Daniel pulled away and took a deep breath before glancing around the garage again. He swallowed down the lust that didn't belong in this place or time.

He'd better get his mind back on the job and off his need to be with Ani.

When it was dark and Daniel was absolutely certain they hadn't been followed, he arranged to trade vehicles with another pair of Deputies, then took Ani to a safe house.

It was a nondescript brownstone, and more importantly, it had exits at the front and back. They were able to park an unmarked car in front of the safe house, place undercover guards in more unmarked cars up and down the street, and they still had an emergency escape route out the back.

When Ani was settled and secure upstairs in a room with two exits, guards posted to either side of her door and at the door to the adjoining room, Daniel asked for a moment alone with McNeal.

Daniel met up with McNeal in the kitchen. As Daniel sat at the table in a chair opposite McNeal, his friend told him that Daniel and Ani likely hadn't run into any cops as they made their escape because the NYPD had been slammed with a shitload of accidents, and even a bank robbery.

As Daniel shook his head, McNeal briefed him on

what had happened with the men in the blue van. There'd been no sign of the sedan once Daniel lost the tail.

"Bastards in the van were armed to the teeth." McNeal turned his chair around so that he was straddling it, his arms folded across the back. "We nailed them. With our men in the rear, along with Hernandez and me, we were able to take them down and send them to their new home with the NYPD."

"Good job." Daniel looked at the plastic bottle of water he hadn't touched yet, and wished it was whiskey. He wasn't off duty as Ani's 24/7 bodyguard, but after today he could use a stiff drink. Something to relieve the tension in his body. Especially with what he was going to ask of McNeal.

Daniel hoped their long-standing friendship would hold out if his friend suspected anything after his request.

He pinched the bridge of his nose, then looked at his friend. "I need you to get our gear from our room at the Martinique."

"No problem." McNeal had a puzzled expression on his face as he took a drink of his own water. He set the bottle down. "Why didn't you just call me?"

Daniel didn't know how the hell to put it, so he stalled by knocking back some of the water in front of him. The ice-cold water rolled down his throat into his empty stomach that growled in response. He sighed as he peeled the label off the bottle. "I've got some real personal items in that room. It's out of sight in one of the bags, but I don't want to take any chances of it being seen. I need you and only you to get everything for Ani and me."

For a long moment McNeal just studied Daniel. Finally, McNeal said, "You're fucking the witness."

Daniel's head ached. McNeal had always had real good instincts. "I know I've compromised my position." This time he took a long swallow of his icy water. Yeah, he'd definitely rather have whiskey. He set the bottle on the table with a thump. "But you've got to let me get Ani through this alive."

McNeal had a real hard look on his face. "You should let another Inspector take over her case."

"I can't let her go this alone." Daniel leaned his forearm on the small, round table and it tilted slightly. "I've got to be there to protect her."

"What about when this is over with?" McNeal said. "What the hell are you going to do then?"

"What I have to." Daniel pushed his hand through his hair. "Goddamnit, Gary, I'm in love with this woman. I'd do anything for her, no matter the cost."

"That includes your job, buddy." McNeal shook his head. "They might put you into another area, but you know you'll be off WITSEC. Permanently."

Daniel looked down at the label he'd torn off the water bottle before returning his gaze to McNeal's. "I've known that from the moment I realized I was in love with her."

McNeal dragged his hand over his face before responding. "You've always been one of the most stand-up guys I've known in the service. I never would have expected this."

"Me, neither." Daniel ground his teeth then said, "I fell hard for her. Real hard. I intended to wait to take it any further until after the trial and she was out of danger. But things got a little out of control."

McNeal shook his head. "I'll leave it up to you to face that music."

A measure of relief escaped Daniel's lungs. "I don't want to put you in a bad spot."

"You're the one in deep." McNeal grabbed his bottle and took another gulp.

Daniel added quietly, "Like I said, I love this woman. Didn't intend for things to get carried so far before it was over with, but it did. A few more days and I'll do what I've got to do."

"I trust you, buddy." McNeal took the key card Daniel had dug out of his pocket and handed him. "I'll get your crap from the hotel and you can take it from there." McNeal got up from his chair and gave Daniel a short nod.

He watched his friend walk across the kitchen and through the closed door that thumped quietly behind him.

Daniel took another drink of his ice water, wishing again that it was one hell of a big shot of whiskey. He shoved his seat back and got to his feet, then headed for the stairs. In the mood he was in, he barely nodded to the Deputy guarding the foot of the stairs.

Damnit. He should have waited to take things so far with Ani, but he'd lost his mind.

When he reached the room, he acknowledged the guards outside Ani's doorway. For appearances' sake,

Ani and Daniel were each in a different bedroom in the safe house, but it was connected through a bathroom.

He entered his own room, locked the door behind him, then strode through the bathroom and looked into Ani's room from the doorway.

She had stripped off her body armor and jeans, and was just in her undershirt. She was curled up on her side on the bed, her eyes closed and her features relaxed. She was asleep.

He moved to her bed and sat on the edge of it. For a long moment he studied her, noting every line, every curve. He took a lock of her hair and wrapped his finger in it, enjoying the silky softness.

She stirred and murmured something in her sleep as he stood and moved to the bureau where she'd left her body armor. He stripped out of his overshirt, then his armor, leaving only his undershirt on, like Ani.

As quietly as he could he eased onto the bed, scooted close to her, and wrapped his arm around her waist as he spooned her back to his chest. She snuggled against him, but he was certain she was still asleep.

Daniel held her as his mind worked through everything that had happened up to this point. The Borenkos were too smart. Even when it had looked like he and Ani had probably bought it when the cars exploded, the Borenkos hadn't given up looking for her.

Tomorrow was Friday and she'd be testifying. He'd get her through all of this mess, and then he'd tell her just how much he cared for her.

The conversation with McNeal churned through his mind. Daniel already knew what he'd have to do as soon as the trial was over—it wasn't a question of if, but a question of when. He had to keep Ani safe, and then he'd do what he had to do.

CHAPTER FOURTEEN

A knock startled Ani and she opened her eyes. The knock came from the room next door—the room where Daniel was supposed to be sleeping—but was loud enough that it had woken her.

She felt Daniel's warmth behind her and was enveloped by his scent that she loved so much. Then his weight shifted as he rolled away and off the bed. The heat of his body left with him and she sighed from the loss of contact.

Ani rubbed her eyes with her fingers as he paused at the foot of the bed. She heard the rustle of stiff cotton as he tugged on his jeans before his feet padded across the tile of the bathroom floor from her room to his to answer the door.

What time was it? Her vision was still a little hazy and she felt like she had grit in her eyes. She pushed herself to a sitting position with her back against the headboard and looked over to the opposite side of the bed where a clock displayed 9:21 P.M. in bold, glowing red numbers. The day had been so long she was surprised that it wasn't a lot later.

Soft light poured in through a window with lacy curtains, breaking up the darkness so that Ani could see to turn on the lamp beside the bed. She blinked in the sudden yellow glow.

She heard Daniel speaking with another man and a thud then another on the floor before the door closed with a loud thump and a click.

Daniel came back into her room, a rumbling sound following in his wake as two carry-on suitcases rolled across the wood floor.

"McNeal got us something to keep all of our things in," he said as he set a suitcase on the bed. "Not to mention he cleaned out the hotel room for us."

The vibration of the suitcase hitting the bed traveled through her. Ani was still a little sleepy and she yawned. "That was nice of him."

She gave Daniel a lazy smile as she watched him. He was so sexy with his rumpled hair and the stubble on his jaw. Beneath his tight black T-shirt his muscles flexed, and she couldn't help a sigh of pleasure. He turned her on just by the way he moved.

Daniel unzipped one case and opened it. The thing was stuffed with all the clothing that had been purchased for her and delivered just this morning. Wow, it felt like days instead of hours.

The pharmacy bag was on top and she could see the red of the condom box through the bag and her face grew hot.

Her gaze met his. "They know," she said, her heart

sinking. Concern for him and his job tightened her chest.

"Only Gary McNeal." Daniel took the box of condoms out and set it on one of the oak nightstands beside the bed. "I'll have to deal with everything later." His eyes met hers. "For now we'll worry about your safety."

She laid her hand over her belly as nervousness caused her stomach to twist like a wet dishrag. "I should never have—"

"Hey." Daniel sat on the bed next to her, close enough that he could settle his palm on her bare thigh. "I knew what I was doing, and I wouldn't go back and change a thing. Understand?"

Ani worried her lower lip then said, "I can't help but feel—"

He placed his hand over her mouth, silencing her. "Do you regret any of our time together?"

She looked up into his eyes. How could she regret anything about being with this man? Except for the fact they'd probably endangered his job.

"Do you?" he asked again.

Slowly, Ani shook her head, her lips sliding across his palm.

"Good." He moved his hand from her mouth, slipped it into her hair and cupped the back of her head. He drew her closer. "I'm a big boy, honey. Nothing happened that I didn't want to happen. I just planned to wait a little longer."

Her eyes widened. "You—"

"Yeah." He brought his mouth so that his lips

nearly brushed hers as he spoke. "I had no intention of letting you go once all of this is over with. I still don't."

Ani's heart pounded hard enough to feel it against her breastbone. All thought evaporated as he caught her mouth in a soft kiss that stole the breath from her lungs. Everything slipped away with that kiss. It took her to new heights, took her to the clouds, took her to the stars and beyond.

Daniel eased her down on the bed so that they were stretched out, lying face-to-face. He hooked his jean-clad thigh over her bare hip as he broke the kiss. He traced her jawline with his fingertip as he smiled at her.

"From the first moment I met you, I knew you were special." He rubbed his thumb over her lips in a soft sensuous movement. "For two years I haven't been able to get you out of my mind, out of my system."

She swallowed, trying to say something but having a difficult time finding the words. The way he was looking at her, the things he was saying to her, the way he was caressing her mouth with his thumb, made her mind go back into those clouds and stars his kiss had taken her to just moments before.

"Talking on the phone with you . . ." Daniel sucked in a deep breath. "It made me want you more than you can imagine. And I'm not talking about sex. I'm talking about you and me." He gave her a crooked grin that caused butterflies to take over every other feeling in her body. Dozens and dozens of butterflies. "But the sex part is great, too."

His expression grew more serious as he started to

stroke her cheek with his thumb and cupped the side of her face in his palm.

She leaned into his touch and closed her eyes. Daniel was saying things she'd dreamed of, but never thought would come true. Never thought *could* come true. She was someone he was assigned to keep safe. He was her protector.

But he was so much more than that.

And now he was her lover.

Her eyes were still closed when his lips met hers and he took her mouth in another tender kiss. Tasting, seeking, claiming . . . loving?

When he backed away she opened her eyes to see him studying her, his brown gaze dark with arousal and his expression so caring. After this past year of talking with him on the phone and sharing so many things about themselves, she felt such an incredible connection to him.

The sexual attraction had always been there, crackling over the telephone lines, but it had been more than that—at least on her part. And it sounded like he'd felt something, too. That he still did.

He seemed to be waiting for her to say something, but no words would come to her. She wanted to say, "I love you, Daniel," but she was afraid to push him. Maybe he wasn't ready for that step. The fact that he cared for her this much was enough for now.

When she didn't say anything, he picked up her hand and brought it to his mouth. She shivered as he pressed his lips to each of her knuckles before turning her hand over and kissing the inside of her wrist.

Desire rolled like a firestorm in her belly, working its way down to the place between her thighs in a slow burn. He moved his lips up her arm from her wrist until he reached the inside of her elbow. She watched the softness on his features as he focused on touching her, tasting her. He darted his tongue along her flesh and she shivered with every lick and kiss.

Daniel's mouth reached her bicep just below the sleeve of her T-shirt and she caught her breath as he nipped her flesh. He raised his head and brought his mouth to hers. He kissed her, darting his tongue inside her mouth and giving a deep groan that sent another thrill throughout her, from head to toe.

Gently he rolled her onto her back so that he was kneeling between her thighs, looking down at her. He grasped the bottom of her T-shirt and pushed it up until her belly was bared and he placed soft kisses all over her skin.

She couldn't stop the soft moans that rose up in her throat. Moisture dampened her underwear and she wondered if he could scent her arousal. He continued to raise her T-shirt in achingly slow movements and slipped it up over her bra.

"Mmmmm . . ." he murmured as he nuzzled her satin bra and her nipples pressed against the thin fabric. "You smell so good. You always smell good." He circled one of her nipples through the satin with his tongue, wetting it and making the nub harder and tighter.

Ani wriggled beneath him and wound her fingers in

his silky brown hair. "You smell good, too." She sucked in a deep breath and let his scent wash through her. Male. Pure male.

He moved his mouth to her other satin-covered nipple, leaving the first one hard against the now damp fabric. Again he circled her nipple then sucked it. She fisted her hands tighter in his hair and arched her back so that her breasts thrust closer to his mouth.

The whimpers and moans rising from her didn't stop, she couldn't stop them. She wanted him to hurry and take her. She wanted it slow and sensual. Fast. Slow.

She wanted him any way she could have him.

Daniel trailed his lips up the curve of her throat to her chin until his mouth rested on hers. Immediately she sighed, waiting for his kiss. Instead of plunging his tongue into her mouth, he gently nipped at her lower lip then traced the edge of her teeth with his tongue. She pulled his head down so that their mouths met more firmly and he gave a soft laugh against her lips before taking her mouth in a slow and sensual kiss.

Ani grasped his hips between her legs, feeling the roughness of his clothing on the insides of her bare thighs. He mimicked thrusting into her, rocking his jean-covered cock against her damp panties and causing more sounds to escape her throat.

When he moved his mouth from hers and trailed kisses along her jawline to her ear, she groaned out loud. He was being so slow and attentive, but she wanted his naked skin against hers. At the same time she loved everything he was doing to her. He dipped his tongue in her ear. Everything he did made her shiver, tremble, squirm with need.

Daniel drew away and gave her his sexy smile that made her heart and body melt. He rested on his haunches as he tugged her T-shirt up and she helped him pull it over her head, leaving her only in her bra and panties. After he tossed her T-shirt over his shoulder, he braced his hands to either side of her arms.

"Do you have any idea of how beautiful you are?" He dipped his head and kissed her softly before raising his head again. "I bet you don't even realize it."

Heat flooded Ani's body. "I'm not—"

His mouth dove down to capture hers in a hard, silencing kiss.

Daniel settled back on his haunches again and reached beneath her back for the clasp of her bra. She arched up so that he could reach it more easily, and he unclasped her bra in a simple movement. The satin slid across her breasts as he pulled it down her arms. Her nipples tightened into hard, aching nubs.

As if fascinated by her breasts, he stared down as he cupped them, squeezed them, and pinched her nipples hard enough that pain mingled with pleasure. Ani wriggled and reached for him again, wanting to draw him down to lick and suck them. She wrapped her arms around his neck and tugged him forward, needing to feel his mouth on her.

His sexy smile thrilled her again as he moved to

one of the taut nubs and slipped it into the warmth of his mouth. She gave a little cry and arched up, thrusting her breast more firmly against his face. He licked harder and sucked harder, and she swore she was going to climax from the sensations spiraling from her nipple to her belly, to her clit.

Too fast, too slow, he moved his mouth to her other nipple and suckled on it. He made low growling noises as if staking his claim on his territory. She loved the sounds he made as he pleasured her.

Daniel kissed her hard again before moving lower, kissing her shoulder before brushing his lips over her breastbone. He worked his way farther down, trailing his lips along the center of her chest to her belly button. She squirmed as he dipped his tongue into her navel. She swore it was connected directly to her sex the way it made her feel deep inside of her.

He moved his mouth over the flatness of her belly to the line of her silky panties. He ran his tongue along the edge of her panties then caught the elastic band in his teeth and tugged down. She smiled at the same time she raised her hips to help him draw her panties lower.

When he reached her mound, he took an audible inhale and groaned before tugging her panties farther down. He grasped her thighs with his palms and slid them along as he removed her panties with his teeth. It was so incredibly sexy having him take her underwear off this way.

Daniel used his hands to slip them off her feet and she was totally naked—and he was still clothed. She didn't want him wearing anything at all. She started to get up, but he was between her thighs again and gently placed his palm between her breasts and pushed her back down on the mattress.

"I'm not finished yet." He traced the inside of one of her thighs with his fingertip. "Spread your legs as wide as you can."

Tingles spread throughout her as she obeyed him. He rewarded her with a smile and adjusted himself on the bed so his head was between her thighs.

In anticipation of his mouth on her clit, she caught her breath. Instead, he blew softly on her folds and she squirmed from the exquisite sensation. He grasped her thighs firmly in his large palms, spreading her wider, then nuzzled the curls of her mound.

Ani clenched the bedspread to either side of her in her fists and bit her lower lip to keep from yelling at him to lick her folds.

Daniel blew on her clit again before he swiped his tongue from the soft skin between her anus and her sex all the way up her folds to her mound.

This time she couldn't help a low cry and found herself begging him for more. "Daniel, please."

He looked up at her and gave her a wicked grin before burying his face against her folds.

She squeezed her legs against his face. His stubble abraded the inside of her thighs and the skin around her folds as he moved his head while licking and sucking her clit.

Ani gripped the covers tighter in her fists and lost herself in the feel of his mouth on her. She grew even more lost when he slipped a couple of his fingers into her core and began pounding his knuckles against her flesh. How she loved that. Him pounding, thrusting, licking, sucking. The only thing better was having him inside her.

Through the haze in her mind, she looked at him and saw him staring up at her. The sight of his head between her thighs as he went down on her sent more thrills through her belly.

The swirling sensation in her body began to tighten inside her, winding up before it would release through her whole body. Tighter and tighter it wound, until she was shaking, her thighs trembling around his face.

She couldn't see his features anymore because her vision blurred. She tilted her head back and let the buildup grip her whole body until she reached higher and higher—

And lost it. The coil inside her released and her body flooded with icy heat, her skin tingling, her core contracting around his fingers, and her clit swollen against his tongue. She bit her lip to keep from crying out and being heard by the guards outside the door.

She gripped his head tight between her thighs as he continued to lick and suck her clit. She thrashed from side to side as her orgasm continued on and on, as if it would never end. Sweat broke out on her forehead and she felt a sheen of perspiration coat her body.

"Okay, okay." Ani twisted in his grip and held back another cry as a wave clenched her abdomen. "Stop, Daniel."

He gave her clit a few more swipes with his tongue,

causing her core to spasm. She was whimpering and begging him to stop the sweet torture when he finally obeyed.

Daniel placed a kiss on the lips of her pussy then eased up so that he was looking down over her, his hands braced to either side of her head.

"You are so gorgeous when you come." He lowered his head until his mouth was close to hers. "With your skin flushed pink and your body trembling."

The scent of her musk on him was strong, heady when mixed with his masculine scent. His lips met hers and he slipped his tongue between her lips and she gave a sated moan. Her taste mingled with his. He kissed her hard, as if he was having a difficult time holding himself back now. His clothing felt rough against her naked body, an erotic sensation that she loved. But she liked it better when they were both naked.

While he continued to kiss her, she tugged at his T-shirt, pulling it out of his jeans. She slipped her hands under his shirt and ran her palms over the hard planes of his abs, to his carved chest. His muscles flexed beneath her hands as they roamed his firm flesh. She brushed his flat nipples and paused to tweak them and he kissed her harder.

Ani pushed his T-shirt farther up his chest so that she could explore his powerful shoulders and the tendons of his neck.

Slowly, still continuing her exploration, she let his T-shirt fall back to his waist as she moved her hands down to the waistband of his jeans. He sucked in his breath as she came close to his erection. But she knew the teasing game, and she was going to make him wait, like he'd done to her. Besides, she was having too much fun.

Not to mention it was really turning her on even more to feel his muscular body beneath her palms and between her thighs.

Daniel groaned as her hands left his waistband and she moved her palms up the soft hair of his forearms to his biceps that bulged and flexed as he shifted above her. He drew away from the kiss and a hungry look burned in his eyes.

"Take off your shirt." She moved her fingers along his waistband again. "I want to see you."

He pushed away from her so that he was on his haunches again and he tugged his T-shirt over his head and flung it aside. She watched the play of muscles beneath his skin with every movement he made. Taking the shirt off had rumpled his hair and he looked sexier than ever.

Ani moistened one of her fingers in her mouth, her eyes on Daniel. She ran her wet finger along the waistband of his jeans and his look grew fiercer. "You know how to play with fire, don't you, honey," he said as he captured her hand in his.

He brought it lower and pressed her palm to his erection. When she ran her fingers over his jeans from the head of his hard cock down to his balls, a soft purring sound rose up within her.

Daniel's growl was louder and he thrust his hips back and forth, his cock hard against her palm.

A feeling of empowerment sizzled through her and she placed both of her hands on his chest and pushed. She rolled him onto his back then heard the thud of their suitcases as the movement caused him to knock the cases off the bed.

They grinned at one another, although his grin seemed a little pained. She straddled him and kissed him with a hunger like nothing she'd ever felt before. Her nipples brushed his bare chest. More moisture released from between her thighs when he pinched and pulled her nipples as they kissed.

She drew away. "No, this is about you."

"Then let me be inside you, honey." His voice was husky as he squeezed her breasts harder.

With a shake of her head, she smiled. "Not yet, Marshal."

She felt his rough stubble beneath her lips as she kissed his jawline, down his neck, until her mouth met the hollow of his throat. He grasped her ass and began to massage it.

Ani stilled for a moment and raised her head. "Just don't touch my back, okay?

"One day you need to share everything with me." His expression was serious. "I said I would wait until you're ready, and I will—but we won't keep anything from each other, okay?"

As he said the words his gut clenched. When Ani found out about her sister—*Christ.* She might not forgive him. He just told her they wouldn't keep anything from one another, and he'd been keeping a secret from her for two years.

After the trial, he kept telling himself. *After the trial when she's safe.*

In the meantime, Ani was driving him out of his mind as she slowly moved down his chest, making small circles with her tongue. He never considered his own flat nipples as erogenous zones, but when she licked and bit at his, it blew that thought all to hell.

He was careful not to touch her back as she moved down, licking a path closer to the button of his jeans. He settled his palms on the indentation of her waist and groaned from the tightness of his cock against its prison.

With a few fumbled attempts, Ani unbuttoned his jeans and looked up at him. Her expression was so sexy as she took the tab of his zipper in her teeth and slowly slid it down. Her mouth passed over his cloth-covered erection and he groaned. Hell, she knew how to get even.

When his zipper was down, she raised her head, grasped the waistband of his jeans in her hands, and tugged. He raised his hips so that she could more easily pull them off. He about came unglued when she lightly bit his cock through his briefs.

He reached for her but she slid farther down, taking his jeans with her. "Damnit, Ani, I need to be inside you."

"You're just going to have to wait." She eased his jeans all the way off and threw them aside.

His cock was hard enough, and he needed her so much that his erection practically vibrated. Her fingertips skimmed the light hair on his legs, to the place where his briefs met the insides of his thighs.

"I'm about to throw you down and bury myself inside you." He clenched his hands in her hair. "I'm not kidding."

She grabbed the waistband of his briefs and gave him a sexy little grin as she started to pull them down. She ran her tongue along his cock as she freed it, then paused to lick his balls.

A growl rose up in his throat and he released her hair as she continued to work the briefs off, so slowly, flicking her tongue along the inside of one of his thighs as she went.

"Come here," he said in a voice that was hoarse and demanding.

She just gave a soft laugh and finished taking his briefs off and ditched them.

Ani got to her feet and he wondered what the hell she was going to do next. She went to one of the suitcases and pulled a condom packet out of the box.

When she returned, she had dropped the wrapper and was holding the condom. While she held on to it, she ran her hands up his calves to his knees, then moved her palms to the insides of his thighs.

Ani climbed back on the bed, looking like a sleek cat with her dark hair, blue eyes, and the slow, sensual way she moved as she made him wait.

He thought he was going to burst when she reached his erection and grasped it in her hand. She placed the condom on the head of his cock and then moved her mouth down to the condom. She wrapped her lips around his erection as she pushed the condom down with her mouth and her hand so slowly and so sensually until his cock was fully sheathed and he was about to lose his mind.

With a sexy smile she looked up at him. But she cried out in obvious surprise when he grasped her forearms and dragged her up his length until she was straddling his hips, her slick folds against his cock. "Now, Ani. I've got to be inside you so damn bad."

"Not yet." She groaned and tilted her head back as she rocked her hips, her clit rubbing his erection. Her folds slid up and down his cock at the same time he moved with her, just not inside her.

She let her head fall forward and her curtain of dark hair caressed his face and chest as she kissed him. He couldn't stand this waiting game. He grasped her face in his hands and kissed her hard and hungry. Ani moaned and matched his kiss. It grew wilder, more intense, and soon their hands were everywhere as they kissed. Touching, squeezing, caressing, grasping.

A low growl rose up in Daniel that he couldn't hold back.

Fuck the wait.

He flipped Ani onto her back and she gasped. He hooked his arms beneath her knees, spreading her thighs wide, his cock pressed against her pussy.

"No fair," she said, even though she was breathless and her eyes were dark with passion.

He knew she wanted this now as much as he did. He could read it in her expression, in the way she looked at him, the way she ran her tongue along her bottom lip in anticipation.

She gave him a little pout. "I was having fun."

"I bet you were." He released one of her legs long enough to place the head of his cock at the entrance to her core. Just enough that he was slightly in and ready to drive into her.

Ani squirmed beneath him and linked her fingers behind his head as she lifted her hips, trying to take him inside her.

"Finished teasing, honey?" He slid in a fraction then retreated.

"Yes." She raised her hips again. "I want you now."

He raised her knees higher, spread her thighs wider, and drove his cock deep inside her pussy.

She gave a strangled cry, obviously holding back from making more noise, and writhed as he held himself still. So hot. So tight. So wet.

"More," she whispered. "Don't stop. Don't wait."

In slow, deliberate strokes, he began to pump his cock in and out of her pussy. Damn, she felt good. So damn good.

The way her core gripped his erection was enough to make him come if he hadn't fought so hard to keep from climaxing.

Slick, so slick. A tightening sensation grew in his groin. His vision swam and darkened and he thought he saw stars. He wasn't going to last much longer.

The sensations spiraling through Ani were like colorful streamers whirling in a storm. The way Daniel had her spread wide, with his arms hooked under her knees, made her feel him deeper than ever.

He thrust faster and harder, his jaw tight and his eyes intense as he focused completely on her. Their slick skin slid against one another and the smell of sex and sweat made those colorful streamers inside her whirl even faster.

The way he felt inside her—it was indescribable. He touched places that pushed her higher and farther. Bright colors twinkled in her mind and she knew it was only a matter of a few more strokes before she would be gone.

She was so close to crying out, "I love you, Daniel." It was all she could do to hold it back.

Instead she let herself completely fall into the place he was taking her. Those streamers of colors and sparkles of light swirled through her mind as she gritted back a cry from the force of her orgasm. All she could see were the colors that were now like an aurora shimmering in her mind.

Her body shook and she was vaguely aware of clinging to Daniel as he continued to thrust and thrust and thrust.

No words would come to her as she started to come down. But a cry did slip from her. He captured her mouth, his kiss grounding her and bringing her back to reality.

She still felt high, like her head would float off, but Daniel's face came back into view. He was sweating and an almost pained expression crossed his face.

"Come, Daniel." She pulled his head down to meet hers, and said against his lips, "Come, now."

He raised his head and she could tell he was holding back a shout as he pressed his hips hard against hers. She felt his cock jerk inside her and her core clamped down on him every time a spasm rocked her.

Finally, he lowered her legs and rested on top of her, holding his weight just enough that he wouldn't hurt her.

He moved his mouth to hers and kissed her again before drawing her onto her side with him and holding her close.

CHAPTER FIFTEEN

Today was the day.

After leaving the safe house under a tight guard, Ani's stomach ached as she was whisked away to a private location. From there she would be escorted to Federal Plaza and the courtroom.

This time five black SUVs waited for them in a designated location. All had blacked-out windows. Ani had a hard time coming to terms with the fact that so many Deputies had to protect her as she was taken to court.

She felt like she was going to throw up. Chills continued to race under her skin, causing her to quiver nonstop.

All of the vehicles had been swept and reswept for explosives. Once the SUVs and the street were declared secure, at least twelve federal agents surrounded her as she was escorted out of the car she arrived in to one of the other vehicles.

She felt exposed in the lot, even surrounded by so

many agents. All of a sudden, New York City seemed cold and unfamiliar, almost hostile. Somewhere in this city, people were hiding and waiting to kill her.

What if the mob fired missiles at the cars again? What if a sniper shot her in the head and dropped her right then and there?

Get a grip. You can do this. You will *do it!*

Like the other Marshals, Daniel wore a black suit and dark glasses. Ani wore one of the dress suits that had been bought for her when the other clothing was purchased. The black suit was loose, the low heels tight. She wore her Kevlar vest beneath the blazer over her blouse. Since she didn't have one of her hair clips, her long dark hair hung in waves around her shoulders.

Daniel helped her into the SUV, and Ani felt grateful for the sudden shelter of the vehicle. She sat between him and another Deputy, while two Deputies took the front seat. She felt a little scrunched between the broad-shouldered men, but well protected. The smell of leather from the seats and the men's aftershave filled the SUV.

As soon as the Deputies in all five vehicles radioed they were ready to move, the SUV Ani was in followed two of the other SUVs into traffic.

She clenched her hands in her lap and wished she could take Daniel's hand and lean into him for comfort. But she remained rigid in her seat, her mind racing through everything they'd been through up until now. The climax.

This was happening. It was really happening.

She was about to go to court to testify against her family's killer. And she was going to testify about the information she had read on her father's computer and what she had overheard as she stood outside her father's office.

Her mouth was dry and her palms sweaty as they made the journey to Federal Plaza. Any moment she expected bullets to fly and shatter the glass. Even though it was supposed to be bulletproof, she was afraid someone would get shot. So many people had died already to protect her—she couldn't stand the thought of anyone else being murdered.

She could almost feel a bullet pierce her own skull, like the one that had killed her father.

The trip seemed to take forever and her heart pounded like mad the entire way. She couldn't focus on anything outside the vehicle. All she could think of was the motorcade escorting her through the city and her upcoming testimony.

When they reached the Marshals' back entrance at the courthouse, she still didn't breathe a sigh of relief. It wasn't until they made it through the parking garage and into the building that she relaxed—but only a little. Within a couple of hours she would have to be strong to face Dmitry Borenko head-on. She had to keep calm no matter what the defense threw her way.

The Deputies escorted Ani to a conference room where she was told she would wait until it was her turn to testify. Four Deputies, including Daniel, stayed in the room with her while the other Deputies either stood outside the room or patrolled the halls.

She felt like she was surrounded by men and women from the *Men in Black* movies.

"What do I do now?" she asked Daniel after the door closed behind the other Deputies.

He pushed his hand through his hair, rumpling it in that sexy way she loved. "All we can do is wait. The other witnesses have finished testifying—neighbors, emergency personnel, doctors, the coroner. Special Agent Michaels, the FBI case agent, is testifying this morning. Once the defense attorney has cross-examined him, it will be your turn."

The jittery, trembling feeling inside her increased. How could she make it through hours of waiting?

Unable to sit, Ani paced the length of the conference room, her heels wobbling a bit on the worn carpet. The smell of dust and neglect made her stomach even queasier. She shoved her long hair over her shoulders in a nervous motion then flexed and unflexed her hands at her sides. She ignored the other Deputies in the room but let her gaze meet Daniel's every now and then.

The Deputies made light conversation, talking about sports, the stock market, a couple of major fugitives who had just been apprehended by the U.S. Marshals Service, among other things she couldn't begin to concentrate on at that moment. Right now she couldn't find interest in anything. She was too jumpy, too keyed up.

When she got tired of pacing, she sat in one of the ratty brown chairs and folded her hands on the dark brown laminate tabletop. The waiting was driving her crazy—she wasn't one to sit and do nothing. But even if she'd had a book to read, she wouldn't have been able to concentrate.

Instead, she battled thoughts of Dmitry Borenko, wondering how he'd look now, after two years. Memories of how he *did* look that horrible night flooded her. He'd acted so casual as he'd shot her father. But those ice-blue eyes had narrowed as he turned when her scream caught his attention, and he'd aimed for her heart.

And then her mother and sister. Oh, God. Hearing them scream. The thump of their bodies against the floor when they dropped.

The memories made her gut clench and tears fill her eyes. She wrapped her arms around her belly and rocked to and fro as she tried to get the thoughts out of her mind.

What seemed like hours and hours later, the door opened and she just about jumped out of her skin. Gary McNeal carried in a tray of food. Smells of mashed potatoes, gravy, beef and the strong smell of coffee met Ani's nose even before the orange plastic tray reached her.

"Hit the lunchroom." McNeal directed his statement to all the Deputies in the room and nodded toward the door. "Judge Steele has ordered a short recess for lunch. She isn't giving us much time." To Daniel he said, "We've got four Deputies ready to relieve you."

Daniel's gaze met Ani's, and his expression was one of concern, caring, and support. He hesitated, then followed McNeal out of the room, along with the other Deputies. Four Deputies came in the door to replace those who'd left.

A sense of panic rose up within Ani and her heart beat faster as she watched Daniel exit. He glanced over his shoulder with an expression that said he didn't want to leave her. She hoped her panic didn't show on her face. She needed to be strong and not lose her self-control. When had she come to rely on him so much for emotional support?

Ani's shoulders slumped a little as she stared down at the plastic-wrapped plate. Her stomach was churning too much to eat, but she peeled the plastic off and the smell of canned corn added to the other scents. In another plastic-wrapped bowl was canned fruit cocktail. There was also a glass of orange juice with plastic wrap covering the top of it, coffee in a plastic-lidded Styrofoam container, a straw, and a bottle of water.

Oh, yum.

The silverware and a paper napkin were bound by a piece of paper that she tore off. She noticed there was no knife.

And to think she could have gone after Dmitry herself with it.

Her lips twisted briefly in amusement at her thought, but the amusement faded almost at once. Her movements were mechanical, and she only messed with the things on the tray to have something to do. Otherwise she would probably have pushed the whole thing away from her. How could anyone expect her to eat right now?

She *was* thirsty, however, even though she'd been supplied with water bottles all morning.

After toying with her food and drinking most of the orange juice, she told one of the Deputies she had to use the bathroom.

Talk about an ordeal. All she had to do was pee, for cripe's sake. But still she knew it was in the interest of her safety as four Deputies accompanied her. Two checked out the bathroom and secured it. Deputy Janet Hernandez stayed in the bathroom with her.

When she returned to the conference room, John Singleton, the prosecuting attorney, was waiting for her.

"Sit, please, Ms. King." He gestured to the chair and she complied.

When he was seated close to her, she smelled his spicy aftershave. Singleton looked at her directly, wasting no time. "I have to be back in court in a few minutes, but I wanted to check in with you. Are you doing okay?"

Ani tucked her hair behind her ear. "How much longer?"

Singleton leaned closer, his forearms braced on the tabletop. "The defense attorney's cross-examination of Special Agent Michaels is taking longer than I anticipated. Michaels has been presenting evidence that corroborates with your sworn statements. But they need your testimony to make it solid. I expect you'll be on the witness stand soon."

Great. Joy. She couldn't wait.

Mental sarcasm aside, she did want to get this over

with and hoped that her testimony would be enough to put this bastard away.

"When you approach the witness stand, do it in a deliberate and unhurried manner," Singleton said as she tried to focus on him through the roaring in her ears. It had started when she realized how close she was to being in the courtroom. "You're making your first impression to the jury. All eyes in the room will be on you from the time you walk into that courtroom," he continued, remaining focused on her. "Stand erect, act confident."

Ani sat straighter in her seat and took a deep breath. "What else?"

"After you take the oath, don't fidget or exhibit any other nervous mannerisms." Singleton glanced at his watch before looking back to her. "If you do, the jury might think you have something to hide or you're having a difficult time remembering the facts."

"I'll never forget." Ani's spine stiffened. "It's all as clear as if it just happened."

Singleton gave her a smile. "That's what I like to hear, Ms. King." His expression turned serious again. "If you don't understand a question, ask for it to be repeated. No matter how much the defense attorney badgers you, do your best to keep your cool."

Ani nodded. She could do this.

"When your testimony and cross-examination are finished and you're allowed to leave the witness stand," Singleton said, "try to look confident, but not overconfident. It will be the last impression you give the jury."

Her stomach did that twisting thing again.

The prosecutor checked his watch. When his gaze met Ani's he said, "It's time I get back to the courtroom." As he stood, he picked up his briefcase that had been on the floor beside his chair. He paused to look at her one more time. "You'll do fine."

She took a deep breath and tried to smile but failed. "I'm ready," she said, even though she wasn't sure she'd ever be completely ready.

Then more waiting.

The fact Daniel wasn't in the room made her feel as if she were alone with her demons. While she waited, she realized how much Daniel's support truly meant to her. How much *he* meant to her.

The door to the conference room opened and she started. She glanced up to see Daniel stride through the doorway and nod to one of the Deputies to let him know he was the man's replacement. A sense of relief and strength filled her as her gaze met his. It was so hard to keep her expression neutral and not express how much he meant to her.

It took a lot of effort to take her gaze from his and study the still full plate in front of her. She took the plastic wrap and tugged it back over the plate and pushed the tray away.

More waiting.

And waiting.

Finally the door opened and McNeal stepped in the doorway. "She's on."

This time Ani was sure she was going to throw up. Her legs shook as she started to stand, and she had to take deep breaths of air—she felt as if she were suffocating.

Daniel moved to her side at once and helped her to her feet, then he released her. She tugged down the jacket of her suit, adjusted her skirt, and rolled her shoulders back. She didn't know whether to push her hair out of her face or let it fall forward over her shoulders, so she settled for letting it stay the way it was.

When she had stalled as long as she could, she took another deep breath and headed for the door.

She was surrounded by Deputy Marshals, Daniel ever present at her side. The Deputies were almost all taller than her and she felt like a little kid wanting to jump up and down to see what was ahead of them.

They escorted her down a hall to an elevator that made a whirring noise as it descended. Her belly dropped with the car as it sailed down. The pounding of her heart grew faster and faster when they exited the elevator and the Deputies escorted her along another corridor. They took her to a tall door and Daniel told her it was a side entrance to the courtroom.

He squeezed her shoulder. "Kick their asses, Ani."

"I've got my heels on." She gave a tremulous smile as she looked up at him. "I'll grind him into the floor."

The corner of his mouth quirked. "Go get 'em."

The Deputy Marshals opened the door and Ani stepped over the threshold with Daniel on one side of her and Gary McNeal on the other side. She was vaguely aware of the smells of wood and carpeting and the coolness of the room's temperature across her skin.

A sea of faces blurred before her eyes and she grew light-headed. She could barely make out the jury to her left and ascertain that the courtroom was packed.

Then her vision cleared and she saw one man and one man alone.

Dmitry Borenko.

The blond man looked so calm and innocent, his expression almost angelic.

Fear stabbed her belly like a knife and she came to a stop.

In her mind she heard the shot.

Saw the hole appear in her father's head.

Heard herself scream.

Then saw those ice-blue eyes. Killer's eyes.

Dmitry turning his gun on her.

The bullet piercing her, close to her heart.

For one moment while she met Dmitry Borenko's eyes in the courtroom, Ani felt herself slipping. Slipping away back to that night.

The horror.

The fear.

A warm hand pressed against her lower back and she realized it was Daniel encouraging her to go forward to the witness stand.

She jerked herself back to reality and shoved away the fear.

And replaced it with anger.

This was the bastard who murdered her father and mother.

The bastard who made sure Jenn was taken from her life.

Hot rage flamed within her. Pain dug into her shoulder wound and her burn scar itched like mad. She tore her gaze from Dmitry's, held her chin just a little higher, and straightened her spine before she reached the witness stand with the Deputies to either side of her.

Everything seemed surreal, like it wasn't happening to her. For over two years she'd been preparing herself for this moment. Never forgetting her family's killer's face. Never forgetting what had been documented on her father's computer.

Ani hoped her expression was composed as she took the single step up and into the witness stand and moved in front of the chair. Daniel and Gary McNeal retreated.

She remained standing as a Bible was thrust in front of her and she was sworn in by the court reporter.

"Place your left hand on the Bible and raise your right hand."

Ani complied.

"Do you swear to tell the truth, the whole truth, and nothing but the truth, so help you God?" the court reporter asked.

Ani took a deep breath. "Yes." Her voice shook a little and she hoped no one noticed.

Judge Steele said, "The witness may be seated."

After Ani sat, Singleton approached the witness stand. "Ms. King, please state your full name for the record."

Ani avoided looking at Borenko. "My name is Anistana Rachel King."

"Thank you, Ms. King." Singleton gave her an encouraging look. "Tell us where you have been for the last two years."

Ani took a deep breath then let out a slow exhale before answering. "For just over two years I've been in the Witness Security Program," she said. "For the first couple of months I was in a burn center in Oregon, followed by a few weeks in rehab. The burns on my back were a result of the fire that also consumed my mother's and father's bodies." Anger at the thoughts of their murders caused her to raise her voice. "When I was released from rehab, I was transferred to a safe house and went through more physical therapy."

Singleton gave her a nod. "Go ahead."

"This past year I've been residing in a small town in Arizona and working in an antique store." More anger from all that she had lost swept through her. "Before I was put into the Witness Security Program I worked as an art curator for a major museum in New York."

"What about family?" the prosecutor asked.

Ani clenched her fingers. "My mother, father, and sister were murdered two years ago by Dmitry Borenko."

"Objection!" the defense attorney said with a huff. "Whether or not my client had anything to do with the deaths of her family members is up to the jury to decide."

"Disregard the witness's statement about whom she believes to be responsible for the deaths of her family members," Judge Steele said to the jury.

After a nod from Singleton, Ani continued. "I do have cousins, aunts, and uncles, but I was forced to cut all ties to family and friends when I entered WIT-SEC. I haven't been allowed any contact whatsoever with my former life." Her face fell. "When I left, I had a cousin who was getting married and another cousin and his wife who were expecting a child. I haven't been allowed to hear any news about them. It's been like my past never existed."

"Your recent injuries." Singleton gestured to her face. "How did you obtain them?"

Her face felt warm every place she was wounded. She hadn't put any makeup on today so she knew her bruises and scratches stood out against her fair skin.

She kept her eyes on Singleton, not sure she could look at anyone else. "I was first cut during an attempt on my life in Tucson, Arizona, from glass that shattered when I was shot at while on my way back to New York City to testify." She swallowed. "The majority of my injuries were the result of an attack on three U.S. Marshal vehicles after my plane landed in New Jersey. The cars exploded and I was flung through the air and hit with shrapnel. From what I understand, the assailants used a rocket-propelled grenade launcher to blow up the vehicles. Seven Deputy U.S. Marshals died in that attack."

Ani paused and Singleton said, "Go on."

"I have lacerations on the backs of my legs and the other cut on my face." She gestured to the bruises on the other side of her face, then pointed to her shoulder. "I also have extensive bruises on my shoulder and hip."

Singleton gave her a sympathetic look as he glanced at the jury and back to her. She focused on him as he continued his direct examination. "In your own words, please tell the court what led to the night of the murders—the things that concerned you the most." After naming the year, he said, "What are the events leading up to the nineteenth of August?"

She tried not to fidget as she started telling the court about the information she had discovered on her father's computer, just as she had during witness prep. Embarrassment at what her father had done and had become was overshadowed by her anger at the Borenkos for murdering him.

As she testified, the defense repeatedly objected to parts of her testimony. From the judge came "sustained," "overruled," and "I'll allow it"—which all made her feel as if she were on an episode of some television show.

After she finished explaining the records she found on the computer on the eighteenth of August, she told the court how angry she was to discover that her father worked with the Russian Mafia.

"He was out of town the day I found the computer files," Ani said, "so I was unable to speak with him about them."

Singleton held his hands behind his back as he stood in front of the witness box. "Now, I know my next questions will be terribly painful for you, but please do your best to bear with me. Can you tell me where you were on the night of August nineteenth, and what you were doing?"

Ani swallowed hard. "I was at my parents' home, 1616 Potter Street, Brooklyn."

The corner of Borenko's mouth quirked so subtly that she was sure it was meant for her and her alone. He was probably seeing her lying on the carpet of her living room, certain he was leaving her for dead.

Her entire body went cold.

Daniel, where was Daniel? Was he close to her? God, how she needed his support. From the corner of her eye, she caught sight of him standing tall by the adjacent wall next to Gary McNeal and her heart rate slowed a bit.

She sucked in her breath and straightened in her seat. She wasn't going to let Borenko know he was shaking her up.

The prosecutor walked her through the events that occurred the night of the murders. Just like he had during her witness prep, he focused on what she'd overheard Dmitry say before asking her to speak about the shootings and the fire. She felt more angry, grew more rigid with every answer, every word she said, and it became harder and harder to keep from breaking down.

But when it came time to tell him about the murders themselves, she just couldn't help it. Tears rolled down her cheeks. It didn't matter that she was supposed to put up a brave front. The memories were too intense, too painful.

"What are the last things you remember?" Singleton asked gently.

His question threw her off. He hadn't asked her that during the prep.

She held up her chin. Her skin felt tight from crying and her eyes felt puffy. "The last thing I remember from that night is my mother's body burning beneath the gasoline-soaked drape. The hole in my father's head. My sister shot, her body on fire, as I pushed her out of the window, trying to save her."

Ani did everything she could to keep any more tears from falling when she said, "And the face of my family's murderer. I'll never forget his face."

Singleton gestured to the courtroom. "Is the man who shot and burned your family in this room?"

Ani clenched her fists in her lap. "Yes." The word came out loud, clear, resolute.

Singleton's features were a dark mask as he asked in a firm tone, "Could you please point him out?"

Ani looked directly at Dmitry and tried to control the trembling—trembling of rage this time. She pointed to him with no hesitation. "That is the man who murdered my family."

"Let the record show," Singleton said as he looked at the jury, his voice ringing through the courtroom, "the witness identified Dmitry Borenko as the assailant."

Finally, when she didn't think she could answer anything else, Singleton said, "No further questions, Your Honor." To the defense attorney he said, "Your witness, counselor."

Ani straightened in her seat and wiped the tears from her eyes with her fingers. *Here it comes*. She couldn't be weak. She had to be self-assured, confident in her testimony.

The defense attorney, Mr. Plutov, threw her off balance with his first question. "Ms. King, are you absolutely certain of what you saw and heard the night of August nineteenth?"

Ani blinked at him. "No question. I saw Dmitry Borenko shoot my father, myself, my mother, and my sister. Then he ordered two men to set our house on fire. I'm the only one who survived."

Mr. Plutov gave her an indulgent smile, and she wanted to claw out his heart. Bastard. He was already enjoying this. "Sometimes, in the heat of the moment, people can become confused, right?"

"Some people, perhaps." With great force of will, Ani reined in her temper and kept her eyes on the slimy fat man in the brown suit. "But not me."

"So you're certain, with no doubts whatsoever, that your entire family died on August nineteenth."

"Objection." The prosecutor got to his feet. "Asked and answered."

Judge Steele, sounding mildly annoyed, said, "Sustained."

Another indulgent, condescending smile from Mr. Plutov.

Ani clenched her fingers together. Plutov's heart would look good on the flagpole outside the courthouse.

His smile was positively gleaming as he asked his next question. "Ms. King, did you identify the bodies of your mother, father, and sister?"

Ani frowned. "I was taken into protective—"

"Yes or no, Ms. King."

After a pause, she said quietly, "No."

The attorney focused his eyes on hers. They were calculating, intense eyes that held no mercy. "Then you do *not* know for certain if they are all dead."

Singleton stood again and braced his hands on the prosecution's table. "Objection, Your Honor."

"Where are you going with this, counselor?" the judge asked the defense attorney.

"My client is on trial for murder, among other things," the defense attorney said smoothly. "It seems reasonable to establish that, indeed, the people in question are dead."

The defense attorney exchanged glances with the Deputy Marshals and looked at Judge Steele. "Sidebar, please, Your Honor."

"Approach the bench."

Both Singleton and the defense attorney went to the judge's bench, Plutov carrying a file folder. The judge took off her glasses, glanced over the documents. Her head snapped up, she looked at Singleton, her expression sharp and angry. She turned and spoke to the attorneys in tones low enough that Ani couldn't hear.

Not that she could hear through the buzzing in her ears.

"I'll allow it." The judge's expression was thunderous as she put her glasses back on.

The two attorneys retreated from the sidebar and Plutov approached Ani again. Her skin tingled from head to toe and she gripped the hem of her skirt with her fists. What was going on?

Plutov looked positively glowing as he stated, "What would you say if I told you that not all of your family died in that fire, Ms. King? What if I told you that your sister is alive and well? Would that, perhaps, cause you to reevaluate your perceptions of what happened on the night of August nineteenth?"

Ani felt as if the blood had drained from her face to the floor of the witness stand.

Jenn? Alive?

Her gaze shot to Daniel's where he stood with Gary McNeal. Neither had any expression on their faces.

Heart pounding in her throat, she turned back to the court.

He's trying to rattle me.

And he's succeeding.

Singleton pinched the bridge of his nose at the prosecution table and looked down for a moment.

He wasn't objecting?

Plutov approached Ani with an open file folder. "Here is the hospital release form for your sister." He handed her a page and it wavered in her hands as she held it. "She was released from the first hospital she was admitted to, nearly a month after you were taken into protective custody." He said his next statement with emphasis. "She did not die the night of the fire."

Ani stared at the date, not quite registering what it said. September 12. Three weeks after the fire.

He took the paper from her hands as she looked up at him, her mind whirling.

"This can't be accurate," Ani said as she let the paper slip through her hands when Plutov took it from her.

"I was told Jenn died on the operating room table two days after the fire." Yet the paper he'd shown her said she'd been checked out almost a month later. There had to be some kind of mistake. It must have been someone else's release paper.

"As a matter of fact," Plutov said as he faced the jury before looking at Ani again. "There isn't a death certificate for your sister, Jennifer Francis King."

Ani felt as if the courtroom were spinning around her. She clenched onto the railing of the witness stand as if it would help stop the dizziness.

Plutov strutted back to the defense table and tossed the file folder onto it before approaching the witness stand again. "It's been two years, Ms. King. How could you not know your sister is still alive?"

Ani looked frantically at Daniel again, but his face showed no emotion. When her gaze returned to Plutov's, her voice shook as she said, "I was told my sister was dead."

The defense attorney's expression was smug. "We have discovered that she, in fact, was released from the hospital in New York City, taken to a burn center in Rochester, and now resides in that city."

Ani's heart pounded and her mind swam. Her stomach convulsed. She was going to throw up. Oh, God, Jenn was alive? All this time she'd been alive? Her emotions were so ramped up she couldn't sort anything out.

Anger at those who hadn't told her the truth.

Confusion—was this real? Was Jenn really alive?

Joy at the thought that her sister hadn't died.

She isn't dead!

Yet disbelief, too. It was too much to hope for.

"Ms. King," came Plutov's voice, jerking her to the present. "If you didn't know your sister is alive, how do you know if your parents are dead?"

"I—I—" Tears rolled down Ani's cheeks. "I saw the bullet hole in my father's forehead. I saw my mother's body encased in fire. Only Jenn and I made it out of the house."

"But you haven't seen the bodies of your parents, have you?"

"Objection, Your Honor." Singleton approached the bench. "We have autopsies that show both Mr. and Mrs. King are, in fact, deceased."

Singleton sighed and looked at Ani before returning his gaze to the judge. "The witness was in the U.S. Marshals Service Witness Security Program and had signed documents that severed her ties completely to her former life. At the time she signed the papers, her sister *had* died on the operating room table. The fact that she had been revived was not revealed to Ms. Anistana King because she had given up the right to any knowledge of her former life by signing the WIT-SEC contracts."

With every word Singleton said, Ani's hair prickled at the nape of her neck and chill bumps broke out on her skin. Her head swam.

The judge glanced at Ani with an almost sympathetic expression in her eyes. She turned back to the courtroom.

"It's four P.M.," the judge said. "Court is adjourned

until nine A.M. Monday morning when the defense will continue its cross-examination of the witness."

Judge Steele stood and chairs scraped the hardwood floor as everyone in the courtroom stood with her. Like a robot, Ani stood but stared blankly ahead, not seeing anything but her sister's face in her mind.

Jenn. Jenn. Jenn.

Oh, God. Her sister was alive.

But it had been kept from her for over two years. Two years of thinking her sister was dead. Two years of believing she'd lost her entire family that night.

Two years of deception.

Daniel and McNeal approached the witness stand. Both had blank expressions on their faces. Had they known?

Had Daniel known?

If he knew, he would have told her, right?

Movements stiff and rigid, she turned and started to take the step down when her knees gave out. Daniel caught her on one side, McNeal on the other.

Her mind still buzzing and churning, she let them escort her out of the room and into the private hallway where the rest of the Deputies were waiting.

Everything was a blur as the convoy brought her to another hotel rather than the safe house. As the five black vehicles made their way through the city from Federal Plaza, the Borenkos were sure to see where she was being taken, and they couldn't allow the location of the safe house to be revealed. The Deputies talked about how they would be doubling her guard and moving her to another safe house once they had the opportunity to, without the Borenkos finding out their new location.

The Deputies managed to get her into the hotel without getting shot at or blown up, and then upstairs to a hotel suite. Daniel, as usual, was the only Deputy Marshal to enter her suite.

When they were in the center of the sitting room, Ani stared up at Daniel. "You knew, didn't you?" she stated as she looked at him, feeling both numb and incredulous. "All this time you've lied to me."

Daniel braced one hand on the television set and scrubbed his free hand through his hair. "I never told you your sister was dead."

Her gaze didn't move from the man she'd thought she loved. "But you let me think she was."

"I'm sorry." Daniel ran his palm down his face. "We had no choice after you signed the papers, honey."

"Don't you ever call me that again." Ani balled her fists at her sides. "You sonofabitch."

He reached for her. "Ani—"

With everything she had, she slammed her fist into Daniel's nose.

CHAPTER SIXTEEN

Yegor smiled as he relaxed in the Red Room of his mansion. He leaned back in his leather recliner, his feet propped up on a footstool. He took another puff on his rare Leon Jimenes Don Fernando and blew out a ring of smoke. He savored the wood and nut flavors of the cigar as he sucked another draw.

He didn't bother to offer Dmitry or Piterskij a cigar as he listened to their report. The smokes were far too fine for such shits as these two.

"Now that Jennifer King has been discovered—that she is alive," Dmitry said with a gloating expression, "I am certain Anistana King will do whatever it takes to see her. And we will make sure she doesn't survive the visit. We will eliminate Jennifer King as well."

"Without a cross-examination of Anistana King by Plutov," Piterskij said, "our defense will argue to have her initial testimony tossed out of court."

Yegor blew a smoke ring at his son. "How did you find this Jennifer King?"

"The woman saw news reports about the trial on the television while she was in public—at a physical therapy center," Piterskij said. "She was overheard speaking to someone during one of her physical therapy sessions, saying that she was concerned about her sister testifying against Dmitry. A receptionist at the PT center was aware of our reward for the death of Anistana King and informed one of our men."

Yegor blew out another smoke ring. "You have the weekend to rid us of the *pizda*."

"Two days is more than we need." Dmitry grinned. "Our men are preparing as we speak. We know the hotel she is staying at and have all entrances and exits covered."

"Very good." Yegor waved him away. "You have much business to take care of."

Piterskij bowed, turned, and strode from Yegor's Red Room.

Dmitry stood with his hands behind his back, his chin raised.

"You"—Yegor pointed to his son with his cigar—"are a worthless *govno*. You have failed and failed, and failed again. I expect nothing from you but success this weekend. Not even the weekend. Today she dies. Today!"

"Yes, Father." Dmitry's jaw tensed. "I will see to it myself."

"I expect you to do no less." Yegor blew another smoke ring into his son's face.

Dmitry did not show the same courtesy as Piterskij by bowing. He simply turned and walked out the door.

The fact they were so close to eliminating the King woman made Yegor's dick harden. He rubbed it through his fine Armani slacks. He knew exactly how to relieve the ache in his groin.

With his cigar still in his mouth, he used the intercom and ordered his maid, Fayina, to the Red Room. By the time she reached him, she had fear in her expression, which only made his excitement more intense.

CHAPTER SEVENTEEN

Ani was still shaking with fury as blood started dripping from Daniel's nose. Her hand hurt from slugging him so hard. But she barely felt the pain as she stared at the man who'd allowed her to think her sister was dead for *over two years.*

He grabbed a couple of tissues from a box on the hotel room's dresser. He wiped the blood from his nose and studied her for a long moment. "I deserved that," he finally said.

Ani ground her teeth. "I want you out of here. I don't care who it is, but I want a different Deputy to remain in the room with me."

"Ani, please listen—"

"You can't say anything to change this, Daniel." Heat made her feel like her head was going to go up in flames. She pointed toward the door. "Go."

He wiped more blood from his nose. "I'll be up for my things later," he said, but his eyes told her he didn't want to leave.

She clenched her hands so hard her knuckles ached. She didn't give a damn what he wanted. "You can send someone else to get your crap for you."

Daniel looked at her one more time before tossing the tissues into a wastebasket beside the dresser. It looked like his nose had stopped bleeding.

He walked to the door. Just as he grabbed the door handle, he glanced over his shoulder. "I'm sorry, Ani. I had no choice."

She responded by turning her back on him and facing the curtained window. His heavy sigh carried back to her, and it wasn't until she heard the loud thump of the door closing that she let the tears fall.

Ani sat on the edge of the bed in her part of the suite and tears flooded her cheeks. After all that had happened she felt so worn out, betrayed, angry, and hurt. Maybe hurt most of all.

She kicked off her heels and padded across the carpet to the box of tissues. After mopping the tears from her eyes and cheeks, she looked at herself in the mirror over the dresser. Her eyes were puffy and red, her complexion pale, and the bruise and cuts dark against her face.

Through all the pain and confusion, a single thought pounded at her and pounded at her, pushing aside everything else.

Jenn's alive! She's alive!

Her tears dried and she stopped sniffling. Excitement and joy washed through her. Jenn hadn't died. She was alive!

A knock at the door startled her and she jerked her attention toward it. Was it that jerk, Daniel?

When Ani reached the door, she peeked through the peephole and saw that it was Deputy Janet Hernandez, who had a duffel bag slung over one of her shoulders. She saw two other Deputies directly across the way, so she knew it was safe. She took a deep breath, opened the door, and let Janet in.

"I want to see my sister now," Ani said the moment Janet walked in.

Janet tossed her duffel on the floor beside one of the beds. She was a petite woman with wide chocolate-brown eyes and an olive complexion.

"We'll arrange it," Janet said, "but not until after the trial when you're safe."

Ani planted her hands on her hips. "You'll arrange it *now*."

Janet had a hard look in her eyes. "You signed the paperwork severing ties with your past life. Daniel was not *allowed* to tell you. That's the fact of the matter."

"Maybe it's too late today." Ani wiped the back of one hand across her wet cheek. "But tomorrow you *will* take me to her. I won't testify any more until I see my sister."

Janet studied Ani. "I'll see what I can do. But I can't promise anything." Janet's short, bobbed hair swung as she shook her head. "You know you have to testify regardless or you'll be held in contempt of court."

Ani glared at her. "Someone better make it happen."

Janet didn't answer and walked to the phone where

she picked up the room service menu. "What do you want to eat?"

She folded her arms across her chest. "Nothing."

"I watched you at the courthouse." Janet set the menu down. "You didn't eat lunch and you need something to keep up your strength."

The reason Ani had lost so much weight since the tragedy was her lack of appetite, and this was one of those times. The thought of food made her want to puke.

"I'm fine." She looked at the phone before meeting Janet's eyes again. "I want to call Jenn and hear her voice. *I want to talk to my sister.*"

"Listen." Janet approached Ani. "Your sister is in danger, too. Jennifer didn't see who shot her, and she doesn't remember anything from that night, so she's not a witness. Because she wasn't a witness she couldn't be put into WITSEC. But she's been under as much protection as we could give her."

Ani felt like she was going to hyperventilate. "Where has she been?"

"As the defense attorney revealed, she's been in Rochester." Janet gave her a pointed look. "Jennifer *did* die on the operating room table but was revived." Janet's overshirt fell to the side and Ani saw her gun, reminding her that this was a U.S. Deputy Marshal she was speaking to.

"After leaving the hospital," Janet continued, "your sister was admitted to the burn center with a new identity. The doctors didn't know if she'd make it for a while, and they never knew her real name or background. Until now, everyone not involved in her care and safety thought she was dead. Even Borenko's people."

"So she's not safe now, because they probably don't know how much she does or doesn't know." Ani's heart started racing. "Will they move her?"

Janet nodded. "She's already been moved to New York City to a safe house and she's under tight guard by our people. We don't think Borenko's men know where she's hidden right now."

Ani plopped down on the edge of the couch in the sitting room of the suite, feeling as if she couldn't stand any longer. "You do what you have to in order to protect us, but I'm not going another day without seeing Jenn. I heard you all talking. You're planning on moving me anyway. Make it the same place as my sister is staying."

Janet looked like she was going to argue but instead she went back to the phone, picked up the menu, and flipped through it. "Cheese potato soup or chicken noodle?"

"Chicken noodle," Ani said without really thinking about it and her stomach rumbled. Smart woman to pick something Ani could probably keep down.

"Milk will help settle your stomach, too," Janet said as she dialed one of the Deputies on her cell phone and placed an order that was big enough for two people. Obviously she planned for Ani to eat more than soup.

Once the Deputy who brought their order had come and gone, Ani managed to get some food down.

She didn't need to be weak or dizzy when she saw Jenn.

The thought of seeing her sister almost made her giddy. After Janet went into the bathroom and changed out of her Kevlar vest and suit, and put on a T-shirt and jeans, the Deputy turned a movie on and kicked back on the couch in the sitting room.

"Do you want to watch this movie with me?" Janet asked as she looked up at Ani. Her lips twisted with wry humor. "*The Fugitive* is on."

Ani shook her head. "No, thanks." She turned and retreated to her part of the suite and looked at the bed, picturing herself snuggled up on it with Daniel.

Just the thought of him made tears bite at her eyes, but she refused to cry. Instead she went into the bathroom and changed out of her suit and body armor into the T-shirt and shorts sleepwear that had been purchased for her along with the rest of the things. Her duffel had been brought up shortly after Janet took Daniel's place.

When she left the bathroom, she crawled into bed. She laid her head on her pillow, the chattering on the television from the sitting room fading into white noise. She squeezed her eyes shut and attempted not to think of her and Daniel making love.

Wasn't working. She turned to her other side, clenched her eyes tighter, trying so hard to rid herself of the images. Daniel kissing her. Touching her. Making love to her.

Betraying her.

Finally, she managed to stop thinking of him and

switched her thoughts to Jenn and remembered the good times they'd had when they were young. Yeah, they'd always had a tight bond even with all the fighting they'd done when they were kids.

Despite everything, Ani smiled. Jenn was alive.

Ani's heart raced as she was loaded onto a stretcher. The paramedics put an air mask over her nose and a blanket up to her chin. Her white wig itched and the air coming in through the mask smelled funny. They taped an IV drip to her hand to make it look like she had one of those needles in her veins.

Daniel and Gary McNeal pushed her to the elevator on the stretcher. They had dressed as paramedics with red jackets over their white shirts and blue pants, their gun belts hidden beneath the jackets.

As soon as the car's doors opened, they hurried her through the hotel on the stretcher and police officers made sure everyone was out of the way.

Outside an ambulance, a firetruck and two police cars blocked off the hotel entrance. Emergency lights flashed in the bright morning sunshine and a crowd gawked as Ani was rushed out to the ambulance. She was surrounded by men and women in uniforms until she was lifted into the back of the vehicle. As soon as Gary and Daniel were inside with her, the doors were shut securely and the ambulance started to move.

Ani's heart still pounded. She'd had no idea this was going to be a huge ordeal when Gary had told her of the plan they'd originally put in place to move her to a safe house. They'd intended to take her to a different one than the one her sister was at, but had decided to let them stay together.

Damn good thing.

Ani had thought they'd just take her out on a stretcher and into an ambulance and they'd be on their way. She didn't think it would involve the FDNY and the NYPD, too.

Daniel lifted the air mask and removed it from Ani's face and she bit her lower lip as his fingers brushed her skin. For one moment her eyes met his and she wanted to cry. She turned her head and looked at Gary instead.

She scratched her forehead where the wig itched her. "I didn't know you were going to have a whole circus involved."

Gary shook his head and grinned. "Parker's idea. I think it worked."

"So far so good." Daniel was up and looking out the small window. "I don't see a—" He snapped his attention to Gary. "I think we've got a tail."

Gary gripped the side of the stretcher. "If we don't go to a hospital, they'll know something's up."

Daniel jerked his head toward the front of the ambulance. "Have them take us to the closest emergency room. We'll deal with these sonsofbitches."

By the tone of Daniel's voice Ani wondered exactly how they planned on doing that. She struggled to think of Daniel as just an Inspector, one of her protectors. She wouldn't let herself look at him.

Gary knocked on the window separating the back

of the ambulance from the front. Ani heard him giving instructions to the two Deputies in the front who were also posing as paramedics.

Without meaning to, her gaze met Daniel's and she saw so much in that one look. Caring, concern, hurt. Yeah, like her, he was hurt.

She turned away from him again. It wasn't possible for him to be hurt as much as she was.

Daniel's heart hammered as he moved to the rear of the ambulance and looked out the back windows. He narrowed his gaze at the black Cutlass that had followed them through the city, straight toward the ER. Shit, yeah, those had to be Borenko's men.

McNeal had the Deputies in the front take their ride straight up to the doors where only ambulances were allowed to park. The Cutlass stayed a few feet back.

Daniel looked to the front of the ambulance where he knew the other men had drawn their weapons. They were ready to swing their doors open and aim at the Cutlass as soon as Daniel gave the word. He moved his hand under his jacket and unholstered his Glock while McNeal drew his own weapon. They stood to either side of the back doors.

Daniel held his position, his heart pounding, adrenaline rushing through his system.

All four doors of the Cutlass opened and four men stepped out—all with weapons.

Daniel was certain the Deputies in the front would see the armed men in their side-view mirrors and be prepared when Daniel gave the order.

"Stay down, Ani," he said. She didn't respond, but she didn't move, either.

"Now!" Daniel shouted as he and McNeal swung the back doors of the ambulance open. They opened the doors just enough so they were able to use them as shields. Daniel popped off the first man who aimed a gun at him. Right between the bastard's eyes.

McNeal got off a shot and took down one of the men.

But then McNeal dropped.

He pitched forward onto the asphalt.

He'd gone completely still.

Fury rushed through Daniel. He fired off a couple of rounds and nailed another one of the men. He heard shots from behind him as the other Deputies joined in the action.

The ping of bullets piercing the ambulance and the sound of gunfire was loud in the morning air.

In moments all gunfire ceased.

Four men lay sprawled on the ground surrounding the Cutlass. But McNeal was down, too.

Two cops rushed out of the ER and shouted, "Drop your weapons!"

"On the job! On the job!" Daniel said as he slowly put his gun on the concrete. "U.S. Marshals. We've got an officer down."

"Back away from the guns," one of the officers shouted. "All three of you. Don't make any sudden moves."

One of the cops got in front of Daniel and the other Deputies while the second police officer trained his gun on the four men on the ground around the Cutlass. That officer spoke into his radio, requesting backup and stating there was a possible officer down.

The cop with the gun trained on Daniel and the other two Deputies had them brace their hands against the ambulance—several feet apart.

After checking out McNeal to make sure he was indeed injured, one of the police officers allowed hospital staff to attend to him.

The cop then patted Daniel down.

"My creds are in my back pocket," Daniel said.

The cop searched Daniel for additional weapons and rid him of the knife strapped to his ankle and everything attached to his belt, including the cell phone. Then the officer reached into the rear pants pocket of Daniel's paramedic uniform. He withdrew Daniel's creds and stepped away.

"Hands behind your head and face me," the cop said.

Daniel ground his teeth. They didn't need this crap right now.

He obeyed and the officer kept his gun trained on him while he used his other hand to examine Daniel's credentials.

He glanced at Daniel's badge and his creds. "I want to see everyone else's, too."

After being patted down, the other two Deputies had their creds taken, too. When the first cop examined them all, he lowered his gun. "What's the situation?"

Daniel explained as much as he could. "Mind if I retrieve my weapon?" Daniel said as a NYPD cruiser came up behind the Cutlass, another one in front of the ambulance, their lights flashing.

As soon as the other officers were on the scene and apprised of the situation, Daniel was allowed to retrieve his Glock and his knife, as were the other Deputies.

Two officers approached the Cutlass, weapons drawn.

When they reached one side of the Cutlass, one cop slammed the driver's door shut with his foot so that two of the downed men were visible. He kicked each man's gun, and they skittered across the asphalt, out of reach. One of the men groaned and stirred.

The officer trained his weapon on the man. "Don't move another muscle, asshole."

When everything was straightened out, heart still pounding, Daniel tucked his gun back into its holster beneath the jacket. Everything had been returned to his belt.

He hurried into where McNeal was being attended to on the ground. To Daniel's relief, McNeal was sitting up and there were no visible signs of bleeding. He had a bullet hole in the center of his shirt and he was breathing heavily. The vest had saved him.

"Scared the shit out of me, McNeal," Daniel said as he crouched by his friend.

McNeal gave a tired smile. "Hurts like hell, but nothing I can't handle."

"I still want you checked out more thoroughly." Daniel shook his head. "You could have a cracked rib or something."

"I'm fine." McNeal held his hand to his chest. "I'll just have a bruise."

"You're staying." Daniel directed the other two Marshals into the front of the ambulance. "We've got to get Ani out of here."

McNeal grumbled a lot more while two emergency room staff helped him to his feet. Daniel gave him the thumbs-up before he closed the ambulance doors.

McNeal flipped him off.

After they'd closed the rear doors, Daniel sat on one of the benches to the side of Ani, who was still lying on the stretcher. He tilted his head back against the inside of the ambulance. Adrenaline still pumped through his body.

Ani pushed herself to a sitting position and flung the white wig onto the metal floor of the ambulance. Her dark hair tumbled around her shoulders and she had an angry expression. She looked so beautiful when she was mad. Hell, she looked beautiful no matter what—especially when her skin was flushed as she climaxed.

He rubbed the bridge of his nose between his thumb and forefinger. Thoughts like that weren't going to get him anywhere.

Ani tore at the bandage around her wrist to get rid of the fake IV and tossed it all aside. She flung her legs over the side of the stretcher so that she was sitting.

The ambulance jostled her as it started moving and she swayed. Daniel leaned forward and caught her by the shoulders to keep her from falling.

They both froze and he saw Ani's chest rise and fall more rapidly as her eyes fixed on his. He slid his palms from her shoulders, down to her forearms, and to her hands that he took in his own.

For just a moment she let him hold her fingers. Her parted lips and her expanded pupils told him that she wanted him, but her expression told him she was still angry and hurt.

She jerked her hands from his, crossed her arms under her breasts, and turned to face the back of the ambulance.

Daniel braced his forearms on his thighs.

"Where are we going?" she asked, her gaze still averted from his. Ani looked so distraught that Daniel wanted to take her into his arms and comfort her, but he knew she'd refuse him.

To hell with that.

He got up and sat on the stretcher beside her. He wrapped one of his arms around her shoulders and she stiffened at once. He pulled her against him.

Ani struggled and tried to push away, but he kept her tight beside him. Her heavenly scent of some kind of exotic flower and woman overshadowed the medicinal smell of the ambulance. She felt warm against him and right. She felt so right.

Gradually she relaxed and her body shook as sobs tore through her. "I'm so tired of this. I don't want anyone else to get hurt."

Daniel kissed the top of her head and felt her shiver in his arms. He released her so that he could head to the back of the ambulance and check out the cars behind them. As he scanned the traffic, he kept his eyes open for any vehicles that might be tailing them.

Looked good.

They reached a designated location where they transferred Ani into an unmarked vehicle with nondescript lead and tail cars to follow them. An ambulance would stick out in the neighborhood where they were taking her.

When they finally reached the safe house, the other two vehicles parked in the front, while the two Deputies driving Daniel and Ani took the back alley. Daniel waited a while to see if they'd been tagged. After about ten minutes of intense scrutiny up and down the alleyway, he was certain no vehicles had followed them.

Still he held his gun ready when the other two Deputies joined him and they rushed Ani into the back entrance of the safe house.

CHAPTER EIGHTEEN

As the three Deputy Marshals, including Daniel, escorted Ani into the safe house, she scrubbed her sweating palms on her jeans. She wore body armor and a black T-shirt as usual.

The Deputies took her through the back door of a plain white carriage house. She found herself trembling so hard that when Daniel put a hand on her shoulder, as if trying to reassure her, she didn't jerk away. He guided her through a kitchen and into a living room where a few men and women were posted at the stairs, exits, and entrances.

They went to the right and then up the stairs. Every step seemed so slow and it felt surreal, like a dream. Like none of this was real.

On the top floor they reached a door with two men stationed to either side of the doorway. They acknowledged Daniel and the other two Deputies with her, obviously knowing them.

Daniel stepped forward and knocked on the door.

It sounded loud in the quietness of the hallway that smelled of new carpet and disinfectant.

For a moment nothing happened. Then she heard the scrape of a chain and the click of a bolt lock just before the door opened. Another man greeted them with a nod.

Ani followed Daniel into a sitting room. It had French doors leading to bedrooms on either side of the room. She moved in front of the men and held her breath.

No Jenn.

The handle of the French door to the right clicked and the door slowly swung open.

Jenn stepped through the doorway, her eyes fixed on Ani.

"Ani?" she said, and took a step forward, her eyes wide.

Ani cleared her throat and nodded. No words came to her.

"Is it really you?" Jenn took another tentative step toward her. "You look so *different*. Skinny."

Ani's eyes filled with tears. "It's me, Jenn."

There was only a moment's pause before Jenn ran and flung her arms around Ani.

Ani sobbed against her sister's neck. "You're alive. I can't believe you're alive."

Jenn was crying so hard, too, that she shook in Ani's arms. "They—the Marshals—said you were in the Witness Security Program and that you weren't allowed to have anything to do with your past. Not until after the trial, at least."

Tears still streaming down her face, Ani stomped her foot. "They had no right to tell me you died. For two years I thought I'd lost you. They had no right!"

Jenn hugged Ani tight again. "What matters now is that we're together."

"Yes." Ani kissed Jenn's cheek that was wet from tears, too. She drew away and they held one another at arm's length. "You look good," Ani said as she reached up and stroked a scar at the side of Jenn's head, pushing her sister's dark hair away from her face with the movement. "We have a lot to talk about."

Ani heard the click of the door and started. She looked around to see that all the Deputy Marshals had left the sitting room, giving Ani and Jenn privacy for their reunion.

Ani took Jenn's hand and walked with her to a love seat where they sat and faced one another.

"You're here." Jenn pushed tears from her cheeks with her fingers. "You're really here."

For a moment neither of them said anything. They just held each other's hands and squeezed them tight.

"I missed you." Jenn broke the silence and released Ani's hand to hold her palm over her heart. "I was so glad you were safe, but I wanted to see you so badly it hurt."

"Even though I signed those papers, I still can't believe they let me think you were dead." Ani released Jenn's other hand and clenched her fists in her lap. "The jerks let me think I lost all of you that night."

Jenn covered Ani's fist with her hand. "They told me it would have endangered us both to break your contract with the program. Borenko's Mob is just too dangerous."

Ani grimaced. "After these past few days, I know that more than you can imagine."

"I'm so glad you're safe. Alive." Jenn's chest rose and fell as she audibly sucked in a breath.

Ani swallowed. "Tell me what happened. The Marshals said that they were informed you weren't going to make it. Then you died on the operating table right before I signed those papers."

"I got shot in the head." Jenn touched the scar. "I was lucky. Really lucky. The bullet angled upward and lodged in the top of my skull. It was touch and go for a while with the swelling, but it didn't cause any permanent damage." She gave a quirky little smile. "Well, there's a lot about that time after the injury that I don't remember, but I don't know if it's caused by the trauma or the damage the bullet did."

In Ani's mind she saw the blood coming from Jenn's head that night, and then the bullet hole in her father's skull. She blinked, trying to force the images from her mind. "I can't believe you survived that," Ani said quietly.

"Hey, you were nearly shot in the heart," Jenn said.

"I was fortunate, too." Ani's healed shoulder wound ached just thinking about the moment the bullet entered her body. "How did you make it through everything?"

"The hospital I was taken to had an extraordinary team of doctors." Jenn rubbed at the scar on the side of her head again. "They had to put me in a medically induced coma for a while, until the swelling of my brain went down. And then I basically died on the operating room table.

"When I came back, they were uncertain I would live. Once they moved me to the burn center in Rochester, they treated my burns. Eight weeks later, I went into rehab, and since then I've gone through extensive physical therapy."

Ani's heart twisted at the thought of what her sister had gone through. For the first time, she looked at what her sister was wearing. Jenn had on a pair of pink sweatpants and a pink T-shirt.

Despite the heaviness in her gut, Ani smiled. "You always did like pink."

"I don't remember you being partial to black." Jenn reached up and slid her fingers over Ani's Kevlar vest. "Or body armor."

Ani sighed. "It gets annoying, sometimes, but it beats the heck out of getting shot."

"What happened?" Jenn let her hand fall away from Ani's vest and rubbed her palm on one of her thighs as if she had an itch.

Ani grimaced. "Other than being chased, shot at, almost blown up, and chased and shot at some more . . . not much."

Jenn looked horrified, her eyes and mouth wide. "You're kidding."

As she shook her head, Ani's thoughts immediately went to Daniel and how many times he'd saved her life. "The Marshals have gone above and beyond duty to keep the Borenkos from killing me."

"Wow." Jenn glanced at the door. "No wonder there are so many of them hanging around."

"Yeah." Ani closed her eyes for a moment before opening them again. "Now that the Russian Mafia knows about you, you're in as much danger as I am. They'll want to get to you so they can get to me." Tears threatened to fall again. "They had to move me anyway, so they brought me to your safe house. I needed to see you. To touch you. To know that you're really here. Alive."

Jenn leaned forward and took Ani into her arms. "I'm so glad we're together." Jenn kissed Ani's cheek before drawing away. "I was so happy when they said you'll be staying with me here."

Ani smiled. "You couldn't tear me away. Even if I have to sleep on the floor!"

With a gesture to each French door, one on either side of the sitting room, Jenn said, "Each room has two double beds. So our ever-present guards have a place to sleep, too."

That mention made Ani think of Daniel and her heart hurt all over again.

"What's wrong?" Jenn touched Ani's shoulder.

Ani shook her head and she didn't have to force a smile when she looked at her very much alive sister. "I'm just happy you're here. I still can't believe it." Her smile faded. "But your burns." Ani swallowed. "They must have been pretty bad."

Jenn said softly, "If you hadn't pulled me from the house I wouldn't have survived." She looked down at her sweatpants and back up to Ani. "It's a small price to pay for one's life."

Ani wiped away a tear. "And here I've been self-conscious about my burn scars and you went through so much worse."

"Hey." Jenn grinned. "I'll show you mine if you show me yours."

Ani smiled at the teasing look on her sister's face. "Mine is nothing compared to what you went through."

Jenn kicked off her jogging shoes and stood. "Brian taught me that there's beauty in everything."

"Who's Brian?" Ani asked as she got to her feet and started unfastening her body armor.

A beautiful smile crossed Jenn's face. "My physical therapist, Brian Derrida. And he's my fiancé."

Ani had just tossed her vest aside. She turned to her sister. "You're getting married?"

"Eventually." Jenn grinned again. "He's wanted to for the past six months, but I thought we should wait for just the right moment." Her face softened. "Like now, now that you're here."

Ani hugged her sister. "I'm so happy for you."

"Me, too." Jenn laughed and stepped back.

She tugged down her sweatpants—she was wearing pink jogging shorts beneath—but when Ani saw her sister's legs her heart nearly wrenched in two. Jenn stepped completely out of her sweatpants. Her once beautiful long legs were completely scarred, the skin twisted and lumpy. Because of her own experience in a burn center, and all the other victims she'd seen there, Ani recognized skin grafts and realized how much pain her sister had faced.

At Ani's shocked expression, Jenn said softly, "Fifty percent of my body. Waist down. It's better than being dead. And you're the reason I'm alive."

Ani hugged Jenn and clung to her for a long time. She didn't want to let her sister go. "I love you, Jenn," she said as the tears flowed. "I love you so much."

"And you know how much I love you back, sis," Jenn whispered. She smiled as she stepped away and drew her sweatpants back on.

After Jenn was dressed again, Ani took off her Kevlar vest and tossed it on the floor. She turned her back to her sister and held her shirt up. Embarrassment made her cheeks hot—not from her scars, but from the fact that she'd been so self-conscious about them. How could she have been afraid to let anyone see hers?

Look how brave Jenn was. She hadn't even hesitated to show Ani her burn scars—and she had a fiancé. Ani shivered as she felt Jenn's fingers lightly touch her skin and trace the scar to the highest point at one of her shoulder blades.

Jenn said in a thoughtful voice, "It almost looks like a phoenix, rising from flames. Just like you did. Almost mortally wounded and yet you still got us both out of there."

Ani took a deep breath, dropped the hem of her T-shirt, and faced her sister. "Now I understand. I won't be embarrassed about my scars anymore."

"Good." Jenn smiled. "We have lots of stuff to catch up on."

Over turkey sandwiches and sodas one of the Deputies brought up for lunch, Ani and Jenn talked about their lives over the past two years. It had taken Jenn a long time to accept her appearance, and she gave credit to her fiancé, who had taught her that what was inside was more important than physical appearance.

"You look like you need to eat a little more," Jenn said to Ani when they finished lunch. "I didn't recognize you. But your eyes and your voice cut through that. And my gut instinct. So why haven't you been eating?"

Now that Ani was so slender, she was about the same size as her sister and she could see herself mirrored in Jenn. They looked so much alike now, it was amazing.

Ani shrugged in response to Jenn's question. "When you all were gone, I just couldn't eat much."

"You're not anorexic, are you?" There was genuine concern in Jenn's voice.

With a smile, Ani shook her head. "Up until these past few days, I've been telling myself I need to eat more. I never lost weight intentionally. It just happened, you know?"

Jenn nodded. "Yeah, I think I do." She cocked her head to the side. "So—did you move on at all? Did you find someone special?"

Ani's skin flushed with heat and she glanced at the door before returning her gaze to her sister's. "There used to be."

"Something tells me I need to hear this." Jenn folded her arms across her chest. "So get on with it."

Heat burned even hotter in Ani's cheeks. "I—I don't know if I can."

"Hey, it's me you're talking to. Your sister, remember?" Jenn leaned forward. "Maybe you've had to keep a lot of secrets these past two years, but now you don't. Right here, right now, it's just the two of us."

"Okay." Ani told her own story about the burn center and being taken to a couple of different safe houses by Daniel before she settled in Bisbee. About how they had talked on the phone so many times and how she slowly fell in love with him.

Jenn frowned. "What do you mean, then, that 'there used to be' a relationship when he's standing right outside that door? Did he do something to you?"

"Daniel kept the fact that you were alive a secret. He knew, but never told me. I didn't find out until I was in court and it was such a shock. Finding out like that—it was horrible." She flexed her hand—her knuckles were still a little sore from punching him. "When we were alone I let him have it by telling him off, then sort of slammed my fist into his nose."

Jenn snorted then burst out laughing. "You *sort of* hit him? Was there blood?"

Ani's mouth quirked into a smile. "Yeah. Hit him pretty hard."

Jenn sobered. "You know that he was just obeying orders, don't you? He couldn't tell you without endangering his job, or you. You signed the papers and they stick to their rules."

"I'm slowly realizing that," Ani admitted. "A part of me doesn't want to forgive him because it feels like a betrayal. But the other part of me knows he didn't have a choice."

"He didn't, Ani. You know that." Jenn put her feet on the coffee table in front of the couch they were sitting on. "So, didya get laid?"

"Jenn!" Ani said in a hushed voice. "He could *really* lose his job right now if anyone found out."

Jenn dropped her feet right off the coffee table. "You did it? With a U.S. Marshal?"

"Quiet!" Ani looked around as if someone might be standing near them, listening. "It just . . . happened. We both wanted it to, I know. But neither of us planned on acting on it until after the trial and all this mess."

"Whoa." Jenn put one foot on the couch and wrapped her arms around her bent knee. "Do you love him?"

Ani looked down at her hands before she met Jenn's gaze. "Yeah, I do."

"Then you can forgive him." Jenn stared at her matter-of-factly. "It's not worth it to let love slip through your hands. So, he could have broken the rules and told you, but he knows his job and he knows how to protect you."

For a moment it all churned in Ani's mind as she looked at her hands. Then it gradually became crystal clear. She'd been shocked and hurt, but Daniel truly hadn't betrayed her. He'd done what he was forced to do.

"You're right," Ani said as she glanced at her sister

again. "Now if I can figure out how to make it up to him."

Jenn snickered. "I'm sure you can think of a way."

Ani shook her head at her sister's teasing then gave a wicked grin. "Oh, I know how to show him just how sorry I am." But then she sobered. "Like we'd even get a chance alone from this point on—at least until after the trial."

"Hmmm . . ." Jenn pursed her lips. "Maybe I can come up with something." She rolled her shoulders as if relieving an ache. "What about when all this is over?"

With a sigh, Ani said, "I don't know. I just don't know."

"From what you've told me of how things have gone between the two of you," Jenn said, "let's just say I'd lay a bet on Daniel's side."

Warmth spread through Ani's chest and butterflies filled her belly at the thought of Daniel loving her as much as she loved him.

Did he?

She'd just have to show him how she felt and he'd have to take it from there.

CHAPTER NINETEEN

While he sat in a lounge chair near the custom-designed, Olympic-sized swimming pool, Yegor caressed the barrel of his Russian Grach pistol. It was much too cold to swim, but he preferred not to make a mess in his home.

The metal ridges of the gun in his lap felt rough beneath his fingers. He picked it up, feeling the weight of it in his hand. It had been a while since he'd used it. He usually left such dirty work to his men.

Like falling off a bicycle, the Americans would say, he thought as he wrapped his hand around the grip.

He looked from the handgun to the six men standing before him. Dmitry, Piterskij, and four of Yegor's front men, including Alkash.

"I am sick of failure after failure after failure." Yegor squeezed the grip of his pistol as he looked directly at Piterskij, then Dmitry. "How many times have you failed to eliminate the King woman?"

Yegor raised the Grach and waved it at both of

them as he spoke. Piterskij and Dmitry both flinched. Dmitry looked like he was going to piss his pants.

Pidoras.

Piterskij recovered and his usual calm expression settled on his features.

"I can tolerate such failures no more." Yegor raised his gun and pointed it at Piterskij. The man's expression of calm vanished.

Just before Yegor squeezed the trigger, he turned the barrel at Alkash. The shot rang out in the late afternoon air. Alkash only had time for a surprised expression before the bullet pierced his forehead and blew out the back of his head.

Alkash's body crumpled to the cool deck beside the pool and Yegor shook his head. "Such a shame, really."

He aimed his gun at Dmitry who trembled like a woman.

Yegor shook his head again and made a tsk-tsk sound. "Before I see you in prison, I will see you dead, just like him. Only slower. With much more pain."

Dmitry's throat worked as he stared at Yegor.

"My granddaughters need a father, not a convict. I will not allow them to live with such an embarrassment. You will show up for trial again, but the King woman must never make it."

Dmitry slowly nodded. "Yes, Father."

"It is good we understand one another." Yegor lowered his handgun and saw the visible relief on his son's face. "As I have told you, I will allow you to stand trial, and as long as you are acquitted, you shall live so that my granddaughters have a father." He waved the Grach as he spoke. "Otherwise, I will make sure you do not live to make it to the prison. Understood?"

"Yes, Father." Dmitry sounded like he had to force the words out.

He made a shooing motion with the gun, waving it at Dmitry and Piterskij. "Go now. Clean up this mess. The smell sickens me."

The remaining three men beside his son and Piterskij each gave Yegor a deep bow of acknowledgment. Yegor's arms strained as he pushed his bulk from the poolside chair. When he was standing he tucked the Grach inside his jacket pocket.

It wouldn't do for his granddaughters to see him with a weapon when he visited them in their playroom.

CHAPTER TWENTY

Jenn spoke with one of the two Deputies guarding their door and told him that she wanted her fiancé, Brian, and to please call Deputy Parker, too. Brian had wanted to leave the sisters alone during their reunion, and was staying in one of the other rooms for the time being.

The Deputy Marshals almost hadn't let Brian accompany Jennifer to the safe house since he wasn't officially "family." But after a quick background check, and with Jenn's insistence, they allowed her fiancé to go with her.

Ani felt jittery and couldn't sit still as she waited in one of the bedrooms. It was on the other side of the sitting room, across from Jenn's room.

Now if Daniel would just come so she could speak with him.

She intended to do a lot more than *speak* with Daniel.

While she waited she paced the length of the room

with its two double beds. It would be where she stayed with Janet Hernandez until after the trial. It was prettier than any of the hotel rooms they'd stayed in, with blue carpeting that was soft beneath her bare feet. It had whitewashed walls, blue comforters, and paintings of seascapes. The place was decorated as if it were on the French Riviera. Much prettier than the other basic, functional safe house.

Her suitcase was sprawled open on one of the beds—she hadn't had a chance to hang anything up and right now she was too nervous. She'd taken what she needed out of the suitcase and left the rest. The box of condoms had ended up buried underneath her clothing because she hadn't sent it to Daniel in his suitcase for some reason. As if she'd known in her heart she would forgive him.

She took a condom out and tucked it into the back pocket of her jeans.

As she paced, she took a deep breath. What if Daniel was mad at her for being so upset with him? By the look in his eyes, she knew she had hurt him, but he'd still been attentive during the ambulance ride.

She rubbed her arms against the goose bumps that prickled her skin.

When she heard the front door open and close she stopped in mid-step and held her breath. Two male voices that she couldn't distinguish. Had Daniel come as Jenn had requested?

A shiver trailed up her spine as she recognized Daniel's deep, sexy voice. Mere moments later there was a light knock on the French doors.

"Ani?" Daniel said from the other side.

She took a deep breath and stood where she'd stopped walking, several lengths away.

"Come in," she said loud enough for him to hear.

The handle turned and the door slowly opened until Daniel stepped through and closed it behind him.

Daniel just stood there and stared at her, waiting for her to speak.

He looked so good. He wore jeans and a black T-shirt under his overshirt that was snug around his muscled physique. He didn't have his body armor on, so she could see his gorgeous bod better. His carved biceps, broad chest, powerful shoulders, and flat stomach that led to trim hips. His "package" was well defined behind his stone-washed jeans and she sighed inwardly.

For a moment neither of them moved nor spoke.

Ani couldn't hold herself back any longer. She ran up to him, flung her arms around his neck, pulled his head down, and kissed him with everything she had.

Daniel seemed startled but recovered pretty quickly. He grasped her ass and pulled her tight against him while he kissed her hard and fierce. His growing erection pressed into her belly. Their kiss became more frantic. She reached between them and unfastened his belt. He released her long enough to take it off and lay everything that had been on it on the bed, including his gun and his cell phone.

Ani wrapped her arms around Daniel's neck and hooked her thighs around his hips.

His mouth was harsh, his kiss rough, his stubble

abrading her skin. Her nipples were hard against his chest, her sex ached, and her panties were damp. She was vaguely aware of him carrying her as he stepped forward until her back was against the wall.

Both of them made hungry sounds of want and need as they thrust their tongues into each other's mouths and meshed their mouths together, licking, sucking, biting. He tasted like he'd just had a glass of iced tea and lemon, along with his wonderful flavor that she loved. And his smell—the way it filled her made her heady.

They were breathing heavily, and Ani gasped and moaned as he began kissing her jaw, moving his mouth toward her ear. She kept her thighs tight around his hips and crossed her ankles behind his ass.

"Does this mean I'm forgiven?" he murmured before nipping her earlobe and causing her to give a small cry.

"*Daniel.*" She tipped her head back against the wall, exposing her neck to him. "If you take me right here, right now, I'll forgive you for anything."

A powerful rumble rose up in Daniel's chest as he moved his lips down her exposed throat. Her thighs were still hooked around his hips as he brought his hands between them and unbuttoned her jeans.

"No condom," he growled, but he didn't stop kissing her throat.

"In my back pocket." She could barely speak as he reached around her and slipped his hands into each of her pockets and pulled out the condom from one of them.

He grinned. "Prepared."

"For you." Those butterflies went crazy in her belly and electricity zinged straight to that place between her thighs. She needed him so much.

Ani let her legs slide down his hips until she was standing. She moaned as he shoved her underwear and jeans down and she helped by stepping out of them. She brought her hands to the button of his jeans, unfastened it, and unzipped as fast as she could. She pushed his briefs and jeans down just enough to free his cock and balls at the same time he shoved her T-shirt and bra up. Cool air brushed her nipples just before his hot mouth latched onto her. He slowly let it slip from his mouth and she whimpered.

The crackle of the condom package opening made her more excited. She looked down to see him roll it on. His gaze met hers. "Wrap your legs around me again, honey."

She did and immediately the head of his erection was poised at the entrance to her core. He grabbed her hands and drew her arms up high over her head, pinning them to the wall, and she whimpered at not being able to touch him. He gripped her wrists in one of his hands and used his other to cup her ass.

The wall was hard behind her back as he thrust his cock deep inside her. She almost cried out at the sheer pleasure of having him back where he belonged. He captured her mouth in a rough kiss and began pounding against her sex, thrusting his cock in and out, hitting that sweet spot so deep it made her squirm.

They never stopped kissing as he took her hard and

fast, as if asserting his dominance over her. Claiming her.

Daniel's jeans were rough against her thighs, heightening her pleasure. His kisses stole her breath away and she grew light-headed the closer she came to orgasm.

The world seemed to spin. All that mattered was having Daniel inside her, his mouth taking hers as their kiss turned rough. As rough as he was thrusting in and out of her channel.

Ani felt herself slipping out of reality. Her orgasm was barreling toward her and she knew she was going to be swept away with it.

Her climax hit her hard. She cried out against Daniel's mouth and he took the rest of the cry in a harsh kiss. She felt like she was spinning, being taken to some other place.

Yet she never stopped feeling Daniel pounding in and out of her and the feel of his kiss, his hand keeping her arms above her head, her nipples brushing his shirt and feeling the hard wall against her back.

Ani couldn't come down from her climax because he was still thrusting, causing her orgasm to go on and on. She almost felt like she was going to pass out from the power of all the sensations she was experiencing, but she didn't want it to stop.

Daniel suddenly jerked and pressed his hips tight against her. He broke their kiss, tilting back his head and letting out a groan while his cock throbbed inside her.

For a moment they stayed there. He lowered his

head and buried his face against her neck at the same time he released her wrists. She wrapped her arms around his neck and clung to him with her thighs still wrapped around his hips. She took deep gulps of air and his breathing was heavy, his chest expanding against hers. Perspiration clung to her skin from the power of their lovemaking and the scent of sex was heavy in the air.

Another groan rumbled in his chest. He raised his head and looked into her eyes before taking her mouth in a short, hard kiss.

Daniel drew away and carried her to the bed and gently laid her on it beside the suitcase. He looked down at her before wrapping the condom in tissue paper and disposing of it in a wastebasket beside the bed. To her disappointment he tucked his cock back into his briefs and fastened his jeans.

He set the suitcase on the floor then eased onto the bed beside her. She rolled onto her side to face him. He wrapped his hand in a lock of her dark hair and she melted at how he was looking at her. He brushed his fingers over her T-shirt-clad nipple and she gasped at the feathering sensation.

Daniel brought his forehead to hers and they looked into each other's eyes. His were such a warm brown that she could easily lose herself in. Always.

For a long time neither one of them spoke. Then he said, "You know, I never intended to let you go. No matter what I had to do to make it up to you."

She drew back and gave him a little grin. "You did one hell of a job doing just that."

He smiled and rubbed noses with hers.

"Seriously," she said, her grin fading as she drew away from him, "I was wrong. You had no choice and were obeying orders. A part of me still feels like you could have told me, but inside I know you did what you had to."

"I wanted to tell you, honey." He stroked her hair away from her face. "Every time we talked about your family and you said how much you missed them, it got harder and harder to not tell you. But your safety—"

"I understand." She sucked in a deep breath. "Now."

"You have no idea how ruthless the Russian Mafia is," Daniel said quietly. "What they've done to you— that's nothing. If they were to capture you instead of just killing you, they could torture you in ways you can't imagine. Including breaking every bone in your body while you were still alive."

Ani shuddered and Daniel drew her closer and gave her a soft kiss. "I'm sorry," he said. "I shouldn't have said anything."

"That's okay, really." She moved closer to him and he hooked his jean-clad thigh over her hip while grasping her waist under her T-shirt.

They both froze as Ani felt his fingers on her scar, but he didn't move his hand.

She took a deep breath. "I'm ready." A tremor went through her as she moved away from him a little and his fingers trailed away from her waist. She turned so that she was lying flat on her stomach, her cheek resting on her folded arms as she looked at him.

Daniel slowly pushed her T-shirt up until it was to her shoulders, his gaze fixed on her back. He rose up to a sitting position and moved his fingers over her skin. She shivered at his touch as he caressed her twisted flesh. Like Jenn had, he traced the scar up to each shoulder blade and back down.

He trailed his fingers over it from her upper back to her ass. "It looks like a phoenix."

With surprise, Ani said, "That's what Jenn thought, too."

He surprised her again as he bent and ran his lips along her scar, slowly kissing his way to the middle of her back, to the dimple at the top of her buttocks, causing her to shiver again.

When he raised his head, he smiled. "You're beautiful, Ani. Everything about you is beautiful."

She scooted onto her side, and Daniel lay beside her again. For a long moment they studied each other.

It was all or nothing. Her chest hurt with the power of her feelings for him. "I love you, Daniel."

His smile was so gentle, so special. "I've loved you for so long I don't know when it started."

Her heart leapt to her throat. She felt a little dizzy and could barely focus on his face.

Daniel had said it.

He loved her, too. Really loved her.

"I think it was from the moment I met you," he continued. "After everything you'd been through, you were so brave and still are. Your intelligence, wit, beauty—everything about you."

She rolled back onto her side as he tugged her T-shirt down. He brought her up against his chest and he smiled. "I could stay like this forever."

Ani returned his smile and snuggled closer to Daniel just as his cell phone rang.

CHAPTER TWENTY-ONE

"One of Yegor Borenko's main men, Alkash, was just found swimming with the fishes in the East River," McNeal said when Daniel answered his cell phone.

Daniel gripped the phone tight as he sat up on the bed, switching his attention from Ani's beautiful eyes to McNeal's words. "What the hell?"

"Personally, I think it's a message to his own people," McNeal said. "They keep screwing up in trying to eliminate our witness. In my opinion, it means efforts are going to be stepped up to find her before Monday morning."

"Jesus Christ." Daniel glanced at Ani who wore a concerned look. "I think she's safe here, with her sister, for the weekend."

"But Monday morning is another story," McNeal said.

"After her testimony Friday, they're going to want her even more." Daniel scrubbed his hand over his face.

"I just want this to be over with and for the bastards to be put behind bars."

"No kidding." McNeal lowered his voice. "Now get your ass out of there. It's getting late and Janet Hernandez needs to stay with Ani."

"Give me a few minutes," Daniel said before he snapped the cell phone shut and stuffed it into its holster on his belt.

"More fun news?" Ani stretched her arms over her head, raising her breasts in a way that made him hard all over again. "This all just keeps getting better and better."

Daniel leaned closer and brushed his lips over hers. "I've got to get out of here."

Ani sighed. "I know. But I wish you didn't have to."

"Same here, honey," he said before he stood and opened the French door to let himself out of the room.

He met with McNeal in the hallway outside Ani's and Jenn's rooms and he nodded to Janet Hernandez who went inside to stay with Ani. Daniel and McNeal strode down the stairs to the first floor.

"I'm off my rotation," McNeal said as they reached the lobby level. "Beer?"

"Damn, I could use one." Daniel's throat was dry. "I don't suppose the fridge is stocked?"

"Jonas brought a twelve-pack for those off duty."

"Good man." Daniel grinned. "Now that I'm no longer Ani's twenty four/seven guard, I'm off my shift, too." He walked beside McNeal until they reached the kitchen, passing a couple of Deputies on guard along the way.

After they'd each grabbed a beer out of the fridge, McNeal leaned his hip against the counter and studied Daniel. "I take it Ani's no longer pissed at you."

"Let's just say that's behind us." Daniel leaned back against the counter and popped the tab of his can. "How are you feeling?"

McNeal rubbed his chest and grimaced. "Hurts like a sonofabitch."

"Damn good thing you were wearing your gear." He shook his head. "Tell me about Alkash."

McNeal took a sip of his beer before setting the can on the counter next to him. "Like I said, he was one of Yegor Borenko's main men."

"How do you know it wasn't a hit by another faction?" Daniel said before he took a long swallow.

"Police informant." McNeal picked up his can and gestured with it as he spoke. "Too bad the informant won't flip and testify against Borenko."

Daniel shook his head. "That would save Ani all the way around."

Sunday morning, Ani woke with warmth in her belly at the thought of Daniel and their make-up session. Janet Hernandez was already out of the other bed and had left the room.

Ani smiled and hummed to herself in the shower before getting dressed. When she left the bedroom, Janet was in the sitting area. The room smelled of coffee, scrambled eggs, and bacon, and her stomach rumbled.

A man sat on a couch. Jenn had her head on his shoulder.

"You must be Brian." Ani reached him as he stood and she extended her hand. He had a smile to die for. He was blond with a dimple in his right cheek and had an athletic build, like a runner. No wonder Jenn had fallen for him.

"It's good to finally meet Jenn's big sis." He released her hand and gestured to one of the chairs where she seated herself before he sat again. "The Deputy Marshals allowed me to come with Jenn, but now won't let me leave, either." He smiled at Jenn and patted her leg. "Not that I want to let her out of my sight.

"But," he added, "I'm sure the two of you could use more time together."

Ani smiled. "Thanks."

He returned her smile before leaving the two of them in the room with Janet.

After eating the breakfast that had been brought up to them from downstairs, Jenn said, "I have some stuff to show you. The FBI gave me a box when I finally came out of rehab. I brought it with me from Rochester."

Ani's jeans felt snug as she followed her sister who was wearing a loose pair of pink sweatpants and a pink top. Janet stayed in the sitting room while Ani went with Jenn into the bedroom she was staying in.

"Have a seat." Jenn gestured to the bed for Ani to sit while Jenn walked over to the closet. She opened the white shuttered doors and knelt. She retrieved a file box and lugged it to the bed. The box smelled faintly of smoke.

"Amazingly enough, some stuff survived the fire." Jenn lifted the lid and set it aside. Ani widened her eyes in surprise. "Dad had a big fireproof safe," Jenn continued. "The police managed to get it open, and this was in it."

Ani's heart beat a little faster at just the thought that some of their past had survived.

"It's not a lot, but some of it is precious." Jenn pulled out a will, titles to their cars, deeds to the property, birth certificates, and Social Security cards. There were many older journals her father had handwritten before he had eventually switched over to using a computer. There were stocks, bonds, old coins, and bills. The kinds of things one would normally keep in a safe.

With a smile, Jenn handed Ani a framed photograph. Tears burned her eyes as she looked at a picture of the four of them the summer they'd gone to Paris. Ani caressed the glass over each one of them in the frame, and a tear splashed onto the glass.

Her parents were smiling and so full of life in the photograph—the person taking the photo had made them all laugh and had captured them with the camera at a good moment. Ani wiped her eyes and set the framed photo on top of all the legal documents. Why her father had put the photo in the safe, she didn't know. Maybe so he'd have it if anything happened to the house.

Next Jenn drew out Ani's and her own baby booties that were in the box, too. They looked at one another and smiled. Who'd have thought their father was so sentimental?

"This is what's really precious." Jenn used both hands to heft the next item out. It was a thick, heavy photo album with red leather binding. "You know how anal Dad was. He probably kept this for posterity."

Ani and Jenn sat side by side as they slowly turned each page of the album. It was amazing. The album started with a few pictures from their mother's and father's childhoods, then photos from when they were dating, on to their wedding. After a few photos of their Mom and Dad, next came pictures of Ani as a baby. It progressed, showing her growing up until she was four and then along came baby Jenn.

There were pictures of them Easter egg hunting, dressing up as ballerinas and princesses for Halloween, opening up Christmas presents, and on and on. Their lives were chronicled all the way to Ani graduating with her bachelor's degree and ended with the trip to Aruba the four of them had taken a month before their parents' deaths.

"I can't believe Dad put this together," Ani said as she caressed the last page of the album. Each picture was in its own protective sleeve against a solid black background.

Ani touched a picture of the four of them in Aruba. A rough, hard shape was behind the photograph. She rubbed the plastic over the picture and pressed down a little more.

"Something's in here," Ani said as she reached in and found a second photo behind the first. In between the two photos, her fingers brushed cool metal. As she touched it, she realized what it was. "A key," she said as she drew it out and looked at Jenn. "It looks like a safe-deposit box key."

Ani clasped the key tight in her hand, feeling its ridges and smoothness. She opened her palm to show the key to Jenn who picked it up and examined it.

"I wonder what he's got in it," Jenn said. "What would Dad keep in a bank safe-deposit box that he wouldn't put in his fireproof safe?"

Jenn handed the key back to Ani who held it between her thumb and forefinger. "Of course it doesn't say the box number *or* the bank." Ani cocked her head. "But considering how predictable Dad was, he only banked at one place our entire lives."

"First National." Jenn fiddled with the key on the mattress.

Ani closed the photo album and set it aside as her thoughts whirled. "What could be so important . . . so important that he wouldn't chance it being found in the house," she repeated. She put her elbows on her jeans and tapped her chin with one of her fingers. "Maybe it's something he wanted to keep from anyone who might know about the safe and try to force him to open it."

Jenn gave her a skeptical look. "That sounds a little far-fetched. A lot far-fetched."

Ani cleared her throat. "It could have something to do with Dad's involvement with the Russian Mafia."

Jenn's face turned bright red. She stood and clenched her fists at her sides. "I still can't believe it, no matter what the FBI says."

Ani rubbed her temples before returning her gaze

to Jenn's furious one. "I was at the door to the office when Dad was talking with three Russian mobsters. I saw them. I heard them." Ani's voice shook. "Dad said he wanted out. He was through working with the Russians. After Dad argued with those men, Dmitry Borenko stood and shot him in the head."

Jenn's expression was a combination of disbelief and horror, her eyes wide and her face pale.

"That's when I screamed. I clearly remember Dmitry seeing me standing in the doorway. I can see him raising the gun and shooting me. I dropped to the floor just as you and Mom rushed into the living room. I'm sure you heard the gunfire and ran in to see what was happening and then Dmitry shot you both."

Jenn wrapped her arms around Ani's waist, tears streaming down her face. "I've known that all along—about Dad—since they told me, but I still don't want to believe it."

"I'd rather not, either." Ani let out a long sigh. "I was shocked and I've never really come to terms with it. You know how Dad kept track of everything down to the last detail. What I heard and saw that night only confirmed what I read on his computer."

"So you'll be able to send him to jail for their murders?" Jenn asked.

"Not only did I witness Dmitry Borenko murder Mom and Dad," Ani said, "but I also have information on money laundering, racketeering, and bribery that could put Borenko away."

Jenn drew away and rubbed her eyes with her

hands. "This whole conversation started because of the key. What are you thinking?"

A little bit of excitement prickled Ani's skin. "Maybe Dad stored some kind of evidence against the Borenkos."

Jenn met Ani's gaze. "That's quite a stretch."

"Not really." Ani clenched the key in her palm and walked back and forth on the carpet in her bare feet. "Dad probably didn't expect to be shot as soon as he said he wasn't going to have anything to do with the Russians anymore."

Ani scrunched her nose before continuing. "Dad might have been planning on telling them he had detailed records that could put them all away if they didn't leave him alone." She gripped the key tighter as she continued to pace. "Dad could have put that information in the safe-deposit box to make sure it was safe. And that he was safe. It would be just like him to do that."

"But they killed him before he could use the threat." Jenn still looked skeptical, but she added, "It's a long shot, but worth checking out."

"It's Sunday, so today's out." Ani stopped pacing and tucked the key into one of the front pockets of her jeans. "Likely the bank won't open until eight tomorrow morning and I have to be in court at nine.

"I need to talk to Daniel." Ani strode through the open French doors of Jenn's bedroom, headed for the sitting room, and went up to Janet.

"I need to see Inspector Parker as soon as possible," Ani said.

Janet nodded. "I'll give him a ring on his cell phone and see if I can get him up here."

While Janet called Daniel, Ani returned to Jenn's bedroom and helped her put away all the things they'd unpacked from the box, minus the key.

When Daniel made it up to the room, he and Ani shared a long look that said so much to her. He broke eye contact first and looked to Janet before returning his gaze to Ani's. "What's up?"

Ani's heart pounded as she dug out the key and handed it to him. She explained her theory and said, "It could be nothing, but Jenn and I can't imagine why Dad would have a safe-deposit box when he put our important documents into the fireproof safe at home. Maybe there's hard evidence on the Borenkos in that safe-deposit box."

Daniel raised his eyebrows with an intrigued expression. "I'll contact Singleton now to get a federal grand jury subpoena. An FBI agent can check out the box," he said.

"Unfortunately," he continued, "no matter what strings we try to pull, we can't get into a bank on a Sunday. But we can get the subpoena to examine the safe-deposit box as soon as the bank's doors open tomorrow."

CHAPTER TWENTY-TWO

Monday morning Ani sat in the witness stand and stared down Dmitry Borenko.

To her surprise, she no longer felt any fear of the man. Only anger and hatred burned deep within her that would never go away. What Dmitry Borenko had done to her family was unforgivable.

Absolutely unforgivable.

Even though Daniel and Janet Hernandez were standing against the adjacent wall, Ani felt their presences, which gave her some comfort. Having Daniel there gave her even more strength than she already had.

God, she hoped something was in that safe-deposit box. Something that would make sure these bastards would pay even more than she was going to make them pay. Singleton had assured her that her testimony would put Dmitry Borenko behind bars, at least for murder and attempted murder, as well as arson, if not money laundering and racketeering. Any additional information that could back her up would be the icing.

As the defense attorney began his cross-examination, Ani clenched her hands in her lap. She spoke as clearly and slowly as possible, trying not to let Plutov rattle her.

First, the defense attorney started with questions about her sister again, which made her want to scream. "Ms. King, please tell the court how it was that you did not know your own sister has been alive these past two years?"

"I was in the Witness Security Program because of the threats on my life." Ani stared directly at Plutov. "I thought my sister had died before I signed the irrevocable papers that would not allow me to have any connection to my former life."

When the defense attorney asked what she could be in danger from, Ani gave him an "Are you an idiot?" look.

Her skin prickled and she felt a little queasy as she prepared to answer his question. What had happened over the past few days—it was amazing she was still alive. The fact that people had died because of the Russian Mafia sickened her further.

She raised her chin. "The Borenkos have had a hit out on me since they discovered that I survived the fire."

Plutov straightened his spine as he turned to Judge Steele. "Move to strike. There is no evidence to support this statement."

Singleton stood. "Special Agent Michaels has already testified to this *fact*."

"Mr. Plutov," the judge said. "I will allow the witness to continue."

Ani moved her gaze to Dmitry Borenko and met his eyes, which held nothing but death. "An FBI agent explained it all to me. He said for my safety I needed to enter the Witness Security Program as soon as possible."

Before Plutov could ask another question, Ani continued, "These past few days, from the time my location was discovered, as I explained earlier, I've been chased, shot at, almost blown up, chased and shot at some more. Wouldn't that tell me that my life has been, and still is, in danger?"

"Irrelevant." Plutov narrowed his gaze at Ani. "Move to strike. The witness has no proof that Dmitry Borenko had any direct involvement in such alleged activities."

Ani's body burned with heat and her words came out in a furious rush. "Then you tell me, Mr. Plutov, who else do you think is trying to kill me, because I'm reasonably certain it's not the Red Cross."

"Objection!" Plutov drew himself up as he whirled to face the judge.

"Sustained." The judge turned her head to face the jury. "Ignore the witness's last statements."

Ani let out a huff of air. She chanced a look at the twelve men and women on the jury. She saw nothing but blank expressions at this moment, which didn't give her a lot of confidence.

"Let's discuss the document you claim you saw on your father's computer," Plutov said, drawing her attention back to him.

Heat continued to burn within Ani. "I didn't *claim*

anything. It's a fact. I saw the document on my father's computer."

Plutov raised an eyebrow. "How could you possibly be sure this was not some story created from your father's imagination?"

"My father kept detailed journals throughout his life." She raised her chin a little and her gaze didn't waver from Plutov's. "He had countless handwritten journals that were destroyed in the fire. He started using the computer to document things once he purchased his first PC."

"That does not answer my question." Plutov gave her one of his sickening, indulgent smiles. "Let me rephrase the question. Could the document you read on his computer be fictitious?"

"No," Ani answered immediately, no question, no doubt in her mind whatsoever.

Plutov braced his hands on the witness stand and practically got in her face. "How do you know this?"

Ani tried not to recoil. At the same time she saw Daniel take a step toward her, a protective expression on his features, as if he were ready to toss Plutov on his ass if he didn't back off.

Apparently Plutov noticed as well because he pushed himself away from the witness stand after a quick glance in Daniel's direction.

"I knew my father well," Ani said in answer to Plutov's last question. "Better than you do."

The defense attorney gave her a condescending look. "Perhaps not well enough to know what you read was a figment of his imagination?"

"He didn't write or even read fiction." Ani clenched her hands tighter in her lap. "He thought it was a waste of time."

"Hmmmm . . ." Plutov studied her with disdain in his gaze. "Did you speak to your father about this document?"

"Before I had a chance to—"

Plutov interrupted. "Yes or no."

Ani tried not to glare. "No."

"Ah." Plutov faced the jury. "So you did not speak with your father to know absolutely whether or not this alleged document was fictitious."

Fury rose up within Ani like a storm. "It would have been difficult to discuss that with my father, considering Dmitry Borenko had just shot him in the head."

"Answer the question!" Plutov's jowls trembled and he looked like he was ready to sprout horns.

Ani was so tense and angry she wanted to *really* explode at him. "FBI agents matched what I remembered reading—"

"Yes or no, Ms. King," Plutov demanded. "Did you speak with your father about the alleged document?"

Ani ground her teeth. "No."

"Then as far as you know," Plutov repeated, this time with a smirk, "the document you claim to have seen was nothing more than a story."

More waves of heat washed through Ani. Plutov was attempting to completely undermine her credibility as a witness. She sucked in a deep breath and steeled her expression. "I also saw and heard Dmitry Borenko speak to my father—"

"Again," Plutov said, his voice booming through the room. "Yes or no. Do you have concrete proof this document existed or that it wasn't in fact, fiction?"

Ani swallowed. She paused a moment and Plutov raised his eyebrows. "No," she finally said, the word barely making it out of her mouth.

"Let the record show," Plutov said to the jury, "that the witness has admitted that this document she speaks of could have been nothing more than a figment of her imagination."

Heat flushed Ani's cheeks. "I did not—"

"Objection!" Singleton's voice rang out. "The fact that the witness has seen this document has already been established, therefore it did, in fact, exist, and is not a figment of Ms. King's imagination as defense counsel would have the jury believe."

"Withdrawn." Plutov looked at Ani, then back to the jury. "Allow me to rephrase," he said. "Let the record show that the witness has admitted to the fact that the document she speaks of could have been fictitious."

"Again, Your Honor, objection." Singleton stood, giving him a more powerful presence. "The witness has already testified as to her belief that her father would not conjure up a document. Defense counsel's tactics are clearly aimed solely at undermining the witness's statements."

The judge threw Plutov an irritated glance. "Move on, Mr. Plutov."

The defense attorney turned his gaze back to Ani. "You also claim you saw my client shoot Mr. Henry

King and Eloise King as well as your very much alive sister, Jennifer King, and yourself."

"Yes," Ani said as loudly as she could. "He murdered my parents."

"Allegedly," the attorney said. He put his hands behind his back and rocked heels to toes. "Apparently your memory is faulty—"

"Allegedly?" Ani interrupted with anger in her tone. "Does Dmitry Borenko have a twin brother? If not"—Ani pointed to Dmitry—"then that's the man I witnessed murder my parents."

Plutov continued as if he hadn't been interrupted. He grilled her, his every question designed to wear her down and to put doubt in the jury's mind as to what she'd seen and heard that night.

The whole ordeal was taking a toll on her, making her feel drained and weak.

"No further questions," Plutov finally said to the judge before heading back to his seat.

Relief poured through Ani and she wanted to collapse against the back of the chair from exhaustion.

The huge double doors to the courtroom opened.

Ani caught her breath and held it when she saw a man in a black suit walk down the aisle between the two rows of benches. He had a piece of paper in his hand.

Was this the FBI agent who had gone to the bank to open the safe-deposit box? If so, had the agent obtained information that would help put Dmitry Borenko behind bars for more than just murder?

The man entered through the swinging wooden gate and handed a piece of paper to the FBI agent seated next to Singleton. The agent glanced at the paper and passed it to Singleton.

The prosecutor nodded. A pleased expression lit his face.

Ani's heart rate picked up and she let her breath out in a rush. The FBI agent must have found something!

Plutov was just about to take his seat when Singleton stood and said, "New documentary information has come into our hands and I request a recess to review the information."

"Objection!" Plutov said. "Whatever this information is, it was clearly not presented in discovery. I insist on being given the opportunity to review it as well."

Singleton's gaze was steady. "As I said, this information has only just been presented to us. We do not yet know if it is relevant, or if we will seek to admit it."

Judge Steele frowned, clearly not pleased at delaying the trial. "We'll recess for one hour while the prosecution has the opportunity to view the new evidence, then we'll have a sidebar in chambers."

"Judge Steele," Singleton said. "We may require computers and screens from Litigation Support so that the jury may view this documentation should I wish to admit it."

The judge gave him a hard look. "Make arrangements as necessary."

Ani's heart raced as she looked from the prosecutor to Special Agent Michaels, to Daniel. They all were seated at the long table in the witness room while Singleton used a laptop to review the documents from a memory stick that had been in the safe-deposit box. He'd already saved all of the key files to his laptop's hard drive.

"A fucking gold mine." Singleton shook his head in obvious amazement as he scrolled through one of the documents. "Wire transfers and corresponding bank account numbers, e-mails, receipts. Not to mention his journal that ends just a month before the murders—when he must have put this all into the safe-deposit box. And this information implicates Yegor Borenko as well."

He laughed and picked up the cell phone that had been in the safe-deposit box, as well as a phone charger. "And text messages. Can you believe it? King saved text messages on his phone that are far more specific than the e-mails."

Singleton looked up at the FBI case agent. "We'll swear out a complaint and get an arrest warrant for Yegor Borenko. Before he catches wind of what we have, we'll be prepared for him."

He turned his attention to Ani. "I'm going to need you to testify once more, but it will be brief in comparison to your other testimony. Of course you will be cross-examined by Plutov.

"I'll have a sidebar in the judge's chambers," Singleton continued. "I'll meet with the judge and defense counsel to let them know I've just received this information and haven't been withholding it from defense during discovery. Arrangements will be made for the defense to review the material, which may delay the trial."

Ani couldn't help but look at him with obvious dismay on her face.

"To avoid having to bring you out of safety again, I'm going to push to have this evidence presented today so that you can finish testifying as soon as possible," Singleton said, not relieving her concerns in the least. "It may not happen, but it's early enough in the day and I'll do my best.

"In the meantime . . ." Singleton smiled as he held up the memory stick and looked at the FBI case agent. "The federal grand jury that's been sitting on the Yegor Borenko case you've been investigating— they'll fucking eat this up."

Ani perched on the witness stand again, her skin vibrating with satisfaction. Singleton had pulled it off and she was going to finish her testimony today. And the documents were going to be entered into evidence and shown to the jury.

Singleton had had his meeting with the defense counsel and the judge in chambers and the judge gave Plutov another hour to read the documents before Singleton entered them into evidence. During that hour, Litigation Support had set up computers and screens for the evidence to be viewed by the jury, prosecution, defense, judge, and witnesses.

Not only would Ani's testimony and the information on that memory stick help convict Dmitry Borenko, but the documents implicated Yegor Borenko. The head of the Russian Mafia family who was ultimately responsible for everything that had happened.

In front of her on the witness stand, to her left side, a computer monitor had been set up to be viewed by the next witness. There were also monitors in front of the judge, prosecutor, defense attorney, and even the defendant. A huge screen was across the room from the jury so that they would be able to view the evidence when it was shown.

Dmitry's glare at Ani had intensified tenfold. She could feel the fury rolling from him in waves, all the way to the witness stand. It made her heart beat faster, but she met his glare with as placid an expression as she could muster. Inside she wanted to smile her satisfaction. The sonofabitch was going down, and he knew it.

Singleton approached the witness stand. To establish where the safe deposit key had come from, Singleton asked Ani how she and her sister had found the key. She explained that it had been hidden in the photo album recovered from the fireproof safe. She told him how she and her sister had determined the bank was the same one their father had banked at as long as they could remember.

When it came time for him to cross-examine her, Plutov approached Ani with narrowed eyes. He spouted questions about the key that made little sense to Ani. They'd found the key. End of story, right? Not according to Plutov. He wanted to know how the key had "magically" appeared and so forth.

"Those documents will prove there's not an ounce of human blood pumping through Dmitry Borenko's veins." She turned her glare on Dmitry. "He's an animal. A disgusting, filthy animal who murdered for greed."

Plutov shouted, "Objection. The witness is expressing emotion here, and not any proven fact."

Judge Steele glanced at the jury. "Sustained. The jury will disregard the witness's last statements."

At the same time Plutov and the judge spoke, a look of total and complete rage overcame Dmitry's features. His face went dark red, his eyes blazing. He stood, and prickling heat flowed over her as she saw his whole body tense and his fists clench.

"Be seated, Mr. Borenko," Judge Steele said in a commanding tone, a firm expression on her features.

Plutov tugged at Dmitry's jacket sleeve. "Sit," the defense attorney hissed loudly enough for Ani to hear.

Ani's body went ice-cold as Dmitry Borenko's eyes filled with hate—and death. The same death she had seen when he'd shot her two years ago.

Dmitry vaulted over the defense table.

He rushed the witness stand.

"Bitch!" he shouted as he reached her.

He wrapped his hands around her throat.

Ani gasped and barely heard the roar in the room as he dug his fingers and nails into her throat. He squeezed so hard she thought her neck would snap.

Vaguely she was aware of someone trying to pry his fingers from her throat.

Despite the bout of dizziness that overcame her, anger and hatred gave her strength.

Using everything she had, Ani took her hand and rammed the hard, fleshy part of her palm into Dmitry's nose. She heard a sickening crack and heard his shout as her hand met his nose, but he didn't let go.

Spots flickered in and out behind her eyes as she heard him grunt and felt his fingers slide from her neck.

She barely had the presence of mind to see Daniel slam his fist into Dmitry's jaw. The man's head snapped to the side and his knees gave out. Only the two Deputy Marshals holding each of his arms kept him from falling.

Blood poured from Dmitry Borenko's nose, down to the white of his shirt. His jaw sported a bright red mark where Daniel's fist had met it.

As Dmitry was dragged away and out through a side door by a pair of Deputies, he struggled and shouted words in Russian that Ani was positive were obscenities.

Her vision started to clear. From behind her, someone was trying to draw her from the witness stand. She had a death hold on the wooden edge of the stand. Her hands and arms ached.

Another person eased her fingers from where she had them clenched so tightly.

"Honey," a voice whispered in her ear, "you're all right. I've got you."

Daniel.

Tears started pouring down her face and she turned and buried her face in his shirt. He didn't try to pull away for the sake of protocol, he just let her sob against him as she gripped his shirt in her fists. Her neck and throat hurt so badly but the emotions of being attacked and finally being finished with testifying were too much.

Daniel held her by the shoulders and whispered so only she could hear. "It's okay now. Everything's okay. You did it, Ani. You did it."

CHAPTER TWENTY-THREE

Yegor growled beneath his breath as his son was taken away. The worthless *govno*. As far as Yegor was concerned, Dmitry was no longer his son, and would be dealt with appropriately while he was in prison.

Yegor heaved himself up from his seat on one of the audience benches. After straightening, and with his backbone rigid, he started to leave the courtroom.

The door was blocked by three men in suits.

He came to an abrupt halt as Singleton's voice rang out through the courtroom. "I have an arrest warrant for Yegor Borenko," the prosecuting attorney said as Yegor was approached by four other men. "For the crimes of murder, bribery, racketeering, money laundering, wire fraud, retaliation against a witness, extortion . . ."

Singleton's voice faded in Yegor's ears as the men he was facing quickly surrounded him, their FBI badges in clear view on their belts. One of the men jerked Yegor's arms behind his back, causing pain to shoot through his shoulders like fire. Cold steel bit into his wrists as he was handcuffed. The officers were forced to use three pairs of cuffs due to his bulk—one on each wrist and one connecting the other pairs.

His fury was so great he shook with it.

Then all he could think about was his beautiful granddaughters and how they would grow up with the shame of their father and grandfather being imprisoned.

For the first time in his life, a tear formed in each of Yegor's eyes.

CHAPTER TWENTY-FOUR

Ani's neck and throat ached from Dmitry's attack. She leaned her head against the back of the couch in the hotel room she'd been sharing with her sister. Jenn sat in a chair opposite Ani, but looked buried in her own thoughts.

Two days ago, it had taken the jury all of thirty minutes to reach a verdict and pronounce Dmitry Borenko guilty on two counts of murder in the first degree, two counts of attempted murder, racketeering, money laundering, wire fraud, bribery . . . So many charges that Ani's head spun with it all. In addition, enough information had been in those documents to indict other members of the same Russian mob family.

And Yegor Borenko, the head of the family ultimately responsible for all that had happened, had been indicted for even more charges than Dmitry had been pronounced guilty of.

Yegor was not allowed to make bail under the circumstances, due to the crimes he was being charged with. He was considered a flight risk as he could easily flee to Mother Russia, and he was a risk to society with his murdering ways.

Ani adjusted her position on the couch. She tried to ignore the constant pain around her neck and throat. Dmitry had dug his fingers into her throat hard enough to leave bruises where every one of his fingers had gripped her.

She brought her knees up to her chin and wrapped her arms around her legs. The attack had shaken her, but ultimately that wasn't what took hold of her thoughts.

No, it was the verdict itself that ran through her mind. She hadn't been sure what to expect when the trial was over.

What she experienced was a sense of closure.

Now that her parents' killers had been put behind bars, she felt she could move on. It would never be the same without her mother and father, but she no longer felt trapped in the time that had held her captive the past two years.

As far as her father being involved with the Mob— she wasn't sure if she could ever reconcile herself to that fact. But she'd had to face it, acknowledge it, and go forward with her life.

Her jeans felt rough beneath her chin, but the couch was soft against her bare feet as she held herself tucked together.

Even with Dmitry probably headed to prison for life and Yegor indicted, the FBI and Marshals still believed that Ani and her sister had to be concerned about Yegor's Mob family. That faction might seek retribution to make her and her sister examples of what would happen to anyone who went up against the Russian Mafia.

The future—she wasn't sure what it held other than a new name and a new location. Again.

Her love for Daniel was deep and had grown stronger every day they had shared. She couldn't imagine life without him, but since she had to stay in the program . . . how could they make things work?

And yesterday he'd left.

Ani sighed. As soon as Dmitry was remanded and Yegor indicted, Daniel made arrangements to fly to Los Angeles. He hadn't explained why, just that he would be back. They'd only had a stolen moment to share a kiss that still made butterflies flutter in her belly every time she thought about it.

But the feeling quickly faded. In order for her and Daniel to remain together, he'd have to enter WITSEC with her and give up his career. She could never ask that of him, and likely it wouldn't be something he'd be willing to do. He'd already told her he'd be taken off WITSEC because of the line he'd crossed. But she knew there were other areas in the U.S. Marshals Service that he could be moved to.

So as far as the two of them—what now?

Daniel sat back in his chair, waiting to see Gorman, his regional superior. Daniel raked his hand through his hair as his gut clenched. He knew what he had to do, but it didn't make it any easier.

As he waited, his mind turned over all that had happened in such a short period of time. Ani was alive. He hadn't failed her.

Not like Judge Moore.

But maybe it was time to make peace with the past.

He still had a burning desire to help others that would never leave him. Not that he wanted it to. It was a part of him and always would be.

When the assistant informed Daniel that Gorman would see him now, Daniel got to his feet and headed to his superior's office. He'd been there before, but not for something like this.

"Parker." The Supervisory Deputy Marshal shook Daniel's hand and gave him a smile as Daniel entered his office. Gorman was fit with an athletic build, sharp blue eyes, and a little gray at his temples. "Good to see you," he said as he walked around to his side of the desk. "Now tell me what's going on."

Daniel seated himself and faced Gorman, a man who wasted no time getting to the point. It was something Daniel had always admired in him.

With no intention of drawing this out any longer than he had to, Daniel said, "I've crossed a line, John." Daniel rubbed his hand over his face as Gorman narrowed his gaze. "I'm out of the Service."

Gorman's eyebrows formed a V as he narrowed his eyes. He leaned forward. "What's going on, Daniel?"

He took a deep breath and eyed Gorman straight-on.

"I've had relations with Anistana King, a witness I've been protecting."

For a moment Gorman just looked at him, before thumping his palm on his desk. His features went hard and unyielding. "You're damn right you're out of WITSEC. Effective immediately. I'll have to transfer you, probably to Criminal Investigations."

Daniel's gaze didn't waver as he sucked in his breath. "I mean I'm leaving the service altogether. I'm marrying the witness."

Gorman rocked back in his chair, shaking his head. "If you intend to go through with this, you know the drill."

Daniel nodded. "Let's get started."

CHAPTER TWENTY-FIVE

As Ani sat in the hotel room, she used the coffee table to finish filling out the paperwork that would reintroduce her to WITSEC under a new identity.

For probably the last time she signed her real name to the documents. *Anistana King.* She'd been through this before, but it didn't make it any easier. She had to change her last name of course, but as before she could still keep Ani as her first name since it was common enough, unlike Anistana.

She and Jenn had been assigned a new Inspector Marshal because they'd decided to relocate to the South. Instead of feeling depressed about leaving her city again, she felt numb. Maybe because she didn't know what was going to happen to her and Daniel.

No, she did.

Now she realized they had been swept up in the moment, that he couldn't give up his career for her and she wouldn't want that.

They would have to part ways, and it was going to

hurt more than she could begin to imagine. He'd been gone for two days, and she wondered if he was also having a hard time with the fact that they had to say goodbye.

Ani glanced up at Jenn and Brian and her heart broke a little more for them. A deep ache settled in her chest because her sister was losing everything. Again.

They both were.

Jenn openly cried as she faced Brian. They were gripping each other's hands. Even Brian seemed to struggle with his emotions, his eyes glazed with the hint of tears.

"I'm so sorry, Jenn." He bowed his head before looking up at her again and meeting her gaze. "I can't leave my family, my friends, my life. I love you more than you can imagine." He looked down again. "I thought I could do it, but I can't."

Jenn straightened and took one of her hands from Brian's to rub it against her eyes as he looked at her again. "I understand." Her voice came out rough from crying. "When I chose to go into WITSEC with my sister, I knew this could happen. But it doesn't make it any easier."

"I know, baby." He released her other hand and captured her face in his palms, then leaned forward and kissed her forehead. When he drew back he brushed her tears away with his thumbs. "This is killing me."

"I'm so sorry." She hiccupped and clasped her hands over his before drawing them away from her face.

"Hey." He took both of her hands again and

gripped them between himself and Jenn. "I'll never regret what you and I have. You'll always be in my heart." His voice sounded like he was trying hard not to cry, too. "I just wish I could keep you here with me. But I can't and we both know that."

Jenn gave a slow nod and sniffed. "You'd better go."

Ani's chest ached even more as she watched them, and tears filled her own eyes. She got up and grabbed a box of tissues off an end table before handing the box to her sister. Jenn released Brian's hands again and clutched the tissue box against her belly.

"I'm sorry," he said again as he got to his feet. "I love you, Jenn."

She broke into further sobs as she looked down at her lap before looking up at him again. "Goodbye, Brian."

A single tear trickled down his cheek but he didn't bother to wipe it away. His chest rose as he sucked in his breath before letting it out in a loud exhale. He turned and walked to the Deputy Marshal waiting in the room who escorted him out.

As soon as the door closed behind him, Jenn totally broke down. She buried her face in her hands and her body shook with the force of her sobs.

Tears streamed freely down Ani's face as she went to her sister and embraced her. Ani stroked Jenn's hair, but said nothing as her sister cried her heart out.

Ani knew then she could never expect Daniel to give up his life to be with her. She wouldn't want to do that to him. Couldn't do that to him. The sooner she returned to the program, the better. She and her sister would go together this time. And somehow they'd make it.

Needing to get away from New York and her memories of Brian, Jenn had insisted on leaving the city to their new destination, their new home. She'd been accompanied by the Deputy Marshal who was the Inspector for the area they were moving to.

Gary McNeal had told Ani that Daniel would be back the day following Jenn's departure. Ani would have gone with her sister, but she had to see Daniel one last time.

Ani was alone in the sitting room of the suite, the Deputy Marshals guarding the door from the outside. They'd left her alone, giving her some time to herself. Right now Ani was glad for that. She needed to think.

A clicking sound came from the door as someone turned the knob. Ani tensed.

The door opened and Daniel was suddenly in the doorway, his big frame filling the space as he looked at her. She didn't move when he closed the door behind him and then just studied her for a long moment.

She stood but didn't go to him. This was it. This was his goodbye.

"Jenn and Brian said goodbye." Ani felt stiff as she looked at Daniel. "He's not going into the program with her."

Daniel scrubbed his hand over his face. "I'd hoped he would."

Ani's shoulders sagged. "Me, too."

The conversation felt tense and formal and Ani just wanted to run into the bedroom and separate herself from Daniel behind a closed door.

But he strode toward her and before she could take a breath he had his arms wrapped around her, holding her tight to his chest. At first she felt stiff in his embrace, but then her body relaxed and she sank into him. He smelled so good as she inhaled his earthy, masculine scent. And he felt so right.

"It's going to be okay, honey," he said against her hair. "It'll take some time, but Jenn will find someone."

"That kind of heartbreak doesn't mend easily." Ani's throat felt thick as she spoke. She placed her hands on his chest, pushed away, and looked up at him. "Sometimes you know that no one can replace the person you love, and your heart will never be the same."

Daniel frowned and wrapped his fingers in her dark curls. "What are you saying, Ani?"

She glanced down at her bare toes before looking up at Daniel again. "You and I—we have to say good-bye now. I don't know how I'm going to get over you. I don't think I ever will."

For a long moment he studied her before shoving his hand into his front jeans pocket. He drew out something that glittered in the room's dim lighting.

When he brought it up, he took her left hand and slipped something on her ring finger. Stunned, barely able to breathe, Ani looked down at her hand to see a beautiful stone that sparkled so brilliantly she had to blink before looking at it again.

"It's a yellow diamond." He continued to hold her hand. "It was passed down from my great-great-grandmother."

"Yellow diamonds are rare," she said, knowing it sounded inane, but too shocked to say anything else. Her body was going hot then cold with confusion.

She looked up at him and he smiled. "Will you marry me, Anistana King—or whatever your name is now?"

She squeezed her eyes shut then opened them again. "You know I can't. WITSEC—everything."

His gaze remained steady. "What do you think of Matthews as a last name?"

Ani blinked. "Uhhh . . ."

Daniel smiled. "I'm asking you to marry me, Ani. It'll be an adjustment, but I've signed the contract, and I'm in the program with you."

Her heart beat faster. "You can't—"

"I can and I did." He settled his arms around her waist. "All you have to do is say yes."

"I don't—I mean, I can't ask—"

Daniel lowered his mouth to hers and silenced her with a sweet kiss. Long, drawn out, precious.

When he pulled away, he was smiling. "It'll take some adjusting to, but I've helped enough people through the program to know how it works."

She searched his eyes. "But your family . . ."

"After being with the Service for so long I know

how to get around without being found." He gripped her tighter around the waist. "I've said my goodbyes to my brothers and Dad. Yeah, it wasn't easy, but they understand that you mean more than anything to me." He placed his forehead against hers. "I won't let you go, Ani."

She squeezed her eyes shut. Her heart was beating hard enough that her breasts ached.

Daniel kissed each of her eyelids. "Now all you have to do is say yes."

The shock of it kept her speechless. He meant it. He was really going to go with her into the program. She looked down at the stone glittering on her finger. A brilliant-cut one-carat yellow diamond nestled in a gold setting. None of this seemed real. Not the ring, not his marriage proposal, not the fact that he was willing to go into WITSEC with her.

He drew away and reached his hand up to stroke her hair and she looked at him.

"It's not that hard to say one little word, honey." His smile met his eyes. "It's simple. Say yes."

Again her throat didn't want to work. "Yes," she finally whispered as her eyes stung with tears. *"Yes."*

Daniel's smile broke into a grin. He picked her up by her ass so that she was clinging to him, her thighs clenching his hips. He kissed her hard this time and she answered just as fiercely. He tasted so good as his tongue delved into her mouth, and he showed her she belonged to him with just that kiss.

She was vaguely aware of him walking toward her

bedroom, then took one of his hands from her just long enough to close the French door behind him. He settled her on the mattress, drew away, and knelt on the carpeting beside the bed.

He picked up her left hand and looked at the ring on her finger and back to her face. "Perfect," he murmured as he leaned in for another kiss. "Just like you."

Ani sighed and let him slowly strip off her clothing. His every touch was reverent and loving. He stroked her with his hands, his gaze, his mouth. She shivered with every brush of his fingers.

When she was naked, he got to his feet and she watched him with a deep, abiding hunger as he shed his clothes in just moments. He was so powerfully built, so handsome, yet so gentle and loving, too.

After finding a condom and setting it on the nightstand, Daniel eased onto the bed beside her so that they were lying face-to-face. He pillowed his head with one of his arms while he used his free hand to stroke her body. He ran his fingertips from her chin, down to her throat.

"I'd like to take another swing at that sonofabitch." He narrowed his brows as he looked at her sore neck. "Are you okay?"

"I'm fine." She slipped her hand down to cup his balls in her palm. "Especially now."

Daniel groaned and closed his eyes as she lightly ran her hand around his powerful erection. She stroked him, teasing him by skimming her fingertips along his length and circling the head before rubbing the bead of pre-come over the slit.

With a low growl, he opened his eyes and practically attacked her as he rolled her onto her back and slid between her thighs. She laughed and held on to his biceps.

"You think torturing me is funny, do you?" A spark lit his eyes and he began moving his cock up and down her wet slit. Slowly. Every movement meant to drive her crazy.

It was too much. Ani gave a soft moan. "Inside me, Daniel. Please."

"Your turn to be teased." He pumped his hips harder so that his erection rubbed her clit enough to make her writhe beneath him.

"Okay, okay." She moved her hands from his biceps down to grasp his muscled ass, loving the way the smooth skin over steel muscles felt beneath her hands. "I won't tease you any more." Then she added under her breath, "This time."

Apparently he chose to ignore her last threat, needing to be inside her as badly as she wanted him. It didn't take him long to sheathe his erection with the condom. She wriggled beneath him, waiting for him to enter her. He gave her one loving look before he drove his cock deep inside her core.

Ani cried out at the feel of him so deep, so thick, so filling. It felt as if it were their first time again, as if everything between them was all new. Maybe it was because this time she knew he was all hers. Forever.

He'd given up so much for her that it nearly brought tears to her eyes again just thinking about it.

Daniel braced himself above her and kept his gaze locked with hers as he moved in and out of her core, with long, deep thrusts. She didn't think he could reach any deeper as his cock rubbed against that spot inside her that made her crazy.

It wasn't long before she could no longer focus on his face. Loud moans came out of her that she couldn't have stopped if she tried. The emotions throughout the day intensified her need for him as did the feelings she was experiencing as he made love to her. Sadness she had felt with her sister and the thought of losing Daniel. Then exhilaration when she realized he was hers. And now tender lovemaking.

She clenched her fingers deeper into his ass and tossed her head from side to side. Her whole body vibrated and she felt the depth of the oncoming orgasm throughout every limb, every part of her being, from her head to her toes. It was almost like an aura of sensation surrounded her.

Ani's orgasm grew and grew until she didn't think she could take any more. Knew she couldn't. A cry built up in her throat.

The force of her climax hit hard and strong and she released the cry as her body was enveloped in heat. The aura of sensation rained down on her, seeping into her every pore.

She tingled everywhere and her abdomen clenched as she bucked against his hips. Her channel clamped down on him with every thrust he made. She was exhausted from the force of her orgasm, but found her energy rising again when she met his gaze and he continued to pound in and out of her.

Daniel could barely hold himself from coming as

he felt Ani's pussy grip his cock like a fist. Sweat broke out on his brow from the force of his restraint, and he clenched his teeth.

It felt so good being inside this woman he loved. He would gladly do anything in the world for her. She meant everything to him.

Again and again he thrust his cock inside Ani until he knew he couldn't take it any longer. He tipped his head back and shouted as his orgasm burst throughout him. It felt like he'd just exploded and he damn near blacked out.

Still buried inside her, Daniel dropped and barely kept from crushing Ani beneath him. He rolled onto his side, holding her tight to him as his cock still pulsed inside her. His breathing was hard and labored, his chest rising and falling against hers.

When he could breathe and see clearly again, he drew apart just enough that he could see her face, but still gripped her hip and held her close. Her dark hair was tousled, her skin flushed, her lips swollen, and her blue eyes heavy lidded and dark with her desire. He drew in a deep breath, taking in her sweet scent mixed with the smell of sex. His hair was damp around his temples.

He rubbed one of her ass cheeks with his palm as he hooked his thigh over hers.

Ani gave him a sated smile. "Matthews, huh?"

Daniel returned her smile and twisted his fingers in her long dark hair. "Yeah."

"Hmmmm . . ." She tilted her head back a little. "Daniel and Ani Matthews?"

"I like that." He tugged on the lock of hair he was holding. "It'll take some getting used to, but we'll make it happen." He leaned in for a kiss before drawing away. "All that matters is spending the rest of our lives together."

She reached up and brushed the back of her hand against his cheek. "I love you, Daniel."

He caught her hand in his. "Honey, you can't possibly love me more than I love you."

EPILOGUE

Ani Matthews grinned as she cradled three-month-old Kyle in her arms while Daniel held Kyle's twin brother, Anthony, over his shoulder and tried to burp him.

So much love filled Ani's heart that she thought she'd burst with it. Kyle cooed against her breasts and she kissed the baby on the top of his head. She'd never get enough of that sweet baby smell, like baby powder and gingersnaps.

Anthony let out a large burp. Ani laughed. Daniel had a towel over his shoulder so the baby's spit-up didn't get on his leather jacket.

Over the playpen hung a mobile of several of Daniel's collector airplanes for the boys to look at. Anthony and Kyle were fascinated when the mobile turned, the planes flying through the air, the little propellers spinning when there was a soft breeze. They were high enough the boys couldn't reach them, just intrigue them.

"Well, Detective Matthews," Ani said as she buckled

Kyle into his baby swing. "Is it time for you to head off to the station?"

"Better get going." He gently handed her Anthony, along with the towel that had been over the leather jacket that covered his firearm. "Got a case that's about to break."

Jenn came out of the kitchen, brushing her hands on her jeans. "The boys' bottles are ready."

"Thanks, sis," Ani said as she passed Anthony on to Jenn, whose long brown hair was held back in a French braid.

For a moment Ani stared after her sister as she walked back to the kitchen through the swinging doors. Jenn stopped by every morning to help Ani with the twins. Jenn's heart was still broken over Brian, but it had been more than a year and she'd started dating again, which Ani took as a good sign.

She left Kyle buckled in the baby swing for a moment while she followed Daniel out to the porch. They lived in a gorgeous antebellum home outside the city limits of Nashville.

With her half of the money she'd inherited from her mother and father, and the restitution the judge had ordered the Borenkos to pay for the murder of her parents, she'd been able to purchase the home. It was a historic and roomy house filled with antiques and art that were precious to her. The Inspector assigned to them had transferred the cash to an account that couldn't be traced.

Even though she wasn't supposed to know anything about any of her past lives, through that same Inspector she'd learned that the Harrisons had been able to sell the statue of Tyrion III to the collector she'd originally contacted. The Harrisons' son was getting the best treatment and therapy money could buy at one of the top burn centers in the country. Her heart still ached for the boy, but he was at least getting the treatment he needed and his family wasn't out on the streets.

Ani had a small gift shop that she and Jenn ran just inside the Nashville city limits. It gave both of them the opportunity to meet people, making them both feel more like they were part of the community.

"Bye, honey," Daniel said, drawing her attention back to him.

She liked giving him her attention. Him, and her beautiful babies, and her sister.

The losses and traumas of her past still ached, but her sweet life with Daniel and her family cushioned her from that pain. Ani had grown into her new name, her new role, and it fit her like Daniel's snug, sexy jeans. She didn't think of herself as that scared, scarred New York girl anymore. She was a strong Southern woman now, just minus the accent.

And she could barely imagine anything happier or warmer, or more secure.

"Bye," she said, then sighed against his lips as he gave her a long, lingering kiss. His taste and masculine scent never failed to fill her with comfort and happiness.

Ani wrapped her arms around his waist and he enveloped her in his embrace. "I love you so much, Daniel."

He raised his head and brushed his knuckles across her cheek. "I love you, honey."

The minute he turned her loose, Ani wanted him back again.

He gave her a sexy grin and a wink, then headed for his Ford Explorer. She watched him go, already thinking about the kiss she'd give him when he got home.

Yes. This is what life should be.

Ani waved at Daniel as he drove away.

This is my gift, my reward, and I won't ever stop being grateful.

When Daniel turned the corner, Ani went inside, eager to play with her babies and chat with her sister, excited about work and definitely looking forward to what evening might bring.

Rich scents of earth and minerals swirled in the cool air brushing Hannah's skin as she walked beside the king. She gripped the strap of her pack tight before releasing some of the tension coiled inside her and letting her hand fall away.

They strode across the great round hall that had many doors around the circumference. Her shoes made soft sounds against the marble, but Garran was as silent as the D'Danann.

Despite the fact that his skin was a grayish blue, the man was gorgeous. It would have been impossible not to appreciate the litheness of his movements, his grace—and power. Power in every flex of his muscles, in the way he held his head, in his very presence. He was a king in every sense of the word.

Garran paused and gestured to the excellent carvings on the walls. "Some of our finest craftsmen created these grand works of art."

The carvings were mostly of male warriors in battle.

Then heat burned Hannah's skin as she slowly looked around the enormous circular hall. Were women kneeling to the men in some of the artwork? *Oh, my goddess.* Most of the Drow women even wore collars.

Hannah's gaze snapped to Garran's. Heat flared up her body and she clenched her hands at her sides. "Don't you dare tell me," she pointed to the carvings, "that Dark Elves treat women as subservient?"

Garran raised an eyebrow. "It is our lifestyle."

"Oh, no." She shook her head as she ground her teeth. "You *cannot* make me believe female Drow enjoy being treated like that."

His shrug was casual. "They would have it no other way."

Hannah considered decking him. Or better yet, using her magic to make *him* a collar—and a leash. "You probably don't give them a choice."

"Certainly we do." He tried taking her by the elbow and guiding her to a door, but she jerked away from his touch. "However, it is a rare thing for a woman to choose not to serve a Master."

A Master?

The thought of Garran on the floor with the magical collar and rope was looking better and better.

He swept his arm out in front of him, indicating they should go through a large arched doorway that spun off from the great hall. "You will see."

Her lips tight with anger, Hannah walked beside Garran as they entered an underground city. For the moment, awe replaced her anger.

Stalactites spotted with glowing lichen projected

down from the great cavern. The entire ceiling sparkled and more lichen caused a blue glow to give a soft light to the city.

Homes clung to rock outcroppings and footpaths wended their ways around the cavern walls. Most of the city spread out across the smooth, obviously well-worn floor of the cavern. Narrow streets wound from one building to the next. It reminded her of the D'Danann village, yet not.

Wonderful aromas spilled from shops that sold bread and other bakery goods, including what smelled like coffeecake. Hannah's mouth watered even though she was still full from dinner.

All she saw were males who gave low nods to Garran as she and Garran passed them. In turn he inclined his head and greeted each person by name. The respect in their gazes and voices, and the way they responded to him with their gestures and expressions, told her how well they thought of their king.

Where are the women?

In between Garran acknowledging every male they walked by, they came across a butcher shop, a place that offered leatherwork, as well as a smithy who made the breast- and shoulderplates most of the warriors wore. It looked like everything one could think of could be found in this underground city.

Except a Starbucks.

She shook her head. First thing she was going to do when life returned to "normal" in San Francisco would be to buy one of those frappuccinos she'd been craving.

Her gaze riveted on a glittering blanket of gems

ahead in a windowless display. Goddess, a fortune in
jewelry was spread out. Diamonds the size of eggs,
rubies as big as a fist.

Gem-encrusted leather collars?

Hannah's head snapped up. She traced her crescent-
and-moon pendant with her fingers before dropping her
hand to her side as she caught sight of a few women on
the path in the direction she and Garran were heading.

The women were so scantily clad they might as well
have been wearing nothing. Practically sheer tops were
so short they exposed the roundness of the underside of
the women's breasts and the filmy material hardly covered their nipples. They also wore short gauzy skirts
that hardly reached the bottoms of their ass cheeks.

Most of the women wore collars.

Collars, for Anu's sake! Like dogs or other ani-
mals, they wore collars and *served a Master*.

Heat filled her as she watched the women. Their
skin was smooth and supple in the cavern's soft lighting, their curves in all the right places—their bodies
virtually perfect.

A couple of the women whispered to each other
when they saw their king with Hannah, and they bowed
to him almost shyly. But otherwise the women smiled,
talked, and laughed among themselves. Despite the fact
they wore collars, they appeared . . . happy.

"Explain to me," Hannah said through gritted
teeth, "why these women allow themselves to be col-
lared and why they are practically naked. Are they
sex slaves or something?"

"The collar means a woman belongs to a Master."

Garran came up short and they stopped in front of the jewelry store as he glanced down at Hannah. His expression softened. "Sex is important to any consenting adult relationship, but our way of life is not 'all about sex,' as you would say."

Hannah braced her hands on her hips as she glared up at him. He was so damned tall she had to tilt her head. "Then what is it about?"

"Come." He touched his hand on her elbow. "We will talk."

One thing Hannah *never* did was cause a scene in public. She clamped her jaws shut as she realized that was what she'd just about done. She blanked her expression and held her carriage high as she usually did.

Garran guided her past a fish market, the scents reminding her of home and the wind off the bay, causing memories of her old life and a twinge in her belly. They strolled beyond the market to a display of wooden figurines and children's toys. Then the smells of fresh fish and wood drifted away as they continued on to what appeared to be a park.

Children wearing rough-spun tunics and pants laughed and played on the flat, moss-covered rock area filled with boulders and stone statues. Hannah couldn't help a smile as she and Garran stopped outside the park and watched the children racing, kicking black leather balls, climbing boulders, or sitting cross-legged on the mossy ground playing with toys. They had wooden dolls and figures, including something that looked like the ugliest troll she could imagine. Some of the male dolls were dressed like warriors wearing breastplates and leather chest straps, and even leather pants. The female dolls tended to have iridescent clothing that shimmered in the blue lichen lighting.

Barbie and G.I. Joe had nothing on these dolls.

Hannah touched one of the smooth boulders surrounding the park. "I never thought about Elves having children."

When she glanced up at Garran, he wore an amused expression. "Did you think we are created from stone?"

"Actually, I had been wondering if *you* were." She turned her attention back to the park. Several women were dressed in a little more clothing than the ladies Hannah had seen in the village, but they still wore collars. They sat on rock benches at various places around the area, many talking as their children played.

A pinging sensation bounced around in Hannah's heart. The mothers looked so happy, as did the children. Hannah hadn't had the kind of childhood where she was allowed to play with other children. She'd been sheltered, watched by a nanny, then sent to boarding schools where fraternization was discouraged.

One of the children threw a baseball-sized black leather ball that overshot the kid he'd been throwing the ball to. It rushed straight for Hannah. Garran snapped his hand up and caught the ball before it would have slammed into her face.

Relief whooshed through her. That would have hurt like hell.

A young boy dressed in a royal blue tunic and pants trotted toward them with a chagrined expression. "I-I didn't mean to—"

Garran squatted so he was eye-level with the boy and handed him the ball. "You have great strength, Jalen." The boy clutched the ball to his chest and looked at Garran with wide blue eyes. Garran placed his hand on the boy's left arm. "Continue your practice, most especially your control. One day you will make a fine warrior."

Jalen nodded hard enough that his blue hair fell into his eyes. "Yes, my lord."

Garran eased to his feet and gestured to the park. "Enjoy your game of *carta*."

The boy nodded again before whirling and bolting to where other boys and girls had stopped playing and were staring at Garran. Some waved and gave shy smiles and Garran acknowledged them with a slight incline of his head.

It was odd seeing Garran as more than a king and a warrior. A strange whirling gripped her insides and she had no idea why.

She let her gaze drift from Garran to the boys and girls. "They're beautiful."

"Children among Dark Elves are rare," he said softly, with what sounded like a touch of longing, and she moved her gaze toward him. "They are much treasured."

The distant look in his eyes surprised her for a moment before she realized he was probably thinking of his own daughter, Rhiannon, who had been raised among humans and kept far from him—in San Francisco. A part of her melted and it took a lot of effort to make herself return to the subject that still bothered her.

"You haven't explained this whole Master/slave thing," she said, and his attention cut to her.

"Our women are not slaves." His words had a hard edge to them and he had an even harder look in his eyes. "It is an exchange of power, protection, and pleasure, if you will."

Hannah frowned. "I'm not following you."

Garran folded his arms and leaned his hip against one of the larger boulders. "Our men are far stronger physically than our women. They rely on us for protection and to provide for them."

She crossed her own arms beneath her breasts and her frown turned into a scowl. "So the males make them walk around with hardly anything on, wearing collars, and calling them *Master*?"

"In turn," Garran continued as his gaze held hers, "the woman holds the power to give the man pleasure."

Her cheeks heated as her anger rose. "So this *is* all about sex."

He shook his head, his silvery-blue hair shimmering in the soft glow given off by the lichen above. "A Drow female who serves a Master has the power to please him in all aspects of his life. Family, home, and yes, sex."

Hannah huffed out her breath. "I don't get it."

Garran took her by the elbow again. They walked along a path and she tried to calm down about the whole woman-serving-a-man thing. *Barbaric*.

He came to a stop in front of another jeweler's display. He glanced at one of the gem-studded collars, then turned his gaze on her. "Wouldn't you enjoy belonging to someone, Hannah Wentworth?"

Belong to someone? Having a Master? More heat flushed over her and her whole body tensed. "I want to talk to you," she said, nearly grinding her teeth as she spoke. "In private."

He winked and smiled, and she thought again about using her magic as a rope and collar.

As the heat in her body ramped up even more, she and Garran walked from the city through a honeycomb of passageways. They entered a dim hallway where arches opened in various directions, and he led her through one of the arches. The whole time they walked, Hannah's temper mounted.

They eventually reached the end of a short hall that led to a door on the right. The sound of rushing water met Hannah's ears as he drew her into a chamber.

A bedroom—likely his. In the far corner, water tumbled from a high rock, spilling into a pool the size of a sauna. Rich tapestries of Drow warriors in battle draped the walls. Rugs lay scattered on the floor in the same rich colors as the tapestries. On one wall hung swords, a quiver of arrows, and a bow, along with other weapons. All would be incredibly expensive in her world. The metals and gems glittered in the soft blue lighting shining from lichen on the ceiling over their heads.

A huge bed that looked as if it had been carved from an enormous round stone commanded the center of the room. "You sleep in a rock?" she muttered. "I shouldn't be surprised."

"Try it." Garran moved closer to her and she felt such power in his presence that it grasped hold of her like a tight embrace. "The bed is quite soft." He reached up and trailed the knuckles of one of his hands down her bare arm. "Almost as soft as your skin."

Immediately a jolt, like spellfire, shot through her body from the places he touched. Goose bumps pebbled her skin and she pushed his hand away as she backed up.

She let her anger replace her awareness of him as a man. Her voice lowered to a growl. "No wonder you were all sent to live underground. All of this woman serving a Master and who holds the power is crap. You're barbaric heathens."

Garran's eyes darkened, no amusement, no teasing left in his gaze. She almost took another step away from him as a chill traced her spine.

"It is not for you or any others to judge our lifestyle." His jaw tightened and the temperature in the room dropped as if winter had shrouded the last whispers of fall. "The Elders are judgmental, hypocritical bastards who had no right to do this to my people."

Hannah swallowed hard as she resisted rubbing her arms from the chill. The realization that he was right hit her like a snowball to her belly, icing her insides. She had always held to the strong belief that no one group had the right to judge what another race did, or to dictate what those people could or could not do, or banish the race because they were different.

As long as it was consensual, this Master thing was really none of her business or anyone else's. If it was true slavery, though, that was a whole different ballgame.